LOVE YOU MORE

Love You More

DEDICATION

For Steve Bobo Jolley

Prologue

With fifteen minutes left before visiting hours are over, Collins barrels through the door to catch an elevator, nearly knocking a nurse over. "Sorry," she says.

"It's all right, honey," the heavyset nurse says. "You must be in a bigger hurry than me."

"I want to see my brother before they stop visiting hours. Assuming he's still awake."

"Which floor is he on, baby?"

"Tenth." Her eyes register a light of awareness when Collins mentions Anderson's floor. She presses the button with the number ten on it and pulls her plump hand away. "You're going to the same floor?"

"No, baby, but you got yourself somebody who needs you more than they need me on my floor." She presses her hand against Collins' hand and steps a little closer. A burst of mint gum slaps against her nostrils. "My shift doesn't start for another fifteen minutes. I'll go back down to the seventh floor after you get off."

"Thank you."

"Anytime, baby. He's lucky to have a big sister like you. Get on in there and visit with your precious angel."

The elevator bings, and the door slides open. Collins slides out in the blink of an eye, waving goodbye to the kind nurse.

"Is he still awake?" she asks one of Anderson's nurses.

"I think so. I just read him a story," she says. "I wasn't sure if you were going to make it tonight or not."

"Sorry, Angela. I had to finish moving my stuff into the dorm." A pang of guilt bangs hard against Collins. "Sword and the Stone?"

"Of course."

"How is he?"

"It was a rough day for him today. Chemo is kicking his butt, but you know him. Always a beautiful smile on his face."

"I better get in there," Collins says. Once she rounds the corner, she sees the glow of his bedroom light. "Guess who!"

"Collins," Anderson says. "You made it. Mom and Dad said you might not make it tonight."

"I wouldn't let that happen."

"Good."

"I have something for you."

His eyes widen as she reaches behind her back. "What is it?"

She tilts her head and taps a finger against her cheek. "I need a kiss first." Since she's his sister and not icky like most girls, Anderson plants his chapped lips against her skin. "Here." A ball cap appears from behind her back like a rabbit from a magician's hat.

Anderson tilts his little head for her to put it on him. The baby blue University of North Carolina hat swallows up his little, bald head. "Awesome." A smile inches across his face. "Can I see?"

"Of course." She grabs a mirror, and once he sees himself, his beautiful smile stretches all the way out like a caterpillar in the afternoon sun.

"I love it. Thanks, Collins."

"How are you feeling today?"

"Better than yesterday. Not as great as tomorrow."

She reaches down and gives him a hug and a kiss. He's nothing more than skin and bones. Paleness creeps into his face and darkness tinges his skin just under his eyes. "That's great, buddy. One day at a time. You'll have this thing beat and be back on your feet in no time." It kills her to watch him struggle day after day. He's tough though. It's not his first time through chemo, and it won't be his last.

"I know." His breathing slows and his eyes sag.

"Nurse Angela told me she read to you tonight?"

"Yeah, she's nice."

"Sorry I'm late."

"It's okay." He lays his tiny hand in hers. "Did you get moved in?"

"Finally."

"Mom and Dad said you had a little more to get unboxed."

"I'm all good now. But I need to decorate this weekend."

He coughs. Collins' hand tightens softly around his. "See my new poster?"

He can't lift his hand, but his eyes move to the far wall of his room. "Nice. Did Mom and Dad bring it tonight?"

"Yeah."

She has no clue about the padded player hanging on his wall, but she knows beyond a shadow of a doubt Anderson does. Anderson is the definition of a sports junkie. For an eight-year-old kid, he knows more about sports than most adults. He gets it from their dad. "You've got to love them Panthers," she says.

"I do."

"Okay, buddy. I'm going to let you get your rest now."

"Collins." Her name barely floats to her ear, the softer side of a whisper. "I love you."

"I love you, too." She plants a kiss against his forehead. A tear edges from her eye, but Anderson doesn't see her wipe it, because his eyes are sealed shut. He'll be asleep before she leaves the room. A nasty combination of chemo and his medication wipe him out. Thank goodness he's only going through one round this time.

Collins makes her way across campus to her dorm, thoughts of Anderson buzzing in her mind like a torrent of wasps. UNC isn't her first choice. It's not even her fifth choice. But it's her only choice. After finding out about his cancer years ago, there was only one choice she could make. Attend the school closest to him.

When she arrives back at the dorm, her new roommate is nowhere in sight. She slaps on her pajamas and crawls into bed. Thoughts of Anderson and UCLA battle in her mind. She shoves her selfishness aside. Anderson wins without a challenge. For better or worse, UNC solidifies its place in her life. She's a Tar Heel just like her Dad. Just like Anderson hopes he'll be one day.

Chapter One

I wring my hands as I wait for my counselor to return. She walked out a few minutes ago without telling me why she called me into her office in the first place. A couple of diplomas in dust-covered frames hang on the wall.

A bowl of candy rests on the corner of her desk, so I reach over and grab a peppermint. When I pull my hand away, my sleeve catches on the side of the oddly-shaped bowl. It slides to the edge of her desk and threatens to jump to the floor and shatter into a million pieces. I catch it just in time, allowing it to live one more day.

"That was a close call," my counselor says as she walks into the office.

"I'm sorry," I say.

"It's okay, Dusty," she says. "But it's a good thing you saved it. My daughter made it for me in art class."

That explains why the clay bowl possesses such an odd and ugly shape. "It's an interesting candy dish." I slide it back to its resting spot.

"I'm not sure what she had in mind, but what you see there is the masterpiece of a first grader."

She slides into her leather chair and lays a piece of paper on the desk in front of me. Seeing the name Dustin Slaughter staring back at me almost seems like the name of a stranger since most people call me Slaughter. It's been that way for as long as I've played football.

"Right now, Dusty," she says, "your chances of getting into a division one university are quite slim."

"Why?" I ask. "I've never failed any classes."

"True, but you're not exactly lighting them up either." She runs her finger down the list of grades, stopping and counting every C. There are a handful of B's scattered throughout and a rare A here and there.

"What kind of grades does it take to get into college?"

This sudden awareness forces my stomach to churn. I need to get out of this place and make something of myself.

"You'd need a B average at a minimum," she says. "You can always get into a junior college."

"But I don't want to go to a junior college," I say. I've seen too many people around this town settle for junior college. It's not for me.

"College is a competitive place, Dusty." She swivels around in her chair and clicks buttons on her keyboard. "Hang on. I have an idea."

The endless series of Cs staring back at me mock me and make me wish I'd paid better attention in school.

"You're a football player, aren't you?"

"I am," I say.

"It says here if you can get into college on a partial scholarship or higher, they'll adjust the GPA necessary. A perk of being a student-athlete."

"But I don't have anyone knocking down my door offering me any scholarships," I say. "It's not like they just hand them out."

She scratches her head. "Y'all play Walker High tomorrow night, don't you?"

"Yes, ma'am," I say.

"I think they're supposed to have some scouts here from UNC tomorrow night."

"For Sully?"

"No," she says. "They're coming to scout the other team. I'm pretty sure I heard your coach tell Principal Adams. You may want to check with him."

"I will at practice today."

"Do you think you can get your grades up just in case?" She picks up my transcript and looks it over. "You're not too far from a B average, Dusty, but you have to earn nothing but A's and B's this year. Mostly A's."

"Not sure," I say. "I've got a chemistry test today. I think I'm doing okay in there. And I've got a paper due tomorrow for English class."

"That's a start." She stands up and walks to the door. My hint to get out of her office and go back to class.

"I'll do my best," I say as I walk out.

If scouts are coming out tomorrow, I have to be ready.

Chapter Two

I'm three reps into my bench presses the next morning when Coach walks in. The lights are off, so it startles him when he flips them on and sees me lying on the bench. "Slaughter," he yells, "what're you doing in here?" Coach only has one volume. Loud!

"Getting in some extra reps, Coach." I sit up on the bench and face him.

Coach scratches his head and checks his watch. "What time did you get here? How'd you get in?"

"Seven. The gym door was open."

"Well, Slaughter," Coach grabs his clipboard from his desk, "there's something we need to talk about."

I cock my head sideways.

"I got word from your chemistry teacher that you failed her test."

"Yeah, sorry Coach. I didn't get a chance to study much for it." What I don't tell him is it's because he keeps us on the field for hours every night and there's never enough time to study, but blaming others has never been my style.

"I'm sorry, son, but I'm going to have to bench you for the first half. I'm starting Woody in your place."

My body goes numb. "Coach, you can't do that. The scouts from UNC are going to be here tonight. It's my only chance to get into college."

"I'm sorry, Slaughter. Rules are rules, and if I break them for you all the other boys will expect the same thing. Just because you're team captain doesn't mean you don't have to follow them."

I want to argue with him but know if I do, he won't hesitate to bench me the entire game, and I can't let that happen. Not if I want to get out of this place.

"Sorry, Coach."

"So am I, Slaughter. So am I," he says and walks away.

I hear old guys in my town bumping gums about the good old days. Glory was theirs when they were gods. Their time to shine.

They talk, and I listen. But that was then and this is now. Most guys wear the uniform for the local factory. If glory days are high school football, and life takes a nosedive to normal after graduation, then I'm already screwed, because my life as the number one running back in the region is far from glorious.

I slam out of the weight room and minutes later stand in the shower and let the cool water splatter off my head and neck and wonder how I'm going to make it through this year. My focus has to be on the field. This game is huge. The biggest one of my life.

Some scouts from UNC are coming to our game. Not to see Sullivan, or me though. I'm almost embarrassed to say it, but they're coming to watch a few guys on the defensive line for Walker High to see if they're good enough to be Tar Heels. It just means I have to get through their defensive line so the scouts will notice me.

I throw my game jersey on after toweling off, grab my books, and head to the library to print out a paper for class. About the time I leave the locker room, Sully and the rest of the guys flood through the door.

Crossing the quad as buses pull in, the brisk morning air that comes with life in the mountains brushes against my face and cools my heated cheeks. It's the kind of cold that lets me see my breath in front of my face like a dim fog.

As always, Jenny Lee gathers inside the commons area with the rest of the cheerleaders clucking like barnyard hens. We've been together for what seems like forever. We met sophomore year and have been with each other ever since. Other than Sully, she's my best friend.

"Hey, babe," she calls out to me. We've been together for so long it surprises me that butterflies still flitter the way they did the first time we met. Her smile makes everything all right.

"Morning," I reach over and give her a peck on the cheek before going to the library.

She stops me. "That's all you're going to say to me?" Her friends all stop whatever they're talking about and stare at me like I just kicked somebody's cat.

"I've got to get to the library and print off my paper for McD."

"Oh yeah," Jenny Lee says. "I forgot to print mine. Will you print it out for me?" She reaches in her bag and pulls out a thumb drive and throws it at me. I would say she threw it to me, except for the fact that she couldn't hit the broad side of a barn, so it plops to the ground about five feet away and skids another ten.

"You better hope it's not broken." I lean over and pick it up.

"Who cares if it is? I'll just tell McDougal it broke and get another one later anyhow." Jenny Lee turns back to the group of girls huddled together and clucks again.

Jenny Lee's more like Sully than me. She comes from money. She almost smells like the crisp, clean scent of freshly printed bills. So when she says it's no big deal and she'll get another one, she's not lying. Twenty dollars is nothing to her, but it means a few early morning hours at my job to me.

I print out both papers. Mine isn't all that great because I didn't get to spend much time on it, but at least it's done.

Life in a small town does have its advantages when you're the number one back and everybody puts their Friday night hopes on your shoulders. It means teachers are a little more lenient with grades and cops will look the other way for little things like drinking and stuff.

But it only lasts as long as you're on the team. After graduation, you're just another one of the slugs trying to make a living. And the cops love to come down hard on the has-beens. My guess is because they're all has-beens too.

"How much?" I ask the lady behind the counter.

"Nothing." She must notice my strange look. "You're the Slaughter kid, aren't you?"

"Yes, ma'am," I say. "I'm Dusty." Her words don't bother me because I've been hearing them most of my life.

At first they said it because they felt sorry for me for being the son of Jason Slaughter. Talk about being punished for the sins of my father. I don't remember much about my dad, because he went to jail for killing a woman in a drunk driving accident when I was six. Not a single scratch on him. I haven't talked to him since I was eight. I'm pretty sure he's never getting out, but even if he does, I don't care.

It's funny, though, how long people can hold a grudge against someone when that someone's daddy kills the preacher's wife on a rainy Sunday evening. One coming home from church and the other from a bar. One goes to heaven and the other to jail.

It's a good thing I know how to carry a piece of pigskin leather filled with air because those same people now ask me if I'm the Slaughter boy for a different reason. Yeah, they all still know Dad's in jail and Mama's pretty much no good either, but because I score touchdowns they seem to forgive me of my parents' sins. Crazy what football in a small town can do for a nobody like me.

"I sure hope you boys can beat the Wildcats." She hands me the last of the printed pages. "I'm tired of seeing them win the trophy every year."

"Me too, ma'am." I say as I leave. "Thanks again for the pages."

"You're welcome, son," she says. "Remember, Wound the Wildcats." Laughter escapes her lips.

The cheerleaders make up a slogan each week that has something to do with beating the other team. They say things like "Rout the Raiders" or "Stomp the Spartans" or "Tear the Titans." Always something to do with killing or hurting the other team. This week we play the Walker Wildcats.

"I will, ma'am." I nod and leave.

I head over to the cafeteria and grab a couple sausage biscuits before going back to the commons to meet up with Jenny Lee and Sully.

"Where have you been?" Sully shouts across the commons.

"Library," I say through crumbles of biscuit. "I have a paper due today."

"She didn't tell me that." Sully nods toward Jenny Lee and the other hens.

"Not a surprise." I grab a spot on the bench next to Jenny Lee and finish what's left of my biscuit.

"You didn't bring me one?" Jenny Lee rolls her eyes and huffs like one of those girls who always gets her way, because she is one of those girls. Pretty easy since her dad is the bank president.

"I didn't know you wanted one." I offer her my second biscuit, and as usual she turns me down.

"You always do that, Dusty." She's the only one who calls me Dusty. Well, besides Mama. "You never think of me anymore."

"What are you talking about? I think of you all the time."

"No, you don't. All you think of is football. Nothing but football. I'm second string in your life."

She's pretty close in her analysis. Football is my primary focus because I want more than what I have now. I want what she and Sully have and will always have. They'll never have to work hard for any of it. Their daddies will take care of them. Sullivan will take over his father's factory one day. He's golden. Jenny Lee hasn't decided what she'll do, but she doesn't have to. When she's got her dad's connections, she can do whatever she wants. I've known Sullivan Ray since the third grade and he's like a brother. When I started dating Jenny Lee, people started treating me different because she has money. I guess I kind of like it.

"Sorry, babe. Just been focused on tonight's game, you know." I put my arm around Jenny Lee and kiss her on the cheek again. "You know the scouts will be here."

"They're not looking at you, Slaughter." Sully slaps me on the back.

"I know, but they'll be looking at the guys I'll be running through like a hot knife through warm butter. That'll make them take notice of me." I don't tell Sully that Coach benched me first half.

"Hot knife through warm butter. Dang son, I like that." Sullivan holds out his knuckles and I bump them. "Charlotte, did you hear Slaughter call their D-line a stick of butter?"

"Yeah, yeah, stick of butter." Charlotte's the captain of the cheerleaders but doesn't seem to care for football at all. It's like she's on the squad because it's a requirement to be popular.

The bell rings to let us know we have two minutes left to get to class. That's another thing Coach makes sure of. We have to be in class every day, unless we're dead or dang near dead. If we show up late to class and Coach finds out about it, he'll have our butts at practice. And if we are late on game day, we sit the bench first half. Since I'm already benched first half, no way I'm going to risk missing the second half. Not with the scouts coming. Maybe next time they'll come out to watch me.

Chapter Three

"You about ready, Slaughter?" Sully splashes a fist full of water on his face.

"Yeah…I'm…ready…" I spit out a mouthful of toothpaste. "I'm ready as I'm gonna be." I rinse the rest of the toothpaste out of my mouth and take my toothbrush back to my locker.

There's been one constant in my life for as long as I've played football. I throw up before every game. Gross, I know. But it's the truth. My nerves twist all up inside me, and I can't help myself. Next thing I know, I'm looking for a trashcan or a toilet. When I was younger, the first thing I found was my helmet, so I blew chunks in it. It didn't take me long, though, before I stopped. Sweat mixed with puke makes for a miserable game, and the stink radiates from my hair for days. Not good.

"Gonna need you to be strong, man. Gotta get big and blow through them Wildcats." Sully grabs his shoulder pads and helmet.

"And that's what I'm going to do! But I'm out the first half."

"What are you talking about?!"

"I didn't do so well on my chemistry test."

Sully curses and then leaves me alone in the locker room. Everybody on the team is used to my silly superstitions, so they don't say much. After I puke, I go to the back of the field house and sit in the corner for a few minutes. I'm not sure if it's praying I do or not, because I'm not sure how I feel about all of the God stuff. I mean, I can't see what the big guy's done for me lately.

No matter what it's called, I find a quiet spot and spend some time alone and think. It's kind of like visualization. Not sure what it is, but it works. At least for me. I see the game in my head before it starts.

About ten minutes later I join the guys as they get ready to take the field. We hide behind the banner the cheerleaders made. The man on the PA system runs through a whole slew of announcements and sponsor mentions. Sully's dad is the biggest sponsor, and I bet we wouldn't have new uniforms if Sully weren't the starting QB.

"Boys, I don't have to tell you what this game means, do I?" Coach's voice, nothing more than a whisper on the wind, barely audible over the roar of the crowd.

"NO, SIR!" The whole team yells back at Coach.

"Then that means I don't have to tell you since this is the home opener, those good people in the stands are expecting four quarters of football, right?"

"NO, SIR!"

"And I'm sure I don't have to tell you when you boys go out on the field, you represent me and the other coaches, your folks, and the fine fans of Coosa County High School."

"NO, SIR!" Coach whips the entire team into a frenzy. Like a group of sharks swimming in circles ready to attack.

"I didn't think so," Coach says. "We have about five minutes before we run through the banner them cheerleaders made for y'all. When we go out on the field, we need to make sure Walker knows whose field this is."

"YES, SIR!"

"Let me remind you we have guests in our house all the way from Chapel Hill. Those scouts came to look at Walker's defensive line, but when they leave, the one thing they're going to remember is how our offense put a hurting on their D-line."

"YES, SIR!"

The voice on the PA blares throughout the stadium and the crowd roars. There isn't much to do in Flatbush, North Carolina, most of the year, but on Friday nights in the fall, the whole town comes out to watch us play. It's been the same way for years, and will be that way forever.

A giant boo roars through the stands as they announce the Wildcats.

Then it's time for us to take the field. "Give it up for the Coosa County Eagles."

All the fans go nuts as Sully and I lead the team through the gate and onto the field. The entire team floods behind us as we break through the giant paper banner and run to the fifty-yard line before we make our way over to our side of the field.

"Sully. Slaughter. Get your butts over here." Coach doesn't care what he says on the field. Nobody can hear him but us, so he lets curse words fly all night long.

"Yeah, Coach?" Sully asks.

"When you boys go out there for the coin toss, if we win it, I want us to receive."

"Got it!" Sully says. "But we need Slaughter to start, Coach. Bench him next game."

"You want to do what I tell you or stand here and argue with me? If you want to argue, I'll get Junior to step up. That'll put both of my captains on the bench."

"No, sir." Sully knows how to play the game, so he closes his big mouth. Coach is the only one I know who can get him to shut up.

"Good. I want us to take the ball first, because I want you boys to go after their defense early. Show those scouts they should've come here to look at y'all and not the Wildcats."

"Dang right," I say as the whistle blows.

We head out to the center of the field. Their captains are already waiting on us.

"Surprised you losers came out here," one of their guys mumbles.

"Up yours," Sully replies with a middle finger.

"You boys want to keep up all the nonsense," the referee warns, "I'll go ahead and throw an unsportsmanlike conduct penalty at both of you."

I yank Sully's jersey to get him to stop. Evidently, the other guy decides to keep quiet too. "We'll get them on the field," I whisper to Sully.

"Heads or tails?" the referee asks. "Visiting team calls."

"Heads," the moron who ran his mouth says.

An oversized coin flips through the air and light glints off of it in short bursts. It hits the turf, bounces up and circles before it falls flat. "It's tails." The referee pockets the coin and looks to me and Sully.

"We'll receive."

"You won't have it long," moron says.

"Just kick the ball." Sully eyes the kid as we walk away.

"It doesn't matter. You're going down." The referee shoots the kid a look but doesn't say anything. I'm sure it's because it's nothing compared to the crap that gets said on the field.

Sully and I walk back over to the sidelines. Coach tells the return team to take the field.

I look around the stadium and pull my helmet over my bushy brown hair before remembering I'm not going in. Electric energy zaps through the metal bleachers and a group of men covered in Tar Heel blue stands near our end zone. I want to be the first person they see popping over the line, but it doesn't look like that's going to happen, so I take a deep breath and set my helmet back on the bench. It's just about the perfect Carolina chill on a September night, and it's killing me not to be going in.

Chapter Four

The whistle blows and Walker's kicker boots the ball high into the air. It isn't deep at all, but it hangs in the air long enough for their team to get halfway down the field. As soon as it plunks into Ingram's hands, they swarm him like an angry hive of bees. This isn't going to be easy.

We take the field with the ball on the twenty-one yard line, and I drown out about as much noise as I can to focus on the game. If I have to sit, I may as well study their defense.

Three and out. The blue wall, as they like to call themselves, is much tougher than they look. They waste no time pounding our O-line into the ground and swarming Sully before he has time to react. By the time they get back to the sideline, Coach is fuming. His plan to stick it to them is a terrible one. Sully limps off the field.

"That's the best you could do, Sully?" Coach yelling at Sully happens so often he expects it. Heck, we all do.

Sully pulls grass from his facemask as he removes his helmet. "I don't think they're human, Coach. Besides, what do you expect without Slaughter?" Sully looks to our offensive line as they struggle for air.

"Get over there with Punkin and figure out what y'all are gonna need to do when we get back on the field."

Punkin is the offensive coordinator. Coach brings him no matter what, because he used to play for Coach over in Texas years ago. He isn't the smartest guy in the world, but he does know offense.

"Take a seat, fellas." Punkin pushes towels off the bench. "We got us a bit of a situation here."

"That's quite an understatement, Punkin." I snatch a Gatorade bottle and squirt some in my mouth. More out of habit than anything else, because I sure haven't done anything from the sideline to work up a sweat.

They go over a few plays and some ideas, but nothing makes much of a difference during the first half. When halftime arrives, it's a miracle Walker's only up on us by two touchdowns. If I don't score soon, I can kiss a scholarship goodbye.

Halftime is over and it's my turn. "Let's go," Sully yells and I follow him onto the field. "You ready?"

"Born ready, Sully. You know that," I say. "Take the snap, drop back, and pitch it to me."

"Right side first," Sully says.

Once we huddle up, it's clear Punkin bit off a chunk of their rear ends. The offensive line wears a look of fury on their faces. Their guys are much bigger than ours and much faster, but our boys are determined.

Sully calls the play and we take our place on the ball. We have decent field position thanks to a good run by Ingram.

The ball snaps and flies through the air. I take off to the right side of the field and Sully pivots on his heels and tosses it out to me. A pack of Wildcats choke the middle like they did most of the first half, so it catches them off-guard when the ball whips out to the side and nobody's there to stop me. I'm ten yards down field when someone flies up and crashes into me like a freight train. We hit the ground hard, but I don't care. A first down and a couple extra yards pump up the lifeless crowd. It's the first thing we've done the whole game to get them excited.

I jog back to the huddle and make sure not to let anyone know their safety got me good. My head still spins when I join the guys. I'll have to keep a better eye on number thirty-seven.

"Nice run," Bean says to me.

"Way to hold 'em off," I say. "Now let's do it again."

Bean stares at Sully. "Dang straight. Let's do this."

Whatever Punkin said to them seems to do the trick. We move the ball down field like we're playing against a peewee team. I get a few more big runs, and our wide receiver blows their safety away for about thirty yards. We have first and ten on the eighteen-yard line.

"It's coming to you." Sully drops to one knee. "You're going to do what you do best, Slaughter. Bust it up the middle."

Sweat pours down our faces, and a cloud of steam rises into the night sky. The big boys suck in huge gulps of air, but they do their job. They're stopping the blue wall from advancing. They haven't been able to push them back yet, but they hold them long enough to give Sully some breathing room. And on a night like tonight, that's all I ask.

"You got it." I hold my hand to the center of the huddle. "I need y'all to make me a hole. It doesn't have to be big."

"You got it," Bean says.

"Eagles on three."

Hands in the middle, we shout in unison and make our way to the line of scrimmage.

As I get ready and the guys head to the line, I look to the men dressed in baby blue. I point at them and give a wink. We're too far away for them to see me, but it makes me feel better.

I line up behind Sully. When he begins the snap count, I take off to the right in a slight jog.

A split second later, I dart for the middle, and Sully meets me with a shuffle pass. I stick the ball tight in the folds of my left arm and cut up field. There isn't much room between the center and left guard.

I bust up the seam and find myself in open field. Since everyone thinks the play is to the right, the entire defense is off balance once I clear the secondary. Daylight stretches for about ten yards, and I run as fast as my legs will carry me. Within seconds, number thirty-two catches up with me, and I stare at grass again.

After popping back up, I jog to the huddle. I don't quite hit the target, but I put us on the seven-yard line.

"Incredible run, Slaughter," Sully says as I put my hands on my knees. "Need a second or two?"

I'm breathing hard, but my juices are flowing. Momentum is on our side. "Nah," I say as I suck in air. "I'm good. Let's do this."

Coach signals a play to Sully. It's a screen pass to our tight end, Wildeman. Sully nods his head and relays the play to us. "Coming to you, Wild Man."

"No, it's not." My words surprise Wildeman, but he knows not to question me. "I'm getting the ball. I got us here, I'm taking it home."

"You sure, Slaughter?"

I look to Sully. "I've never been more sure in my life."

"Coach is gonna chew me out, you know?"

"Let me worry about that." Sully knows me well enough to know when I'm in the zone.

"We've got this boys," Sully says.

Nobody says a word.

"Fox." Sully grabs Jeremy Fox's facemask and pulls him toward him. "You need to get to the far corner of the end zone quick and give me a target. Make them think you're getting the ball. Got it?"

Fox nods. My guess is he's about as nervous as the rest of us. Not Sully though. He never gets nervous. A lifetime of getting his way will do that to a guy, I guess.

"Slaughter." Sully looks at me but knows better than to grab my facemask. "We've got those scouts here from UNC, and I have one question for you before I snap the ball."

"What's that, Sully?"

"You ready to show them what we've got? You ready to change your life?"

The one thing I have on my mind at the moment is running into the end zone and right up to the scouts. Time they know who Dusty Slaughter is.

"Let's do this."

The play clock winds down, so we hustle to the line. Everything goes as planned and the center snaps the ball. Sully pitches it out to me, and I cut for the corner. Unfortunately for me, Walker's defense doesn't fall for anything.

I find myself facing an ocean of blue jerseys, which forces me to jump over the guy diving for my ankles and into the crowd around the two-yard line. Instead, a shoulder slams like an anvil against my chest. I'm at the top of the pile of blue like on a wave about to crash against the shore. As I go down, I'm hit by someone else and it spins me around. Somehow, my feet find the ground and I break free from the pile, my back toward the end zone. I turn and run.

The stadium erupts. Touchdown!

When I look to the corner, my world crashes down around me. The scouts are gone.

Chapter Five

"You played such a good game, boys!" Coach's face drains of all emotion. He doesn't yell like he normally does. It's hard to tell if he's upset or not. "I asked you boys to come out here against the number one team in the state and make us proud."

We all stare at Coach.

"And y'all did that. Look at them folks in the stands cheering you boys on."

I turn around and see a stadium full of fans.

"Tonight's game ball goes to Octavio for his last-second field goal which put us over the top."

My mouth hits the floor, but I don't say anything. Best game of my life and not a word.

"Get on home and rest up," Coach says. "Be back in the weight room first thing Monday morning."

The team scatters like cockroaches in bright light. Most head to the parking lot, but I go back to the field house. Another part of my ritual.

"You want me to wait on you?" Sully asks as he pulls his shoulder pads over his head.

"Nah, I'll meet y'all there."

When I get inside the field house, I pull off my equipment, jump into the shower, and get the stench of sweat and grass off me the best I can.

After I finish my shower and put on an almost-clean shirt and pair of jeans, I grab my bag and head to my dented green Accord. It's a pile, but even with rust spots and a rear door window made of clear plastic and duct tape, it gets me back and forth. At least for now.

We all meet up at the town square after every game. It's more fun when we win, because most of the town comes to the square to hang out. When we're there, they treat us like superstars.

I pull the green monster into an empty spot and hop out. Jenny Lee is already waiting on me when I walk up.

"Great game, babe." She plants her soft lips against mine. She refuses to be seen in the green monster. Says it's a piece of crap and doesn't want to be caught dead in it.

"It was all right." I wait for some more praise. My feelings are still a little bruised from not getting the game ball.

"If it weren't for you, Walker would've beaten y'all like a drum."

"And Sully." Charlotte pops up behind Jenny Lee out of the clear blue.

"Yeah, him too." Jenny Lee wraps her fingers in mine. "But you have to admit, Charlotte, if it weren't for my big stud here, Sully wouldn't have anything. You saw the first half."

Charlotte shrugs her shoulder but doesn't contradict Jenny Lee. "Where's Sully?"

About the time she asks the question, Sully pulls up in his convertible. It's too cold to have the top down, but a little cold weather never stops Sully. Especially when he's got an audience. He works a crowd like a ringmaster at the circus.

"Hey, you." Sully picks Charlotte up and kisses her. "What're y'all hanging around over here for? Let's go eat."

The square's crowded but we're able to worm our way through. Sully and I get a few slaps on the back from some of the old guys. A couple little kids ask us to sign their shirts. Same crap we used to do when we were their age.

We push into Fazzio's Pizza. It's jam packed, but there's one table in the back still open. The girls scooch in first.

"What ya want to drink?" A kid from our school asks. I don't remember his name, but I recognize him from chemistry class.

"Water for me." It's about all I have money for at the moment.

"How rude." Jenny Lee punches me in the arm. "You're such a brute. Don't you know you're supposed to let the ladies order first? Honestly, Dusty, what will I ever do with you? If you're ever going to win over my dad, you have to learn some manners."

Jenny Lee knows her daddy will never approve of me. He made it crystal clear the first time I stepped on her porch. He told me he'd bust my jaw if I ever set foot on his porch again. I could tell he was serious, so I've never been back to her house since. I wish things were different, though. We both do. It tears me up inside knowing how much it bothers her that her daddy doesn't like me.

Sully tries to lighten the mood. "If you and Charlotte would stop flapping your gums and order something, Slaughter wouldn't have to order first."

"Don't get in the middle of their stuff, Sullivan." Charlotte's a sweet girl and always tries to make sure nobody fights, but she's about as dim as a blown-out bulb.

The kid from chemistry class waits in silence for everyone to order. "I can come back if you need a minute to figure things out."

Jenny Lee refuses to let him go. "Bring me a Coke."

"Make that three," Charlotte says.

"I think we'll need a minute to look over the menu," Sully tells the kid. Then he looks to Charlotte. She pulls Sully's hand into hers.

We order a large everything pizza and just like always, it's incredible. Sully and I almost devour the entire thing before Charlotte and Jenny Lee finish their first slice.

"Y'all are a bunch of savages," Jenny Lee says as she reaches for a second slice. "Do you want to share it with me, Char?"

"Sounds good."

"We're not savages." A piece of green pepper dangles from Sully's lip as he tries to talk and swallow at the same time. It doesn't help his case. "We're gladiators. Warriors!" He shoves the pepper back into his mouth and chews. "Ain't that right, Slaughter?"

"Yep, we're warriors all right." Right now I don't feel much like a warrior. My body's about as weak as it can be. I've been running on fumes, and it's catching up to me. And though my eyes are heavy, I fight the sleep that threatens to come.

"What's wrong with you?" Jenny Lee strokes my forehead.

"He's pouting because the precious scouts from UNC didn't come talk to him. To tell him how awesome he is."

Sully laughs as I roll my eyes.

"You don't need to worry about those scouts, babe," Jenny Lee says as she pushes her bottom lip out like a sad child. "We all know how good you are. Besides, they'll be other scouts looking at you before you know it."

I'm not so sure about that. It's hard enough to get attention as it is, much less when you're short and play for a small town school in the middle of nowhere North Carolina. Being three hours away from Chapel Hill might as well be on the moon. Nobody ever drags their butts up to Coosa County unless they're lost or selling drugs.

We finish the pizza and get ready to pay. I pull out my wallet and cringe when I realize I only have twenty dollars left to my name and don't get paid for another week. I need the money for gas, but I owe for Jenny Lee and me.

"Here's my half, plus tip." I slide fifteen bucks across the table.

Sully scoops it up and pays the kid.

"I need to get home, guys." I gulp down the rest of my water, along with a lemon seed I accidentally chomp down on and spit out.

"Gross, Dusty," Jenny Lee says. "Have some manners and use this." She hands me a napkin, and I spit the remainder of the seed into it. "That's a good boy."

"You're going to domesticate him yet, Jenny Lee." Charlotte tries to be cute, but I ignore her.

"I need to get home," I say as I stand up. "I need to get to sleep." I reach down and kiss Jenny Lee.

"Already?" Jenny Lee asks.

"I've got to work in the morning."

"You're not coming to hang at my house?" Sully asks.

"Nope. Maybe tomorrow."

"Call me in the morning, Dusty." Jenny Lee blows me a kiss, and I leave.

Chapter Six

After making the fifteen-mile drive up the mountain, I pull up to what I call home. It's nothing more than a clapboard shack I've lived in for as long as I can remember. The walls are as thin as paper and some windows are made from the same plastic that's on my car.

When I walk inside, the room's pitch black, except for the glow from a wood heater in the front room. It's our only source of heat. Mama's asleep in the corner on a recliner that should've been taken to the dump a decade ago. Stuffing peeks out from several places, and the arms are full of burn holes from where Mama falls asleep with a lit cigarette. I'm surprised she hasn't burned down what little bit of a house we have.

"Mama," I call out to her as I flip on the light. "Mama, you awake?"

It's easy to see she's far from awake. I pick up the empty bottle on the ground next to her and toss it in the trash. I don't know why I bother because I know Mama will just find more pills and liquor. She hasn't been the same since the accident. I hate her for it most of the time, but I hate him more for getting her started. First the liquor. Now the pills. I've tried to get her to stop taking them so many times, and each time I do she tells me she will never touch them again. I learned years ago she isn't strong enough to give them up.

I put my finger on Mama's neck to check for a pulse. It's faint but there. I know I'll come home one day and find her dead. It worries me that if I do find her dead it won't bother me much.

Grabbing a nearby blanket, I lay it over her. I bend down to kiss her on the forehead, and when I do she shuffles in the chair. I think I hear her say, "I love you, Dusty," as she rolls over.

I splash water on my face and brush my teeth before setting the alarm for four o'clock a.m. I'll get a few hours' sleep before work. I took a job last spring at Sully's dad's factory. It's only a couple of hours before school, but it's all I can get right now. With studying in the morning and practices in the afternoon, it's about the only time I can work.

Cleaning toilets and taking out trash isn't my idea of heaven, but as they say, beggars can't be choosers. Until I can get my scholarship, I'll do whatever I have to. That's why most nights I'm in bed by ten. Jenny Lee doesn't understand why I go to bed so early, but then again, she's never had to work a day in her life. That's not my life and never will be.

Things used to be good. We never had money, but we had each other. At least that's what my dad always said. I remember one Christmas when they surprised me with my first bicycle. Dad spent all day teaching me how to ride it in the melting snow while Mama sat on the front porch drinking hot chocolate. That's the best memory I have of Mama and Daddy. It wasn't long after that the sheriff came to the house to tell Mama he was in jail. All I remember is Mama collapsing to the floor in tears when he told us a woman was dead. It was the worst day of my life.

Mama took me to the trial and they said guilty. None of it made any sense, but I remember my dad telling me I was the man of the house now because he was going to be gone for a long time. The last thing he whispered in my ear before telling me he loved me was to take care of Mama. He told me I'm all she has in the world now that he's going to prison. I guess that's the reason I can't leave her now no matter how much I hate her sometimes. I'll never forgive him for leaving us.

*****

It feels like I just put my head against the pillow when my alarm jolts me from sleep. I shake the grogginess from my eyes and get dressed. The mountain chill creeps through the cracks in the floor.

The roads are empty as the green monster clatters down the road back to town. It takes me about half an hour to get to work.

"Hey, Dusty," the night guard says as I pull up to the entrance.

"Nice job last night."

"Thanks, Bill."

"Go on in," Bill says as he lifts the arm for me to drive through.

Saturday mornings are much slower than the rest of the week, so when I walk in only Mr. Franklin's there to greet me.

"Great game last night, Dusty," Mr. Franklin says. "You kept us in it."

Mr. Franklin played offensive lineman twenty years ago. Before I was even born. But to hear him tell his stories, it's like it happened yesterday. One of the many dreamers stuck in the nightmare of Flatbush.

"Thanks, Mr. Franklin." I grab my time card and punch in. "We finally took out Walker."

"Yeah, the Gonzalez kid had one heck of a kick."

My jaw tightens when I hear Octavio's name. "Yeah, it was a good one."

"If it wasn't for that kid's leg, we wouldn't have won."

I don't remind him if it weren't for my three touchdowns, we wouldn't have won either. "No, sir, I s'pose not."

"I just wish Coach would've put my boy in for more than a minute." Mr. Franklin pours a pile of sugar into a Styrofoam cup before he adds coffee.

"Yeah, but he played well." Alex Franklin's a pretty good player for a freshman. He's the one freshman Coach trusts to help protect Sully when Bean has to rest. It's because he's about as big as Mr. Franklin, who happens to be the size of a small house.

"Anyhow, great game. You better grab some gloves. One of the toilets is plugged up."

An appropriate start to the next chapter of my life. A toilet bowl full of crap, and I'm the one left to try to figure out how to clean it up.

Chapter Seven

Mr. Franklin let me put in a few extra hours this morning, so it's fifteen minutes to ten when my head finds my pillow again. After I catch up on some needed hours of sleep, I crawl out of bed and make my way to the kitchen. I already know before I open the refrigerator there won't be any food. At least nothing edible.

I claw around in the pantry and find some stale crackers. It isn't much, but it'll have to do.

My phone rings from the other room. I don't rush to answer it because I'm sure it's Jenny Lee and though I love her, I don't feel much like talking. It goes to voicemail.

"How'd you do last night?" Mama comes through the front door.

"We won."

"But how'd you do?"

"I got three touchdowns."

"You're going to make it out of here, ain't you baby?"

I flip on the TV but don't say anything to Mama. She looks like she's still pretty high and won't remember anyhow.

"Promise me, son." Mama stands in front of me, her eyes hollow and skin thin like paper. The blue veins in her arms are visible.

"Promise you what, Mama?"

"You'll do better than me and your dad ever did. Promise me you'll get out of this place. Make somethin' of yourself."

If Mama knew how much I wanted out of this miserable town. If she stayed sober long enough to notice half of what I've been doing the past few years, then she'd know my whole life's about doing better. About being something she'll never be.

She's still Mama, and no matter how bad I hate her sometimes, I still love her. "I promise Mama."

Mama wanders off to her room. My guess is so she can pop another pill. It disgusts me, but there isn't anything I can do about it. If I turn her in, she'll go to jail. That won't do either one of us any good. So I keep my mouth shut and deal with it.

My phone chirps again to let me know I have a message. When I pick up the phone, the number is one I don't recognize. It's a Chapel Hill area code.

A man's voice speaks into my ear. My eyes grow wide when I realize it's one of the scouts from UNC.

"Holy crap," I scream. "I can't believe it."

"What's wrong, baby?" Mama asks from the other room.

"Nothin', Mama. I'm fine."

I listen to the message again to make sure it's not a dream. It's UNC. I take a deep breath before I dial the number. After the first ring, I hang up. My body shakes too much to even speak. I settle myself and press dial again. Three rings. Then four.

"Hello," a deep voice calls to me from the other end of the line.

"Uhh…Mr. Walcott, please." My voice cracks slightly.

"Who's calling?"

"I'm Dusty Slaughter, sir." I hold my breath and wait for a response.

"Dusty Slaughter?" He asks like he's never heard of me. It makes me think I've dialed the wrong number. "Oh, yeah, here you are. Thanks for calling me back, son."

"You're welcome."

"I've been moving down this list of possible prospects and can't remember who all I've called this morning. Give me a second, will ya?"

"Sure, take your time."

"Gotcha." I can hear papers shuffle. "Dusty…do you mind if I call you Dusty?"

"Most people call me Slaughter, but Dusty's fine, sir."

"Well, Dusty, let me get to the point. I'm the guy who calls folks in when our scouts find someone who they think might be a good fit for our organization."

"Okay."

"I got an email this morning from a scout who says he saw you play last night somewhere up north of here."

"Flatbush. Yes, sir."

"Well, it seems whatever you did last night impressed him enough for me to call you to see if you can get yourself down here to Chapel Hill next Saturday."

I swallow hard before answering. The right answer is to say yes, but I don't have the money to get there and back and I won't get paid before next Saturday.

"You there, son? I need an answer from you because I got other boys I need to call."

"Uhhh…sorry, sir. Yeah, that'll be fine. I'll be there next Saturday. Tell me when and where."

"I'll be in touch with the details by midweek. For now, just sit tight."

"Uhhh…Yes, sir." He's crazy if he thinks I'll be able to sit tight. This is the best thing to happen to me in my entire life. How can I just sit tight?

"Great, and congratulations for getting noticed. That's the easy part. Saturday's the day you better come ready to impress."

"Yes, sir, I won't let you down."

"I'm not the one you need to worry about. The coaches are the ones you need to impress."

"I will, sir. Thanks again."

"Good luck."

Without another word, the phone goes dead. I run into Mama's room and give her a hug. She's so frail I'm afraid she will shatter in my arms like glass. "I'm going to make it Mama. I promise. I'm going to get us out of here one day."

"That's good, baby. Now leave me be. I got some things I need to tend to."

She knows I know all about her problem, but for some reason she pretends I don't. I guess it makes her feel better if she acts like nothing's going on. At least then she can let herself believe she isn't letting me down.

Chapter Eight

The first of the week drags by as I anticipate the call about details for Saturday. Wednesday passes and nothing. No call. No letter. No email. Nothing.

When I'm just about to give up, a call comes in Thursday night as I drive home from practice. It's Mr. Walcott. I pull over to write down the directions and the name of the guy I'm supposed to ask for when I get there. Mr. Walcott gets right to the point and ends the conversation abruptly.

Panic sets in as I rack my brain to figure out how I'll be able to pull it off. I try not to worry about it and don't mention it to Mama when I get home. Wouldn't do any good anyhow, because she's already out of it by the time I walk in the door. She's sprawled out on her recliner as usual. I pour out what's left of the liquor, and then check to make sure she has a pulse. After I toss some wood in the burner and lay a blanket over her withered body, I kiss Mama on the forehead soft as a butterfly wing. She doesn't even stir.

A few hours later, I'm back at work. Mr. Franklin greets me as he always does. "You're a bit early this morning, aren't you, Dusty?"

"Couldn't sleep."

"What's troubling you?"

"Nothing. Couldn't sleep is all."

"Dusty, you can talk to me." Mr. Franklin's seated and nods to another chair at the table. "You've been working here for about four or five months now, right?"

"About that." I say.

"You haven't missed a day of work or even been one minute late."

"No, sir, I haven't."

"I know you don't like cleaning toilets any more than I do, so for you to put up with this job this long tells me a little bit about you."

I take a seat at the long break room table across from Mr. Franklin. "And what's that?"

"You've got a fire in your belly that won't seem to burn out."

"Something like that, I s'pose."

"You aren't anything like Jason." Mr. Franklin's eyes narrow into tiny little slivers.

It takes me a moment to register what he says. My first instinct is to punch him for talking bad about my dad, but what I do is agree with him and nod.

"I bet you didn't know your father and I used to be friends, did you?"

I shake my head.

"He played football with me." Mr. Franklin stands up and goes to the coffee maker. "Bet you didn't know that either, did you?"

Again I shake my head, but he can't see me because he's facing the other way.

He mixes up his sugar and coffee without saying a word. He sits back at the table and blows the hot liquid for a few seconds. "He played the same position you play."

"He did?" I cock my head sideways and try to figure out if Mr. Franklin's messing with me or not.

"He did. He was pretty talented, too."

"What happened to him?"

"Well, your father didn't have the drive you have. Didn't see a way out of this place. Like so many of us over the years. This factory was all there was in this town. Before it was a light factory, it was a parts manufacturer for Chevrolet, until they closed it. That was a few years before Mr. Ray bought it."

"What does any of this have to do with my dad?"

"Your dad was a good ballplayer. I'm not saying he was good enough for the pros, but he had talent."

A weak smile crosses my face for a moment.

"When he and your mama got together, he didn't much care for football anymore. He was crazy about your mama."

"I've never thought about him and Mama much before."

"Our senior year, he got your mama pregnant with you. When he found out he was going to be a dad, he didn't take it so well."

"Geez, thanks a lot."

"I don't mean it like that." Mr. Franklin takes a sip of coffee. "Jason never was the responsible kind, so when he found out he would have to settle down and marry your mama, he didn't know what to do."

"He didn't have to marry her."

"Oh yes he did." Mr. Franklin pinched the bridge of his nose. "Living in a small town like this, you couldn't get a girl pregnant and not step up to make an honest woman of her. Too many people in town would've talked. He loved her and I think he was planning to marry her anyhow. Just not so soon."

"So he quit playing football?"

"Yep. Nobody knew why your mom and dad dropped out of school until after graduation and your mama had you, but he up and quit the football team and went to work. He worked every day of his life after he found out. Up until the time he went to…" Mr. Franklin stops himself. "Well, you know."

"I never knew much about him. I always just thought he was a bum."

"Your dad was a good man, but having so much responsibility at such a young age drove him to drinking. Once he caught the bug, he couldn't shake it."

"Why are you telling me all this?"

Mr. Franklin shifts in his chair and shakes his head. "Because you've got way more talent than he ever did even if you don't have the size, and I don't want you to mess it up. I know your life hasn't been easy, but you need to know you have a chance none of the rest of us ever have. You can get out of here. You don't want to end up like me, do you? Or heaven forbid, like your father?"

"No, sir, I don't."

"Then why don't you tell me what's troubling you and let me see if I can help. I wasn't there to help Jason. The least I can do is help you."

Mr. Franklin's words hang heavy in the air. I never thought about Dad as someone who was ever like me. I always knew him as the drunk driving, alcoholic, preacher's wife-killing bum. It takes me a few minutes to gather my thoughts together. I wipe the threat of a tear forming in my eyes away with my sleeve.

"I have a chance to go tryout with the Tar Heels this Saturday."

"Wow, Dusty, that's fantastic. Why has that gotten you down?"

"'Cause we don't get paid until next week, and I don't have but five bucks to my name."

"Is that all?"

"Isn't that enough?"

"Tell you what," Mr. Franklin says. "Why don't you let me pay for your trip down to Chapel Hill and back?"

"I can pay you back after I cash my check."

"Nonsense." Mr. Franklin reaches into his back pocket and pulls out his wallet. He removes five twenties and lays them on the table. "I'm giving you this money, and I don't want to hear another word about it.

"But let me…"

"Tell you what." Mr. Franklin slides the money closer to me, and I take it. "You can do some odd jobs for me around my house for the next few Saturdays if you want. Sound good?"

"Yes sir." A lump forms in my throat. "I don't know what to say, Mr. Franklin."

"You don't have to say a thing, son."

"I promise I'll pay you back."

"Dusty, listen to me. I don't want your money. I don't want anything from you, except one thing."

"Anything. You name it."

"All I want from you is to ask you go down to that school and show them who we are. Show them you've got heart as big as the state of North Carolina and all you need is a chance. I want you to go down to UNC and get yourself the scholarship none of the rest of us ever thought possible."

A tear creeps down Mr. Franklin's cheek. He stands up from the table and dumps what's left of his coffee into the sink. "Now go punch in and get to work."

Chapter Nine

Our game comes and goes. We blow Eastside out of the water, but I came out of the game early because I twisted my ankle. I iced it most of the night, but it's still swollen and sore.

I put in a few hours at the plant before I head to UNC. When I'm done, I clock out and walk over to the green monster. Mr. Franklin follows.

"Good luck, son."

"Thanks." I turn the key but nothing happens.

Mr. Franklin walks to the front of the car. "Pop the hood."

"It does this sometimes. It'll eventually crank."

"Just pop the hood. Let me take a look."

It's always something. Nothing ever seems to go right. If I don't get on the road soon, I'll be late.

"I don't think this thing is going to make it. Looks like you need a new battery." Mr. Franklin closes the hood. "Better take my truck."

I crinkle my nose. "What?"

"Take my truck. I'll get my wife to pick me up. And while you're gone I'll get a new battery for you."

"It'll crank eventually, sir."

"Maybe it will and maybe it won't, but you need to get on the road now, don't you?"

I nod.

"Then take my truck. I'll add the battery to your tab."

"Okay," I say.

"Here you go." Mr. Franklin hands me a set of keys. "Now she ain't much, but she's all I've got, so be careful with her."

"I will. I promise."

"You remember what you owe me, don't you?" Mr. Franklin leans against the hood of his truck.

"I'll make you proud."

"You be careful."

"I will. And I'll drop it back off here when I get back. I'll put the keys on top of the tire."

"Sounds like a plan." Mr. Franklin walks toward the door. "Now get out of here."

After I lay the directions on the seat next to me, I pull out of the parking lot and head for Chapel Hill. Once I make it off the mountain and onto the interstate, the ride's much smoother.

My heart flutters when I realize this'll be the farthest from home I've ever been. And I'm doing it all by myself. Which isn't a surprise, though, because I've been doing things by myself my entire life.

As the truck motors along the highway, buildings start to show themselves in the early morning sun. Buildings taller than any in Flatbush. Taller than any I've ever seen in my life. Beads of nervous sweat form on my forehead, and the steering wheel slips in my hands.

Instinct forces me to pull off the highway and into a convenience store parking lot. After putting the truck in park, I jump out and pace around for a few minutes. My head swims with confusion and doubt. My breathing becomes labored, so I double over and press my hands against my legs and try to catch my breath.

"You okay there?" A man stares at me as he pumps gas.

"I'm…I'm…" The words are slow to come. "I'm fine, sir."

He makes his way closer to me, and I notice his wife as she gets out of the passenger side of the car. "You don't look like you're fine."

"Do you want me to call nine-one-one, Walter? Is he okay?" The lady I assume to be his wife comes around the back of the car with a cell phone in her hand.

"I don't need you to call nobody," I say. "I'm fine."

When I open my eyes, Walter's black leather shoes stare up at me. He puts his hand on my shoulder. "Son." Walter seems a bit nervous. "Are you on drugs?"

Drugs? Seriously? That's his first question? "No, sir, I'm not on drugs." I've managed to control my breathing and stand to look him in the eye. He's wearing a nice suit with a blue tie.

"Then what is it?"

Walter's wife is beside him now, wearing a beautiful dress. "Is he okay, Walter?"

"He says he's fine."

After sucking in as much air as possible, I'm almost back to normal. "I'm just nervous."

Walter cocks his head sideways. "Nervous? Nervous about what?"

I cut my eyes toward Chapel Hill and the massive buildings staring back at me.

Walter's face twists in confusion. "What are you talking about, young man?"

"The buildings. The Tar Heels. Football. Life." I'm certain Walter and his wife think I'm insane. They don't understand who I am and how overwhelming all of this is. I didn't understand it until just now.

"Are you sure you're not on drugs."

I laugh at his assumption. "No, sir, I'm not on drugs. I've never touched them in my life." After seeing what they do to Mama, there isn't any way in the world I'll ever put anything in my body stronger than a beer. And when I think of Dad and what Mr. Franklin said, I wonder if I even need that.

"Are you sure you don't want me to call the authorities, Walter?" Walter's wife looks panicked.

"I appreciate it, ma'am, but I'm fine. Well, at least I will be fine." I point into the city. "See, ma'am, I come from a town called Flatbush up along the border. Way up in the mountains. And to be perfectly honest with you, I've never been to the big city before. I've never even left Flatbush."

"What brings you all the way down to Chapel Hill then?" Walter whispers into his wife's ear and she makes her way to the store.

"The University of North Carolina saw me play last weekend and asked me to come down today to workout with their team. The coaches want to see if I have what it takes, is what the man on the phone said."

"Well, young man, it sounds like something to be proud of."

"I s'pose so, sir. It's just I get a touch of nerves before games. Puking and everything. On top of it all, I twisted my ankle last night. And since this is way more important to me than a game, I feel like I'm about to pass out. At least I did. I'm okay now."

"It's understandable you'd be anxious. Who wouldn't be in your situation?" He rubs the goatee on his chin. "Let me ask you a question?"

"Shoot."

"You must be a pretty good football player if they asked you down."

"I reckon."

"Then here's my advice for you. Go to the football field and let the coaches see just why you were invited. Life's a lot like football, son. You have to give it one hundred and ten percent until the final horn sounds. It's how I do my job and how I run my life."

His words seep into my brain. "I know you're right, but you don't know where I come from. I've never seen a place as big as this. We don't have too many people in my whole town."

"Can you play?"

"Yes, sir."

"Are you tough?"

"Yes, sir." His wife walks up and hands me a soda. "Thanks."

"Then it doesn't matter where you are. As long as you know who you are, the location's irrelevant. Trust in yourself and work hard. Eventually, others will trust in you too."

His advice punches me in the gut. Nothing in my life has ever gone right. The only person I have in this world I can count on is me.

"Thank you, sir. I believe I'm ready to head on in."

"That's good. Tell me your name."

"My name's Dusty Slaughter, but most people just call me Slaughter."

"Well, Slaughter, I better see you on TV in the next couple of years." A smile stretches across his face. "I'm a Tar Heel myself. I've been on the campus most of my life."

"Cool."

"Maybe after today, you and I will be brothers in blue."

"I sure hope so, sir." I reach my hand out and shake his. "Thanks for the talk." I mean it genuinely. If he wasn't there, I may have turned around and driven right back to Flatbush. "Ma'am," I call out as his wife is halfway to the car. "Thanks again for the soda."

"I'm just glad you're all right." She leaves the two of us alone and gets back into their Mercedes.

"Thanks again, Walter."

"Anytime, Slaughter. And I'm serious when I say I want to see you soon. My wife and I go to every home game and will be looking for you."

"Yes, sir. I'll do my best today. I promise."

"That's all anyone can ask of you."

He shakes my hand again and heads back over to his car. After Walter puts the gas nozzle back in its spot, he and his wife leave.

Chapter Ten

What seems like forever passes, and I pull onto the campus of the University of North Carolina. There's a sign that reads Kenan Football Stadium written in powder blue with an arrow pointing to the right.

After I take a moment to collect myself, I hop out of Mr. Franklin's truck and make my way to the front gate. A guard checks my name and sends me inside.

I head toward the elevator, butterflies fluttering all through my body. Once I get to the third floor, the door opens into one of the fanciest lobbies I've ever seen. The marble floor is so polished I'm afraid to step on it.

After I wander around and soak everything in, I make my way to the recruit's room. There's a guy wearing a light blue windbreaker and UNC hat. He doesn't look much older than me. I assume he's a student.

"Are you here for squad day?"

"Yes, sir." It occurs to me too late that I don't have to call him sir, but I just can't help myself. One thing Mama did right was make sure I say 'yes, sir' and 'no, sir.' It seems to have no impact on him.

"Go on inside. You're early but that's okay. There are some doughnuts and juice, along with coffee if you want." The kid opens the door. "Coaches will be here soon."

"Okay."

"Over there's the food," the kid points to the other side of the room.

"Thank you."

A couple of guys walk in as I'm pouring orange juice into a paper cup. "Is this the right place?" one of the biggest guys I've ever seen asks.

"It is. Have some food." The kid tucks a banana in his jacket pocket and snags a bottle of water. "I better get back out there."

"What's up, dude?" The mountain stands next to me and plows into the food. "I'm Tommy. And this is Mike."

"I'm Dusty."

Tommy drops a giant hand against my shoulder and almost knocks my juice to the floor. About the same time, a group of guys lumber into the room. They all vary in size, but I'm still the shortest of the group. I've never worried too much about being five-foot-ten before, because not too many guys on the team are much taller than me. Sully's the tallest at six-foot-two, but all of the guys here so far are Sully's height or taller. Tommy has to be close to six-six or more.

I find a seat at one of the tables and eat my doughnut. A few minutes later they take us down to get suited up and the game is on.

The rest of the day is a never-ending series of running plays and drills. They bust our butts the entire time and only let us stop once for lunch.

"Hit the showers," Coach Taylor yells after blowing his whistle. "Then meet us in the team meeting room."

He didn't do or say much as we worked out. He stood on the sideline with a tablet and took notes.

"Not bad, Dusty." Tommy slaps me on the helmet.

"You either," I say. "You can call me Slaughter. That's what all my friends call me."

"You're super quick for a little guy," Mike says to me.

"Tough, too." Tommy pulls his helmet off of his sweaty head. "I've hit bigger guys than you and put them out of the game."

"Believe me, I thought about it, but that's not my style. If I ain't dead, I ain't comin' off the field."

"You're all right, Slaughter."

After a long, hot shower, I dress and head upstairs. The massive bruise on my side hurts like crazy and my ankle is swollen to the size of an orange, so I walk a little funny to ease the pain.

Coach Taylor comes in and tells us all to take a seat.

"First of all," Coach Taylor says. "I want to thank you all for coming out to Chapel Hill today." He pushes a button and a screen flickers to life. "I want you boys to see yourself today, so we're going to watch a little film."

We watch a highlight reel of sorts. A lanky black kid catches his pass, and I scurry like a mouse from Tommy and the others. I'm impressed with my run, even though it isn't the play the quarterback called.

The film moves along and clips of all of us flash on the screen. Some look better than others. It closes on the play where Tommy knocks stars into my head. Great, I have to leave with that image stuck in my mind.

The lights come back on and Coach Taylor takes the podium. "You all did a fine job and should be proud you were given this opportunity. We don't invite just anybody to come work with our boys. Only the ones we think have some potential. So if you don't get a call from us in the next week or so, hold your head high. At least you made it this far."

His words aren't comforting, and all I can think of is Tommy slamming me into the ground. Is that what these coaches think of me? That I'm some little guy who can't hack it at this level?

"When you leave in just a few minutes, the guys in the back have something for you."

We all turn around and see more students wearing blue windbreakers holding blue bags in their hands.

"You boys be careful as you head home."

Coach Taylor grabs his tablet and ducks out a side door. The other coaches follow him. I stand and make my way to the rear door, grabbing my parting gift as I pass. I don't care what's in the bag unless it's a scholarship to play football. Since I know it isn't, I sling the Tar Heel cinch bag over my shoulder and leave.

"Mr. Slaughter," someone calls out as I drink about a gallon of water from the fountain. "Do you have a minute?"

I stop drinking long enough to see Coach Taylor standing in the doorway. "Sure," I say.

"Come in here for a second." He pushes open the door and leads me into his office.

"Okay."

"Mr. Slaughter, I need to ask you something that's been bothering me all day."

This is not good. "Sure, ask anything."

"Mr. Slaughter, when the quarterback called your play you deviated from it." I nod. "Can you tell me why you didn't run the play he called?"

Coach Taylor puts me in a tight spot. I don't want to say it was because three giants were barreling down on me and sound like a sissy, but I also didn't want to sound like I know more than the quarterback.

"Well, Coach, it's like this." My stomach knots up but I continue. "When I realized the defense read the play, I had to do something quick."

"So you ran backwards and headed to the other side of the field?"

"Yes, sir."

"Why?"

"Instinct, sir."

"Instinct?

"Yes, sir. The entire line had shifted, and I knew the left side would be weak. I'm fast enough to cut and run before the defense realizes it. Plus, I'm short enough to hide behind some of the offensive linemen long enough to get around the corner."

Coach narrows his eyes but doesn't say a word. After a long pause, he says, "Slaughter, I've got to be honest with you. When I saw you step onto the field, I thought the scouts had lost their ever-loving minds."

Talk about making a guy feel good. "Uhhhh…thanks?"

"I'm sorry, son. It's just that you're pretty small for a halfback."

"True."

"But I have to tell you when I saw you react under pressure like that, it made me stand up and take notice."

"That's good."

"After watching you for another hour or so, I decided to head upstairs to pull your stats." He sits on the edge of a massive wooden desk. "I have to say, son, your stats are quite impressive."

"Thank you. I'm the number one back in our region, sir."

"Yeah, I saw that, but did you realize that you're number eleven in the entire state for rushing yards?"

"No sir, I didn't have a clue." It surprises me when he tells me this.

He flips through the pages in his hand before laying them on the desk.

"Son, I'm going to be honest with you. It's not our practice to say anything to you boys while you're here. After you leave, if we're interested you'll get a call. If we're not, the phone will never ring."

"I understand, sir."

"But I'm going to go out on a limb here and let you know I think we have a place for you on our team."

My jaw falls to the floor. It's all I can do to contain myself. "Are you serious, sir? Is this a joke?"

"I'm serious as a heart attack, and I never joke. Not about football."

"Thank you, sir. Thank you." I reach out a hand to shake his.

"Don't get too excited just yet. I still have to run the film and your numbers by the other coaches, but from what I've seen from you, and what I know we will need next season, you'd make a good fit."

"I understand. I promise I won't let you down."

"I believe that, son." Coach stands and walks me to the door. "We'll be in touch."

"You don't know what this means to me, sir."

"Oh, I think I do."

"Sir?" The film is still fresh in my mind. "Can you tell me why you ended the highlight reel with my face buried in grass?"

He lets out a chuckle. "Absolutely. It was the third play of the day, and that Tommy kid took you down harder than anyone I've ever seen taken down on one of these days."

"Yeah, I lived it."

Coach laughs. "You got right back up, knocked the grass and dirt out of your helmet and went right back to the line. You've got heart. I've seen guys bigger than you take a hit like that and walk off the field to take a break."

"Believe me, I wanted to."

"But you didn't, and that's what's important."

"So why did you leave it to the end?"

"Because all the boys in the room with you know what you did. They may not ever admit it, but it left them questioning themselves. Wondering if they'd given their all on this field while they were here. If they didn't give their all, they will not get a call. Plain and simple."

A goofy smile forms on my face. "Thanks, Coach."

"You're welcome. Now you know how to get out of here, right?"

"Yes, sir."

"Great. We'll be in touch. Oh yeah, ice your ankle when you get home."

Chapter Eleven

The sun has already dipped behind the Carolina Mountains, and I'm doing my best to stay awake the last hour home. It's all I can do to stay awake.

I pull off the highway at a truck stop, park, and go in for a cup of coffee and a fill-up. I'm not much of a coffee drinker, but I need it to get me through the last sixty miles.

Back on the road, I flip on the radio and turn it up. Mr. Franklin listens to country music like everyone else in Flatbush. An old Merle Haggard song plays, but I don't bother changing the channel. With a twist of the knob, Merle sings as loud as the poor speakers can go.

It's closing in on midnight, and I'm about to explode. The closer I get to home, the more pumped I am to tell Sully how things went today. I replay the day in my head like the highlight reel they had us watch. Pride washes over me once it dawns on me that I walked into a stadium in a city I've never been to and held my own against guys from all over North Carolina.

Another sip of coffee drains the cup. The window is down and cool air blows against my face. The nip in the air tells me we're in for a cold winter.

After stopping by the factory and swapping Mr. Franklin's truck for the green monster, I head over to Sully's for the party.

The guard looks down on me like always. I give a slight nod and he presses the button to open the gate. Football is the great equalizer. No matter who you are, rich or poor, when it comes to football, especially on a winning team, it's like we're all the same. I guess that's why I love it so much. When I'm on the team, I matter.

I park on the street and walk up the driveway to his house. As I near the house, I see empty beer cans scattered across his manicured lawn. Of course, Sully doesn't manicure anything. He has gardeners for stuff like that.

"Slaughter," a voice calls out from behind the tree. As a kid named Danny leans his head around to get a better look, I head toward the door

"Better be careful, Danny. You might freeze to death out here in the cold."

"It ain't that cold.

I've never seen Danny with a girl, but whatever. I head along the sidewalk toward the basement as he yells *partay* at the top of his lungs. Good thing Sully's neighbors aren't close enough to hear Danny or the music blaring from inside the house.

A few girls dance in a group as guys stand around and watch.

"Seen Sully?" I ask one of the girls. By the looks of it, she's not the right person to ask.

"Hey, Slaughter." She moves closer to me. "You all by yourself?"

"Hey, Kelsie. Looks like you're having a good time."

Kelsie asks as she grabs my arm and squeezes. "I'm single again. Me and Danny broke up. Want to take me out tomorrow?" She's had a crush on me forever, but when I compare her to my love for Jenny Lee there's no contest.

"I'm good right now, Kelsie." I push her hand away for the second time. "Thanks for the offer."

"Slaughter, where have you been?"

"What's going on, Franco?"

"Franco? Seriously?"

His real name is Sam, but the first time I ever met the kid he called me Sully instead of Slaughter. So for the past year I've been calling him a different name every time I see him.

"I've been busy today. Any idea where Sully is? Or Jenny Lee and Charlotte?"

"Charlotte's over there." He points to the couch where Charlotte lies passed out. "Not sure where Sully is. He was around here earlier."

"How about Jenny Lee?"

"I think she left. I haven't seen her in a while."

I wade through the sea of bodies and look around for Sully. When I don't see him, I head upstairs. Sully's never been to my house even though I've been to his too many times to count. He knows I'm poor but doesn't care. Around here, most people don't have two pennies to rub together. I joke all the time they should call it Flatbroke, North Carolina, instead of Flatbush.

The house is quiet and dark. The thump of the music in the basement below becomes a dull beat vibrating through the floor.

"Sully," I call out as I open the refrigerator for a bottle of water. "Sully, you up here?"

Nothing but silence. He must be upstairs doing something in his room. Before I head up, I go to the bathroom and empty out the coffee that's been threatening for the past half hour.

I top the stairs and see a flicker of light coming from underneath his door. A nightlight maybe, which means he's not in his room either. As I head down the stairs, a faint sound catches my ear. I listen to make sure it's him. He's in his room after all.

I head back up the steps and down the hall to his room. "Sully, you're not going to believe this," I say as I fling open his bedroom door. I stand in the doorway blown away by what I see.

Chapter Twelve

"Crap!" Sully shouts as he jumps from his bed. I stand paralyzed, stuck between the urge to collapse and the desire to knock the ever-loving snot out of him.

Jenny Lee jumps up but doesn't see me at first. A few moments earlier she was making out with Sully. Her head cocks sideways when she sees me standing in the doorway. "Dusty, listen." She snatches her jacket and comes toward me. "I didn't mean for it to happen. Don't go."

Without a word, I glare at the two of them. The guy who's supposed to be my best friend and my girlfriend. Sully scrambles to get his shirt on as Jenny Lee cries.

I leave through the front door. Sully chases after me. "Slaughter, wait up, man. You have to believe me. I didn't mean for you to see us."

My car gets closer, and I refuse to turn around. I'm afraid if I do, I may end up killing him.

He stands in his yard screaming my name as I crank up the green monster. He throws his head back and runs his hands through his hair. Jenny Lee stands on the front porch with tears streaming down her face.

As I drive away, I curse myself for being so stupid. I trusted them and look what happens. Just like everyone I've trusted, they let me down. Jenny Lee has no problem getting hot and heavy with my best friend, while his girlfriend is passed out downstairs.

I want to puke. My head swims and my pulse quickens. I slow down at the guard gate just enough to give the gate time to open. I mash the gas pedal to the rusted floorboard before it's fully opened and speed away.

Adrenaline courses through my body stronger than any football game I've ever played. It's like my life just got ripped away like a Band-Aid. They're supposed to be my friends. To care about me. I'm supposed to be able to trust them.

Things jumble up in my head as I drive around town in circles, wasting gas. I take the curves in the winding road faster than I know I should, but I don't care. I want to get home and get some sleep. To sleep for days and forget about what I just saw. There's no excuse that can ever make up for what they did to me. It doesn't matter how much they had to drink.

Sully is like my brother, and Jenny Lee has my heart. At least she had my heart. I would do anything for that girl. I loved her from the moment Sully introduced me to her. Life with her is easy most of the time. She was so happy when she introduced me to her dad, because I'm the big football star. The sadness that washed over her face when he told her she better not go out with a bum like me ever again just about crushed me. It was then that I decided I'd show him. I'd show them all I am somebody.

There's an old pickup truck creeping up the hill in front of me, so I whip the green monster around it without even thinking. He blasts his horn and flashes his lights at me, but I don't give a crap. The beauty of the day shatters with the betrayal of the night, and it's all I can do not to cry. I fight the urge but can't hold back the flood of emotion cascading over me. Tears stream down my face and block my vision. I reach into the other seat to grab an old t-shirt to wipe off my face and when I do, there's a car pointed right at me. I grab the wheel and sling the car back into my lane. As soon as I straighten back out, the front tire pops and I lose control.

The green monster skids to the outside edge of the road. I grip the steering wheel tight and jerk the car back on the road. It slingshots me into the other lane and I careen sideways along the centerline. The tires lose their grip and cause me to spin in circles. I slam the brakes hard, but it does no good because I have no control over the green monster. It spins me a final time and spits me off the side of the mountain.

The front end catches a tree and explodes. The sound of crunching metal is louder than anything I've ever heard. Glass shatters and peppers me hard against my face. The car falls for what seems like forever, before landing hard. It rolls over and the roof squeezes in on me like an accordion.

Something presses against my leg and refuses to let go.

I hear a voice from above. "Are you okay?" It sounds like a woman's voice but it's hard to tell.

When everything settles, I realize I'm upside down, staring at my collapsed roof. I can no longer feel my body as I hang limp in the seatbelt.

"I've called the police," the voice calls out again. "Just hang on. Help's on the way."

My head spins and blood drips from my face. It pools on the roof below. It's all I can do to breathe, and my chest hurts when I do. Everything starts to spin and my eyes get heavy. I give everything I have to stay awake, but it's no use. There's nothing I can do but hope somebody gets to me soon.

I think of Mama and then nothing.

Chapter Thirteen

A flicker of light registers in my brain. My eyes press tight like they've been glued shut and it's all I can do to open them even the slightest bit. I think I hear voices, but they sound as if they're in a tube. What sounds like talking is hard to understand.

My brain feels like a scrambled egg, and it's close to impossible for me to piece things together. There's a tightness in my throat making it hard to breathe. It all feels like a dream, like I'm not real.

"Get Dr. Riddell." I hear the same muffled voice more clearly now. "I think he's waking up."

Now I'm certain I can hear her. I think she's talking about me, but I'm not sure. I strain to open my eyes, but all that's there is a sliver smaller than an onion skin. The bright light assaults my eyes.

Cold hands press against my neck. Small hands of a woman. I reach up to touch her with one arm, but it won't move. My body feels frozen. Helpless.

"We need to get it out of him before he wakes." A man enters the room. His voice familiar somehow.

Cold hands squeeze me as pressure increases in my throat. The urge to throw up hits me but nothing will come. It's hard to breathe as the pressure in my throat threatens to suffocate me. Another hand presses against me and tugs at whatever it is I'm choking on. For a few seconds I can no longer breathe, and then all of a sudden a rush of air. I suck in as much as I can and feel my mouth dry like a desert. Immediately, someone places chips of ice in my mouth. I'm too weak to do anything other than let them melt on my tongue.

"Can you hear me?" the same familiar voice asks.

I can hear him and try to speak but nothing comes. In my mind, I'm screaming as loud as I can, but my tongue doesn't move. Why can't they hear me?

Someone takes my hand. "If you can hear me, squeeze my hand." I squeeze as hard as I can. "His grip is weak," the man says, "but he definitely moved his fingers."

"That's wonderful," the woman says. "You hang in there, Dustin. Everything's goin' to be all right now."

She must be talking to me. She calls me Dustin. Is it my name? Dustin?

The name doesn't roll off of my tongue easily. I repeat Dustin in my head over and over again to see if I can remember who Dustin is. My mind is blank.

She pushes more ice into my mouth. It's cold, but feels good. My tongue starts to work. "Wa....ter..." I groan.

"Ice chips is all you can have now, honey," the lady says as she presses more into my mouth.

My eyes open a bit more and I see a thick black woman leaning over me. Her eyes wait for mine to open. "That's it, honey," she says. "Take your time. Miss Bernice is here to help you."

"His vitals are looking good," the man says. I can't see him, but his voice seems to be coming from behind me.

Miss Bernice plops some drops in my eyes. I jerk away and automatic reflex closes them soon after. The soothing liquid burns for a moment, but it helps erase the clouds in my eyes. "Where…am…I?"

"Why, baby, you're at the North Carolina Children's Hospital at Chapel Hill. Been here for goin' on three weeks."

Did I hear her right? Did she say three weeks? "What happened?" I struggle to find my voice.

"You just relax, child. Dr. Riddell will be with you soon enough."

I cut my eyes to the left to see if I can get a look at the man behind me. It's no use, because I can't move my head at all. I look down the bed and see nothing but a white sheet covering me.

"His vitals look good. I'll need to consult with the neurologist to determine if his brain swelling has been reduced." The man talking moves close enough for me to see him. I'm confused because he looks familiar somehow. A man I've seen before but can't quite place. "Dustin, I'm Dr. Riddell. I was on rotation the night you were brought in. I've been assigned your case."

My brain races to put pieces together. I recognize this man but still can't remember who he is.

"Dustin, when I told you I hoped to see you again, I didn't mean under these circumstances. I wanted to see you playing football."

Football. UNC. Things start to swirl together like vegetable soup. Memories flicker in the back of my mind. "I'm a football player." My words are slow, but they are clear.

The doctor nods his head, but wears a sad look. "You are, Dustin. And when you're a little better, you and I will have a talk about football and everything that's happened to you."

"How do you…" I struggle to talk. My throat burns with soreness.

Miss Bernice puts more ice on my tongue. "It's okay, baby. You don't have to do no talkin' now."

But I want to talk. To figure out who I am and what's going on. The doctor is still leaning over me with a stethoscope pressed to my chest. It's cold. "How do you…know me?" My voice strains to rise above a scratchy whisper.

"We met when you were on your way to work out with the Tar Heels."

I scan my memory for his face. For anything. Slowly a vision appears in my head. A gas station parking lot, about to puke. A man and his wife. I picture the doctor without his white jacket and realize Walter is standing above me. "You're Walter."

"I am. Dr. Walter Riddell."

"What happened?"

"We have plenty of time for that, son. You need to get some rest. Miss Bernice here is going to get the order in to get you over to the neurology unit so they can do a CT scan on you later this afternoon. We need to take a look at your brain and make sure it isn't damaged."

He pulls the stethoscope off my chest and pulls the sheet back up to my neck. His cologne hints of the faintest scent of sweetness.

"You're a tough kid, Dustin, but you need your rest. You've got a long road ahead of you, but we're going to get you through this."

He leaves without another word. Miss Bernice stands beside me, holding my hand. "We've tried to get in touch with your mother but haven't had any luck," she says as she lays a hand on my shoulder. "Some of your friends have been by to see you, baby." She points to a shelf off to my left.

I cut my eyes to the side and see several bouquets of flowers, a few teddy bears, and one football. The flowers are wilted. "They're dead."

Miss Bernice sighs. "They came every day for a solid week, Dustin, but you've been here three weeks now. I imagine it's hard for them to make the trip every day." She steps over to the shelf. "They brought you a football," she says as she picks it up. "I believe all your teammates signed it for you, baby."

She places the ball in my lap. My hand inches over to grip it the best I can. Names are scattered all over it with words like "get well" and "see you soon." I spin the ball around and run my eyes over each name, reading all the little notes they've written. One catches my attention and triggers a memory. It says, "So sorry, bro. See you soon." The signature says, "Sully."

The memory of Sully running after me slams hard against my brain. I push the ball away, and Miss Bernice catches it before it falls to the floor. "Everything okay, honey?"

When I refuse to speak, Miss Bernice puts the ball back on the shelf but doesn't push the issue. Sully. His image burns in my mind. The look on his face when I walked in on him and Jenny Lee. A tear rolls from my eye as memories flood like a tidal wave. Everything falls into place. Walter. The tryout. The party. The betrayal. The crash.

Even though I hate myself for wanting to know, I can't help myself. I need to know, so with a quivering lip, I ask Miss Bernice, "Did she come?"

Chapter Fourteen

Miss Bernice leaves me alone, but not before putting one of the teddy bears in my lap. Beside it, she places a card. "She cried every day for a week. If you need anything, baby, you just press this button." Miss Bernice puts a cord with a red button on it in my lap next to the bear, pats my hand, and leaves.

I'm alone with memories of a girl I loved. Someone I thought loved me. The brown bear looks back at me with sad eyes as if it knows how I'm feeling. I pick it up with the one hand that wants to work. The bear feels soft against my skin. It's bigger than the football, with a head that's too large for its body. Its arms come together around the stomach and hold a red heart with the words "I Love You Beary Much!"

Another tear rolls down my face.

The envelope beside the bear has Slaughter written on it. My last name. It's strange, though, because Jenny Lee never calls me anything other than Dusty. I lift the sheet and find a cast covering my right arm. I drop the card and press the call button for Miss Bernice.

Within seconds, the plump woman hurries through the door. "What is it, baby? You okay?"

"I need…help." I push the card on the sheet.

Miss Bernice reaches for the card. "That's all, honey? Miss Bernice is goin' to take care of you." I like the way she talks to me. Like a grandmother who loves me. Miss Bernice digs one of her plump fingers into the envelope and rips it open. She pulls the letter out and puts it in my good hand. "Here you go, baby."

Alone in the room again, I hold my breath and start reading the words as they stare back at me.

Dusty,

I don't know what to say. I don't know if there is anything I can say to let you know how sorry I am. I've cried every night for the past week. I've come down every day hoping you'd wake up. You never did. The doctors all said the same thing. You may not ever wake up. It tears me up inside to think you could be gone forever. If I could go back and change things I would. You have to believe me. I never meant for this to happen. I never meant for you to get hurt. It was stupid. I was stupid.

I press the letter next to my chest, unable to keep reading. Tears continue to roll down my face. Every word I read makes me sad and angry at the same time. Part of me wants to rip the letter to shreds and toss it to the ground like she did to my heart. But I'm not strong enough. Something won't let me.

You have to know Sullivan feels terrible. He blames himself for your accident. He hasn't been the same all week. He won't even look at me or talk to me. I think he blames me, too. Dusty, you need to know I do care about you. And I blame myself for all of this. This will be the last time I come down for a while. I hate seeing you strapped up to all of the machines with a tube down your throat to keep you alive. You're the strongest guy I know and seeing you like this…so helpless and alone…breaks my heart. I've asked Miss Bernice to call me when you wake up. I know you're going to wake up. Just know I'm so sorry and miss you so much. I'm going to leave Wesley bear with you to look after you until you do.

Until….

Jenny Lee

I reach for the buzzer again and press it over and over. Miss Bernice must've been just on the other side of the door, because she's through it in no time. Without saying a word, she reaches for a cloth and wipes my face. After a few minutes, she takes a deep breath and speaks. "You know you gonna be all right, don't ya' honey?" I remain stiff-faced. "The Good Lord done looked out for you, and Miss Bernice is gonna look out for you, too."

A weak smile moves across my face. "Thank you," I whisper.

She reaches down and gives me a hug. I break into uncontrollable sobs and my body convulses in wild fits. My world has fallen apart all around me. People I trusted and cared for have let me down, and

I'm all alone in this empty hospital room. Everyone expected me to die, but I didn't. I'm still here, even though I wish I wasn't. The pain presses down on me and threatens to shove me through the mattress below.

"You can't…" My chest heaves and I gasp for air. "Don't call… her."

Miss Bernice pulls me into her ample chest and rubs my forehead. "Now, now, baby. You gonna be all right. Miss Bernice is here."

"I don't…want to see…her."

"I know you're confused, baby, but that girl been down to see you every day for a week, and I promised her I'd call. I'm sorry, honey, but Miss Bernice don't tell no lies."

"But she…"

"Shhh…just breathe. Don't talk."

Miss Bernice holds me in her arms and rocks me back and forth. She sings a song I've never heard before. I like it and within seconds I calm back down and determine then and there that I'll not shed another tear over anything that happened. I will not give them the satisfaction.

Her soft whisper finds my ear. "Listen, honey. I told the pretty little girl I'd call her when you wake up, but it don't mean I have to call her today. You get some rest, and you and I are goin' to talk about a few things before I call her. There's something you need to know."

Chapter Fifteen

The sun sinks out of sight and another nurse shows up to take Miss Bernice's place. She tells me to call her Nurse Johnson. She's younger, much younger, and looks like she's brand new. She's kind of pretty, but the uniform she wears doesn't help.

"Want me to flip on the TV?" she asks. A simple nod and she flips it on. She stands on her tiptoes to reach it. Cute butt. "Here's the controller." Nurse Johnson puts a wired remote control in my hand. "All you have to do is push these two buttons to change channels. These two for the volume."

I'm the lone patient in the room, so I don't guess I'll disturb anyone when I turn it up. I have to turn the TV up higher than normal just to hear it because my head is wrapped from ear to ear. "What day is it?"

"Wednesday." She grabs a clipboard and starts writing something on the pages. As she walks over to one of the many machines, I hear chirping behind me as she presses buttons. Then she writes down more stuff on the clipboard. "You're doing well," she says to me as she plops the clipboard into the holder at the foot of my bed. "In a few minutes we're going to roll you to the neuro ward for the CT scan ordered for you earlier today. From my experience, I'd bet your swelling has gone down considerably."

Since she doesn't look much older than me, I guess her experience is somewhat limited. It doesn't matter though because I like her. If I've got to be here, at least I've got nice nurses. And this one isn't bad to look at.

"I'll be back to check on you after they get done with you. I'll see if you're up for a little soup by then."

She closes the door. Food is the last thing on my mind until she mentions it. Now I'm hungry and want to eat.

I flip channels for about half an hour. Then there's a knock on the door. "Come in." My strained voice struggles to be heard, but it doesn't stop the nurses from coming in. A couple of dudes stand beside my bed. One pumps his foot on something and the bed shifts. The other picks up the clipboard and scribbles on the pages before tossing it back into the holder.

Minutes later, I'm in another room. "Sorry, buddy," one of the guys says. "Now listen. We're going to inject you with this special kind of dye. It's going to feel weird and make you get all hot inside. And it may make you want to throw up, but do your best to avoid it if you can."

Both men disappear and reappear in a room separated by glass. The table inches toward the giant ring. A buzz and then a voice echoes in my ears. "Dustin, I need you to be as still as a rock when I tell you, okay?"

I give him a thumbs up.

"Okay, here we go." It's hard to tell who is talking over the intercom, but I don't think it's either of the guys. "Try to stay as still as possible." I do. "And hold." I do that, too. It seems like hours pass until one of the guys breaks the silence and says, "Okay, you can move." I'm more than happy to. "How are you feeling?"

I tilt my hand back and forth like so-so. The chemicals they put in my body feel strange. Warm, but not in a good way.

After about half an hour of testing, they wheel me back into the room, lock the brakes on my bed, and wish me good luck. From what I can tell, I'm going to need a lot more than luck.

There are reruns of a show I've only seen once or twice on the TV. I turn up the volume to drown out the voices in my head. Nurse Johnson slips through the door with a tray.

"Is it loud enough for you?"

I fumble with the remote and hit mute but don't say anything.

"Are you hungry?" she asks. I nod. "I've got some beef broth for you."

It's not even close to fine dining, but I take what I can get. She spoons a little bit of the soup into my mouth. It's hot, and I pull away.

"Sorry, Dustin. I'll cool it down for you." She blows on the soup a spoonful at a time. Gradually, it cools enough for me to eat. It's bland, but it's something. "Dustin, tell me a little bit about yourself."

I tell her about playing football and the tryouts at UNC.

Her smile changes to a show of sadness for some reason.

"You've got a girlfriend, I bet."

It isn't exactly a question, but I shake my head no over and over again.

"Sorry, I didn't mean to upset you. I just thought the girl that came every day was your girlfriend."

"She was," I say, "but not anymore."

"Oops. Didn't mean to open a wound." She tosses the spoon in the empty bowl and places it on the tray. "Want a little bit of juice?"

"Please." She leaks a bit of orange juice into my mouth. It tastes like heaven. After I guzzle down the juice, she wipes my mouth with a napkin. "You get some sleep now. Dr. Riddell will be here first thing in the morning to let you know what's going on."

"Okay."

She leaves and I turn the volume back up. I can't concentrate on anything except that night. It replays over and over in my head up to the point where I speed away from Sully's house. The last thing I remember is him standing in the yard yelling for me to stop. When I think about where I am, I wish I had listened.

Chapter Sixteen

The next day, a nurse wakes me up way too early. I expect Miss Bernice to come in at any moment, but she never does. She's been replaced by a new nurse who is all business. She and another lady take my bed from room to room, test to test, but neither one of them says much. Nothing more than what's necessary as part of their job.

By lunchtime, my stomach growls. "When can I eat?" My throat feels much better, and my voice somewhat stronger.

"I'm afraid it'll be a few more hours. Most of the tests they're running have to be on an empty stomach." The nurse finishes her paperwork and leaves me alone in my room again. She didn't even bother handing me the TV remote.

All I can think of is the scene replaying in my head. I do my best to wipe it away, but it keeps playing over and over again, like a movie stuck in a loop. At least the television helps distract me some.

The final moments of that night are engrained in my memory. As I struggle to forget about Jenny Lee, Walter walks in.

"How's it going, Dustin?"

He's such a nice man and I don't want to upset him, but I feel like I need to tell him that nobody calls me Dustin. It feels weird. "Walter," I say but he stops me.

"Dustin, I'm afraid that while you're in the hospital and are a patient of mine, you'll need to call me Dr. Riddell. It's one of those formalities that has to remain intact. Otherwise, the nurses and other hospital staff may get lax."

I totally get it. If I hadn't met him already and known him as Walter, I would've already been calling him doctor. This is a good chance to tell him what I'd like him to call me. "No problem, Doc." He eyes me. "I mean, Dr. Riddell. Ummm…Dr. Riddell, nobody calls me Dustin. I've never been called that as long as I can remember."

"Oh?" He sits in the chair next to my bed.

"Most people call me Slaughter. The only people who call me Dusty are Mama and…" I freeze. Dr. Riddell looks at me funny. "Only Mama."

"I'll be happy to call you Slaughter. Not a problem at all. Great football name anyhow."

"Yeah."

"Speaking of your mother," Dr. Riddell says, "we tried to get her to come down, but she wouldn't. She did, however, give us permission to treat you for as long as we need to."

It doesn't surprise me that Mama won't come down to the hospital. "Yeah, she's pretty busy," I say, even though I'm sure he doesn't believe me.

"That brings me to another question, Slaughter." Dr. Riddell tosses one leg over the other and leans back in the metal-framed chair. "So do you remember anything?"

"Well…yeah…I guess so."

"You remember your family and childhood and friends and such?"

Friends? At this point I'm not even sure I know what friends are. They're certainly not people who make out with your girlfriend when you're not there.

"Yes, sir. I remember."

"That's a good sign." Dr. Riddell leans forward with his arms resting on his knees. "We'll have the results back later today or tomorrow on your brain function scans. I'm hopeful that things are normal."

"There is one thing, though."

"What's that Slaughter?" Dr. Riddell takes a long pause and chews on his lip.

"I don't remember much about the accident."

"You don't?"

I shake my head.

"Not everything?"

"No, not all of it."

"What's the last thing you do remember?"

I don't want to go into detail about what I do remember, so I decide to keep my answer short about leaving the party. "I remember swerving away from headlights and the crunch of the car squeezing against my leg.

"That's it?"

"And I remember the sound of the glass breaking and hanging upside down in my car. That's the last thing." I feel like I'm letting Walter down. "I am trying to remember, Dr. Riddell. I promise."

"Slaughter, don't beat yourself up about it. It's not at all uncommon to forget some things after a traumatic accident involving a brain injury. I'm just pleased as punch that you remember everything else. We were afraid for about a week or so there, that you'd lost all brain function. We didn't know if you'd even come out of your coma."

I close my eyes and let a deep puff of air escape. It's not easy hearing that I was in a coma and almost didn't even wake up.

The same nurse comes through the door with a tray of food and sets it on the table next to me. Soup and juice again. This time there are a few crackers. "I'll come back," she says.

"Let me ask you another question, and I need you to be honest with me."

"Okay. Anything."

"Were you drinking alcohol that night? In all the chaos nobody thought to get a blood sample for testing. Believe me, someone's head is going to roll for that mistake."

"I didn't have a drop." Maybe if I did drink there'd be more of an excuse for my accident. "Everyone else was, but I just got to the party, stayed about a half an hour, then left. I swear."

"I believe you, son."

"Will I eventually remember how it all happened?"

"That's hard to say. You might, or it could be a memory lost forever."

"Can you at least tell me about the accident? The parts that you know about?"

"Yeah, I suppose I can." Walter leans back in his chair again like a man about to tell a story to his kids. "Pretty simple. You were on one of the mountain roads, lost control and dropped about twenty-five feet after hitting a darned big oak tree."

"My car?"

"It doesn't look like a car any longer. It hit and rolled over several times, and eventually came to rest on the roof. Like you said, you hung upside down for a good long while. It took the paramedics a considerable amount of time to get to you."

"Sounds terrible."

"Let me just put it this way. If they hadn't gotten you on the helicopter when they did. If they'd been another ten or fifteen minutes getting you to me." He stops like someone who has a secret that he doesn't want to share.

I make it easy for him. "I'd be in the ground instead of this gown?"

"Well, I don't want to think about it like that, but yeah, you'd have died."

"I got lucky, I guess."

"That's enough for today." Dr. Riddell gets up and moves to the door.

It's pretty clear that I'm busted up. A cast on my right arm. My left leg is in some funny contraption, and my chest is killing me. But nobody has told me what's wrong with me. "Dr. Riddell?" He looks over his shoulder and waits for me to speak. "How long will I be in these casts? When can I get back on the field?" It's a pretty stupid question, I know, because the season is almost over, but I have to ask.

"We'll talk about all of that soon enough. Let's wait until all the tests come back."

Something in the way he speaks lets me know it's not good.

Chapter Seventeen

I'm sick of being stuck in this bed and unable to move. The good news is that my voice is back to normal and the bandages have been removed from my head. They let me look at myself in the mirror, and it doesn't look as bad as I expected. Several cuts from where the glass splattered against my face, but all in all, not too bad. Walter says that I'm lucky and most gashes will heal nicely, though he thinks that the one on my forehead will leave a scar after the stitches are removed. I just tell him it'll make me look tougher on the field.

Every time I bring up football or getting some exercise or having the casts removed, his behavior changes. His smile washes away, and all he tells me is that we need to hope for the best. Problem is that he won't tell me what the worst is. I've got a few ideas. I'm pretty certain the rest of the season is toast. I'll workout even harder during spring training to be ready for UNC.

That reminds me that the coaches at UNC were going to call me. I press the call button.

"What do you need, Dusty?" I ask Nurse Johnson to call me by my last name. Heck, I ask everyone to call me that.

"Do you know anything about whether or not I got a call from UNC?"

"Not a clue. I can check the nurses' station to see if you have any messages."

"They don't know I'm here." I push the end of a wire coat hanger into the contraption on my leg and scratch. "It would be on my cell."

"Give me a sec'." She zips out and back again. "They said you don't have a cell phone here."

"What's that supposed to mean?" The hanger is poking my leg in all the right places. "It was in my car."

"I guess they didn't recover your phone from the accident scene." She pulls the pillow from underneath my head and fluffs it before putting it back. "That's not uncommon in auto accidents, I'm afraid. Things get slung all over the place."

"All right." I stop scratching my leg but leave the hanger right where it is.

"You need anything else before you go to sleep?"

"Yeah, can you tell me what day it is?"

"Sunday," Nurse Johnson says. "Now get some sleep."

It's hard to rest. Lying around in a hospital bed is the single-most boring thing I've ever done. Not much goes on around this place, and being stuck in a bed makes it even worse. I fidget through the night and fall asleep sometime before morning, I think, but can't be sure. There aren't any clocks in my room either.

"Rise and shine, honey!" Miss Bernice makes one heck of an entrance, and I nearly jump out of bed. "Careful. I don't want you to break anything." She finds her comment more amusing than I do and lets out a big ol' belly laugh.

"Miss Bernice." I wipe the sleep from my eyes and am slow to speak. "What time is it?"

"Early, baby. Six-thirty." She pulls the curtain back to let the sun stream through the dirty window. "You got yourself a big day today."

"I do?"

"Child, yes. You're on the road to recovery, baby." She whips around to the foot of the bed, grabs my chart, writes something, and puts it back. I wish someone would tell me what all the writing means, but they never do.

She's gone before I open my eyes good. The best thing to happen to me in a few days is to have Miss Bernice come through my door. Although, it would've been nice of her to wait a few more hours.

She's back a few minutes later with a plate of eggs, some fruit, a piece of toast, and some apple juice. For a larger woman she sure moves fast.

"You must be hungry this mornin', Dustin."

"Super hungry," I say as I shove pieces of scrambled eggs in my mouth. "And you can call me Slaughter, Miss Bernice."

"It ain't polite to talk with your mouth full, baby. Didn't your mama teach you that?" She gives me one of those looks with one eyebrow raised. What Miss Bernice doesn't know is that Mama never taught me much of anything. I had to teach myself. "And what's with all this Slaughter business?"

"Sorry, Miss Bernice," I say, after washing down the egg with a swig of juice. "It's my last name. It's what most people call me."

"Most? Not all?"

"No, ma'am. Mama and…" I freeze again, refusing to say her name. "Mama calls me Dusty."

Miss Bernice squints her eyes, gives me a look of suspicion and says, "Ummm hmmm."

"I'm serious. I've never been called Dustin. Ever."

"How about I call you Dusty then, like your mama does? And whoever else it is you don't want to talk about."

"That'd be fine."

"I'm probably going to call you baby or honey most of the time, though. It's what I call all my babies."

That I believe.

She moves around the room like a hummingbird, flitting from here to there. Jotting down notes as she looks at the various monitors they keep me plugged into.

"Did you call her yet?"

"Who, baby?"

"You know who. You just want me to say it."

"That pretty little girlfriend of yours?"

"She ain't my girlfriend no more."

"I know, baby." Miss Bernice sits in the chair beside my bed. "That's what I need to talk to you about. See, I promised that girl I'd call her when you woke up, and Miss Bernice don't tell no lies. But after I told her that, I heard her and that boy who came to see you a few times talking one night." She scratches her head. "Come to think of it, I think that was the last time either of them came to check on you."

"What'd he look like?"

"He's a good lookin' boy, but not near as handsome as you, honey."

"Sully."

"Yeah, that sounds about right. Anyhow, they got to talkin' and didn't pay no attention to ol' Bernice when I come walkin' in to check on you."

"What were they talking about?" I push the tray of half eaten food off to the side and raise the bed a little more to get a better look at Miss Bernice.

"He was saying that it's gotta stop and she was asking him why. He didn't give specifics, honey, but I put the pieces together and figured things out. Not hard to do when you're my age."

Miss Bernice knows that I know what they were talking about, too.

"They acted like it wasn't the first time, but he wants it to be the last. She wasn't going for it, though. Said that she'd tell his girlfriend if he don't tell her first. That girl don't seem like she's too nice. Not nice enough for my baby." Miss Bernice pats my hand.

"Thanks, Miss Bernice."

"Tell me something else, baby."

Miss Bernice has a way of making me want to spill my guts about everything. "Anything."

"Them folks ain't much like me and you, is they?"

"What's that s'posed to mean?"

"They smell like they're made out of money. Me and you ain't."

If she only knew how right she is about me.

"Yeah, I thought so." She stands up. "That boy seems like he's hurting though."

"He should be."

"I know you're hurting, too, baby. I don't know all the details about what went on that night, but I believe I pieced together a pretty good picture, and it don't do nobody no good to hold on to hate in their hearts."

"Yeah, okay." It isn't exactly hate floating around in my heart, but it isn't exactly love either. Somewhere closer to I don't ever want to see them again. But since Miss Bernice don't tell no lies, I guess I'm going to have no choice in the matter. Not like I can get up and run away.

"Take it one day at a time, baby." She reaches out her hand and rubs my forehead. "Forget all that mess for now and worry about Dusty. You got to take care of him first."

I give her a half-hearted nod.

"They're goin' to take you down to Dr. Riddell around nine. I'm goin' to make my rounds then come back later to get you put into your new wheelchair."

Miss Bernice pauses a minute so her words can sink into my thick skull. "Wheelchair?"

"Starting today, you're going to be mobile. And you're going into a different room."

"But you'll check on me?"

"Yes, baby. I don't let none of my children stay in this hospital without checking on them." She pats my good leg. "'Sides, you're going to be mobile. You can come check on me." She lets out another big ol' belly laugh that makes me smile.

Chapter Eighteen

Thank goodness I have a TV, or I'd be bored for the two hours they make me wait before coming to get me.

The same two male nurses that took me for scans come through the door pushing a wheelchair. Miss Bernice pours in right behind them. "Told you we're goin' to get you rollin', baby. Kyle and Dave are goin' to take care of you."

"Hey, Dustin," Kyle says.

Miss Bernice corrects him. "Call him Slaughter."

Dave looks at the paperwork in his hand. "Cool last name. I didn't put two and two together when we came to get you the other day."

"I bet you thought it was about how bad my accident was."

"No way, Slaughter," Kyle says. "You aren't that bad."

"We've seen way worse," Dave says.

"They're goin' to put you down in that chair and wheel you over to Dr. Riddell's office." Miss Bernice stands beside me all excited like I'm about to open a birthday present and she just has to watch.

"I'm not going to lie to you," Dave says as he starts unhooking me. "Some of this is going to hurt."

"We're going to try to be gentle and let the bed down as low as we can, but it's not going to be easy." Kyle steps on something that starts lowering my bed. "We're going to need your help, Slaughter." He pauses and repeats my last name. "I like the sound of that."

Miss Bernice slaps her palms together and presses them to her lips like she's praying. "It's okay, Miss Bernice. Don't you worry none. I'm tough."

"I worry about all my babies, baby."

She holds her breath as Kyle and Dave jostle me around. I help the best I can, but my body still aches all over. I bite my lip to help ease the pain. It helps some, but not enough.

After what seems like forever, I'm in the chair and ready to roll. The chair has a long platform to support my leg, since the contraption on it won't bend. Kyle pushes me along the hallway. "Much busier this morning."

"Always is on a Monday, baby." Miss Bernice asks them to stop for a second. They do. "Listen, honey." Her voice gets serious all of a sudden. "When you go talk to Dr. Riddell, I want you to understand that you're going to get better. Got it?"

I'm confused, but I say yes.

"You got pretty banged up in that car wreck of yours, and we weren't sure if you were goin' to make it."

I nod again.

"So when Dr. Riddell tells you about your injuries, I want you to know that you're goin' to make it through your recovery just fine." She puts my hand in hers.

She's starting to scare me a little bit. "I know it's going to take some time. I'll be fine."

"Okay, baby." She lets go of my hand and looks at Kyle. "Y'all go on now."

Without another word, Kyle and Dave whisk me away to Dr. Riddell's office. There's a plaque on his door that reads, DR. WALTER RIDDELL, TRAUMA SURGEON.

A quick knock on the door, but they don't wait for an answer. Kyle opens it up and Dave wheels me in. Walter's sitting behind a giant wooden desk, wearing a blue shirt with a red tie.

"Slaughter. Welcome to my office." He stands and walks around the oversized desk and shakes my good hand. "Gentlemen, will you shut the door on the way out?"

"See you later, Slaughter." Kyle says as he pulls the door shut.

"Slaughter, I've got to discuss a few things before we get started on your road to recovery."

Walter's tone is deathly serious. He sits back down, and I stare at the diplomas hanging on the wall behind him.

"Here at the Children's Hospital, we are obligated to take care of your injuries whether or not you can pay. We have some generous donors who help the hospital offset some of its costs."

"That's good, 'cause I'm sure you already know I don't have a dime."

Dr. Riddell doesn't even bother acknowledging my comment and keeps on talking. "As I told you before, we reached out to your mother. Your coach came to us and said he's tried to get your mom to come down, but she won't. He didn't elaborate as to why, and quite frankly, it's none of my business. My business is putting kids like you back together."

Coach knows why, but I'm glad he didn't air our dirty laundry. "Okay. And?"

"What I'm trying to tell you is that even though you're family can't pay, you're still my patient, and it's my job to make sure you're put back together as best we can before you leave here."

"Are you saying I'm going to be here for months?"

"That's precisely what I'm saying. Now that you're awake, your coach has gone ahead and made arrangements for someone from your school to come work with you each week, so you can stay on track to graduate."

If Coach has done that, then the whole school must know I'm awake now. Miss Bernice doesn't even have to call Jenny Lee to tell her, because the gossip will spread like wildfire.

"I need to lay out a map of where we are and where we're going for the next few months."

"That would be great. I feel like I'm in the dark."

"I need you to understand that you're alive, and that's the best thing ever, but your injuries are extensive and will require some major rehabilitation."

"Not a problem. I can work out every day if necessary. I'll do whatever I can to get back on the field. UNC said I did great and they were going to call. I bet they already did, but my phone got lost in the accident."

"Slaughter, I need you to listen to me."

He leans forward in his seat and stares at me with steel blue eyes. Everything about Walter becomes serious.

"I'm listening."

"You're not going to be on the football field."

"I know it won't be soon, but—"

Dr. Riddell holds up a hand. "It won't be at all, Dustin."

My head gets light and the room spins. I feel like I'm floating or falling or something. My breathing stops and my pulse quickens. I must've misunderstood him. "What do you mean, at all?"

"What I'm trying to tell you, Dustin, is that your leg was badly damaged in the accident, and I worked as hard as I could to save it."

"Save it?"

"It was almost severed in two."

The leg sticking straight out and swallowed up by some sort of giant cast with rods poking out looks back at me and laughs. I can't feel anything from the knee down, but I never imagined anything like that.

"But it's not?"

"No, we were able to reattach it and blood is flowing, so it'll begin to heal. But, Dustin, I'm not sure you'll be able to walk on it again. You will never run on it."

Walter's words hit me like a sledgehammer slamming into my chest. I can't breathe or think. I can't even look at him for several long minutes. He waits patiently as I gather my thoughts and find the words.

"Dr. Riddell," I say, but he stops me.

"Call me Walter in here."

"Walter, you and I had a real strange encounter." He nods in agreement. "I'm not the religious kind, and I don't know what all that means, but I do know one thing." He sits in silence and waits for me to continue. "I'm a fighter. Have been my whole life. Had no other choice, because my dad's in jail, and Mama's an addict." Walter has no reaction whatsoever. It makes me wonder if he already knows. "My only shot out of that rat hole of a town is football, and if that's gone, I don't have anything. I'm going to end up cleaning crap out of the toilet at the local factory for the rest of my life."

"Dusty, there are many other things besides football for you to explore."

"That's where you're wrong. Football's all I've got," I scream. He waits for me to get everything out of my system. "I'm going to work my butt off and show you and everyone else here that I will walk again. I'll run. And I will play football."

"Dusty, I don't know what that encounter in the gas station parking lot means either, but I'm going to tell you one thing. When they wheeled you into the ER that night, on the one overnight shift of the month I have to pull in rotation and it was you, I have to tell you that I made it my mission to make sure you lived. That was my primary goal. The leg was secondary. Thankfully, we saved it. I believe I was meant to be there for you that Saturday morning. And again the same night."

His words make me feel better, but I don't think he believes that I will walk again.

"Thanks, Walter," I say. "I think I just want to go to my room and think about everything."

"I understand."

Chapter Nineteen

Weeks pass, and I get better at moving around the hospital. They took the cast off my arm a week ago. My leg is still wrapped up tight, but I go to physical therapy once a day for an hour to work on strengthening my injured arm. It got pretty chewed up from the wreck, and I have a few scars that will never go away. Good thing for me one's at the shoulder, so it won't be noticeable most of the time. The one on my hand will be permanent, Dr. Riddell says, though it'll weaken with time.

I'm now able to use both hands to wheel myself around and can get in and out of my bed by myself, too. It's not easy, because the bed is still kind of high, but I manage.

Miss Bernice comes to check on me every day. At least on the days she's here. She told me a couple of weeks ago that she did call Jenny Lee and told her I was up and about. Jenny Lee still hasn't visited.

It makes me wonder why not. Nobody from school stops by to check on me. The lady that comes once a week to give me new school work and take the work I've completed back is pretty nice, though.

Between all of the schoolwork and rehab, I stay pretty busy, but Miss Bernice brought me one of those artist's sketchbooks and some pencils. She tells me that in her experience, drawing—or in my case, doodling—can help in the recovery. My right hand got ripped up a bit and needed stitches. Dr. Riddell says my fine motor skills have been impacted. I'm not sure what it all means, but Miss Bernice says the pencils will help. "If nothing else," she says, "it'll help your brain heal." And she doesn't mean from the wreck. She's talking about the dark times I have here. When I don't feel like getting out of bed.

I'm not much of an artist, but I give it a whirl. Some of the stuff I draw starts to look like what it's supposed to. My room. An apple. A bird. Little things like that.

I'm in the middle of creating a masterpiece when Miss Bernice walks in and busts me.

She looks over my shoulder because I made the mistake of being parked with my back to the door. "Now, honey, what you drawin' there?"

I press the sketchbook to my chest. "Just a drawing. Nothing special."

"You tellin' me that ol' Bernice ain't nothin' special?"

She knows. That lady has the eyes of a hawk.

"I was just tryin' to—"

She holds out a hand. "I've already seen it. Might as well let me get a good look at it, Michelangelo."

I reluctantly let her have the sketchbook.

"You're quite an artist, baby." Miss Bernice puts her glasses on. They hang on one of those chains when she isn't reading anything.

"Yeah, yeah." She looks at me over the top of her glasses. "I didn't mean nothin' by it, Miss Bernice."

"What're you talkin' 'bout, baby." She hands the drawing back to me. "You've got talent. This is a beautiful nurse. If I didn't know better, I'd think you drew a picture of me." She gives a devious grin because she knows it's a picture of her.

"You like it?"

"Yeah, baby, I like it. You've got some real artistic blood in them veins of yours."

"I might do some doodling, but I'm no artist."

"Well, you may not be no Picasso, but you got some talent. More than me. 'Sides, that woman you drew is beautiful, if I say so myself." She plops down in the chair beside me. "How's your rehab goin'?"

"All right, I reckon."

"Dr. Riddell's nurse says you're workin' real hard."

"I am, but I don't know what good it's doing me. At least not until they get this thing off my leg." I slap the contraption. "That's when the real rehab starts. I need to get back on that field, Miss Bernice. It's all I've got."

"I know, baby, but I want you to understand one thing."

"What's that?"

"You need to be thankful you're alive. Be glad the man upstairs spared you."

"If I can't walk or play football, then what good is it? I'll be stuck in this stupid wheelchair forever."

"Just be positive, and good things'll come."

"If I'm not able to play football, then nothing good can come."

"Let's just get you walkin' again and go from there." She presses her hands on the rails of the chair to help lift herself to her feet. "You know there's life after football."

"Not for me, there isn't."

Miss Bernice chuckles before leaving me alone. It's getting close to dinnertime, and I'm hungry. The food isn't great, but I'm at least eating real food now.

"How's it going, Slaughter?" A voice booms from behind me, and I immediately know who it is.

Without turning around I say, "Hey, Coach."

I put the sketchpad down and spin my chair to see him. "Your doctor says you're doin' much better."

My eyes fall to the contraption surrounding my left leg. "A few more weeks, and I get to remove this painful thing and see how my leg is."

Coach drops his eyes to the floor. "Yeah, I heard about that. I'm sorry, Slaughter."

"It's okay, Coach. I'll be on the field by spring."

"Son, the doctor says that your football days are over." Coach points to the chair across the room. "Mind if I sit?"

"Not at all. Mi casa es su casa." Coach takes a seat. "I guess my Spanish homework is kicking in."

Coach gives an unimpressive laugh. "Slaughter, I think you need to take a good look at the reality of what you're facing."

"I am, Coach. I'm getting back on that field by spring."

Coach lets out a slight huff. "Dusty, I need you to understand what's goin' on here. The doctor says you're lucky to be alive to start with."

"Yeah, yeah, he told me the same thing."

"Then I assume he told you that you'd be lucky to walk again. And that's the best case scenario."

"Yeah, but they don't know, Coach. You know me." Coach nods. "You know how hard I work. You know that if anybody can do it, it's me."

"I know, Slaughter, but I'm afraid you're not hearin' what that doctor's tellin' you."

"I've heard it all." I throw the sketchbook across the room. "I'm sick of people telling me I'm lucky to be alive. Lucky if I walk again. And I sure don't want to hear that football is over."

"Believe me, son, I understand."

"No, you don't. Nobody understands." Coach stares at me. "Coach, you know me. You know my life. If I don't have football, then I don't have anything. I'll be another bum working at Sully's dad's factory. I can't do that. I want more than that."

Coach takes a long pause before saying anything. "I know you don't, son. I know. But you're going to have to understand that your life has changed. You're going to have to realize that football…at least as a player…is out of the question."

"What're you saying? Coaching?"

"At least you'll be close to the game you love."

Coach's words swirl around in my head. "Not good enough, Coach. I'm a player. The best player in North Carolina. I'm going places."

"You were, Dusty." Coach calls me Dusty for the second time. I can't remember a time he's ever called me Dusty. "The coaches from UNC called me a couple of weeks ago."

"Yeah? What did they say?"

"They said they wanted you. They had a scholarship they needed to talk to you about, and tried to get in touch with you several times on your phone but only got your voicemail."

"What'd you tell them, Coach?"

Coach's voice softens like I've never heard before. "I told them the truth. I told them you got into a bad wreck the night of your workout with them."

"Did you tell them I'd be back soon?"

"Like I said, Dusty, I told them the truth." It's clear that Coach is having a hard time with all of this. His eyes go dim and his breathing slows.

"What did they say?"

"The coach said they were terribly sorry to hear about it, and that you're in their prayers."

"That's it? I'm in their prayers?"

"What else do you want, Dusty?" Coach's voice trembles as he speaks. "They withdrew their offer for a scholarship, son."

I drop my head into my hands and fight the urge to scream or cry or whatever it'd take to make this pain and misery go away. Instead, I sit in silence.

"You have to understand, Dusty."

"I don't have to understand anything. I don't have to understand why my father killed the preacher's wife. I don't have to understand why Mama loves pills and alcohol more than her own flesh and blood. And I sure don't have to understand why this happened to me."

Coach stands and moves next to my chair. My face is still buried in my hands. I feel his meaty paw on my head. "Son, I know you're about to lose your mind with all of this. Believe me, I get it a lot more than you think. You're a good kid, Dusty, and you're turning into one heck of a great man. And I know you've been dealt a horrible hand, but you've got to fight through all of this. You're going to get through this, I promise. I know it doesn't seem like it now, but you will."

I look at Coach. "For what? What will I have when I *get through this*?"

"Dusty, I wish I knew. Heck, son, I'm just a football coach. The only answers I have are on that field."

"That's me too, Coach."

"But you're young and have your whole life ahead of you."

"What kind of life will it be if I can't walk?"

"Then that's your first challenge. Work as hard as you can and get on your feet. One foot in front of the other, son. Something will happen."

Coach is doing his best to cheer me up. He's a good man, and I'm sure it stinks as much for him as it does for me, so I change the subject and ask about how the team's doing. He tells me of the first game they lost after my accident, but after that, they won every game they played. He tells me how he broke down when he heard about my accident, and how he'll never find another player who has as much heart for the game as I do.

Before he leaves, he agrees to send down the game footage for me to watch.

He starts for the door but stops to take one last look. "Remember what I said, son. Get on your feet. And then worry about the next step."

Coach vanishes from the doorway, leaving me with the memories of my old life.

Chapter Twenty

I'm sick and tired of the scenery on my floor, so I wheel myself to the elevator before anyone can say anything.

I press buttons and head up a few floors because I have no idea where to go. The tenth floor catches my attention with its bright colors, so I wheel myself out of the elevator and take a peek around. I push myself down a hall and pass several rooms with kids in each of them. Makes sense, considering I'm in a kid's hospital.

Something catches my eye as I pass one particular room. I back up and see a kid with a Tar Heel hat on his bald head. It catches me off guard when I realize which floor I'm on. My stare must've caught the baldheaded kid in the blue Tar Heel hat by surprise, too, because he looks up and without cracking a smile says, "Take a picture, it'll last longer."

My jaw drops to the floor, and words will not come.

"Well?" He lets the book he's reading fall into his lap.

"Uhhh…I'm…" I don't know what to say. "I'm sorry, I didn't mean…" I fumble with the wheels on my chair. "It's just that I noticed your hat."

The kid cuts his eyes up to the bill. "You like the Tar Heels?"

The conversation with Coach is fresh on my mind, along with the dream that shattered like my leg. "Yeah, I love them. Always have."

"I never miss a game. I'm going to school there when I get old enough."

"Yeah?"

"Definitely. My sister goes there now. She's a freshman."

"I'm Dusty. Dusty Slaughter, but you can call me Slaughter. That's what most people call me."

"I'm Anderson Thacker, but I like Andy. Nobody calls me Andy, though. Mom and Dad always say if that's what they wanted to call me they would've named me Andy. My parents are weird."

"Nice to meet you, Andy." I notice that Andy is wearing a blue bathrobe, darker blue than Tar Heel blue, over pajamas with all kinds of balls on them. Soccer balls, footballs, baseballs, basketballs, and tennis balls. "You like sports?" I ask as I point to his pajamas.

"Love them."

"Me too," I say. "Which sports to you play?"

Andy gives me a strange look. Almost like he's embarrassed to say anything. "I've never played sports."

"Never?"

"Nope." He pulls his hat off and rubs his bald head. "I've never been healthy enough to learn, but I love to watch."

"Sorry about that."

"Do you play anything?" Andy asks, then immediately catches himself. "I'm sorry. I didn't notice your leg."

It strikes me as funny that this kid doesn't notice the big cast on my leg as it sticks out in front of me like a sword. "It's all right, Andy. This is new." I pat my leg, trying to make him feel better. He obviously has things much worse than me. "I'm a football player." I correct myself. "I was a football player."

"You'll play again one day, right?"

I love his confidence, but I'm starting to believe what Coach and Walter keep telling me. "I'm not sure, buddy. My doctor and Coach say that my playing days are over."

"That stinks."

"More than you know. I worked out with UNC a few weeks ago, and they were going to offer me a scholarship."

"They changed their minds?"

"Once they found out about my leg, Coach says they withdrew their offer. I just found out about an hour ago."

"I'm sorry, Slaughter." Andy gets up from his seat and crosses over to me and sticks out his hand like a grownup. "Nice to meet you, Slaughter."

"Nice to meet you, too, Andy." I shake his tiny little hand. "How old are you?"

"Eight. I'll be nine just before Thanksgiving." He smiles. "Small for my age, huh?"

Even though he is, I lie and say, "Nah, man." I grab his tiny little arm. "Feel these muscles. Almost as big as mine."

His smile grows even bigger. "Think so?"

"Man, I know so."

"You're not on my floor are you, Slaughter?"

"Nope. Got bored on the seventh floor, so I went exploring."

He laughs. "It can get boring around here. That's for sure. I've been here forever."

"How long?"

"This time, I've been here for a month. But I'm here all the time it seems. I get better then I get worse. I'm feeling pretty good right now, so I hope Mom and Dad will take me home soon."

"Do they come to see you?"

"Every day. They just left. My sister comes about three or four times a week, too. That is, when she's not too busy studying for school."

"That's good."

"What about your parents?"

There is no way I can tell this kid about my parents. I want to lie but can't bring myself to mislead him. "They don't come around too much."

"Can I tell you a secret, Slaughter?" Andy lowers his voice like everyone is listening. "I like that name, by the way. Sounds tough."

"Thanks."

"That's not what I was going to say, though. Sorry about that." He lowers his voice again. "I kind of wish Mom and Dad didn't come all the time to see me."

I can't understand why he wouldn't want to see his parents. I can't imagine being eight years old and living in a hospital for weeks or months at a time. Seems like it would get scary or lonely or whatever it gets for an eight year old.

"You don't?" I whisper back.

He continues to keep his voice down so nobody else will hear. "It makes them sad when they're here. Mom always cries before she leaves."

My heart sinks a little when I think about what he says. "That must be tough."

"Hey," he says much louder. "Want to watch the Tar Heel game with me? It comes on at six."

"For sure. Where do you watch it?"

"In the TV room, silly."

He walks over to the bookshelf and places the little book in his hand back on the shelf.

"You like to read?"

"Yeah, I come here all the time. They always have lots of good books. The bad thing is they never have books about sports or anything." He's back at my wheelchair. "But it's okay, because I love to read. It helps me escape from this hospital, even if it is only in my imagination."

"Makes sense."

"Come on."

I follow Andy down the hall. As I roll along, a nurse exits a room off to the right. "Anderson, what are you doing? Who is this?"

"My friend Slaughter," he says as if we've been best buds for years.

"Slaughter, huh?" She stares at me hard. "Which floor are you supposed to be on, Slaughter?"

"Seven."

"How'd you get here?"

"He was bored and went exploring. He found me." Andy is in good spirits for a boy in his condition. "We're going to watch the Tar Heels destroy the Yellow Jackets."

The nurse purses her lips, and I get ready to be told to get back to my floor. "Georgia Tech doesn't stand a chance against our boys do they, Anderson?"

"No way, Angela. My sister is going to be at the game. Did I tell you that?"

"No, sir, you did not. Is that why she didn't come see you today?"

"I think so, but I don't know."

"Slaughter, what's your real name?"

"It's Dustin Slaughter, ma'am."

"He goes by Slaughter, Angela. Isn't that cool?"

"Absolutely. The coolest, but I have to make sure they know where Dus—" Andy waves a correcting finger at Angela. "I need to let them know that Slaughter is up here and make sure it's all right."

"Thanks, Angela."

"You boys go watch the game, and I'll be back in a little bit after I go downstairs and talk to his nurses."

"Come on, Slaughter, let's get a seat before the other kids get here."

"I don't have to be in a rush." I pop a wheelie in my chair. "I've already got a place to sit."

Angela and Andy both laugh.

Chapter Twenty-One

Their room is pretty cool. A few couches, some books, a table with puzzles, and a chest of toys in the corner. The Jackets lead the Tar Heels by a touchdown at the half. Andy is about to come unglued. I've never seen a kid as into football as this kid is. He quotes stats on the players, like their rushing yards, touchdowns, passing and receiving yards. I compare the stats he spits out to my own numbers and wonder how I'd do if I had the chance to take the field during a real game.

"Want a Coke, Slaughter?" Andy hops off of the oversized leather couch. "I'm thirsty and have to go to the bathroom."

"I could use a drink."

"Guess you're not in trouble, since Angela didn't come back and throw you out."

"Guess not." Andy stands in front of me doing the pee-pee dance. "Better get a move on before you bust a pipe."

He disappears, leaving me with about six other kids around his age. Some have hair and others don't. A little girl named Katie comes over to me and pokes my cast. She can't be much older than five or six.

"Why do you wear this?" Her green eyes squint together slightly. She wears a purple bandana with sparkly stones on it and drags a pink blankie behind her.

"Cause my leg's busted up."

"How?"

"I was in a car wreck." About the time I answer her question, Andy is back with a couple of plastic cups of Coke.

"Did it hurt?" Katie asks as Andy hands me my cup.

"To tell you the truth, Katie, I can't remember much of the wreck." She looks at me funny. "My brain can't remember it."

"Does this one hurt?" Katie puts her hand on my good knee.

"Nope. This one is good as new."

She almost knocks the soda all over my chest as she climbs onto my knee and situates herself in my lap. "Why does he call you Slaughter?"

"That's my name."

"Sounds funny," Katie says as she twists her fingers around my shaggy hair. My heart sinks and I wonder what she must think about being bald. The answer seems obvious, so I don't say anything. Holding her in my lap reminds me how blessed I am.

"It does, doesn't it, but it's my name." Andy points his finger at Katie and then at his head and rotates it in a circle letting me know that he thinks she's crazy.

"Second half, Slaughter," Andy says as he tosses his empty cup in the trash and hops back onto the couch. The other kids settle back in to watch the game, but Katie stays right where she is. And I let her.

The kids hoot and holler as the ball goes up one side of the field, gets kicked off and heads down the other. Neither team scores during the third quarter. North Carolina intercepts the ball within the first minute of the fourth quarter and converts it into a pick six. A quick field goal and the Heels tie it up. A couple of the other boys have fallen asleep, while the others settle in.

Not Andy, though. His eyes glisten with excitement as he watches the Heels. He grips my hand as the final minutes wind down. Every time they snap the ball, he squeezes tighter and tighter.

With about a minute or so to go, they toss the ball into the end zone to the tight end. He's wide open and cradles the ball easily for a touchdown. "Yes," Andy says in a hushed voice.

Angela enters the TV room to let them know it's time to go to bed. "Who won?" she asks.

Without hesitation, Andy says, "We did. Of course."

"That's great. Last I saw they were tied."

"Just won with seconds to go. It was awesome."

She wakes up the two sleeping boys and tells them all to head to their rooms.

"Slaughter, will you be here tomorrow?"

"Not sure, buddy. It depends on what they have for me to do."

"But tomorrow's Sunday. That's a free day, isn't it?"

"Hmmm…good point. I'll see what I can do."

Angela huddles the kids together and hands them off to a couple other nurses who take them back to their rooms.

"Looks like this one's had a rough day," Angela says and points to Katie.

Katie fell asleep in my arms soon after halftime, her little fingers in my hair the whole time.

"She's pretty new here," Angela says. "Still trying to make friends and understand what's going on with her."

"How come?"

"This is her first go at chemo. She just lost her hair last week. I think she's having a hard time dealing with it."

There is nothing I can say to that.

"Looks like she's found a new friend, though." Angela reaches down to pick her up, and I realize she means me.

"She's a sweet girl."

"I checked with your nurses, and they said they don't care if you want to come up here sometimes."

"That's cool."

"You know, it might be good for you to spend some time with these little guys. They're great. If I had to go through all they have to go through, I don't know if I could be as strong as they are. They keep getting kicked down by that miserable disease and every single time they do, they get right back up, put a smile on their precious little faces, and move on to another day."

Again, there are no words.

"Anderson likes you, too." Katie shifts a little in Angela's arms, but Angela pats her back to get her to fall asleep. "I popped in a few times to take a peek. You're great with these kids."

"I'm not sure about that."

"Trust me. You are. You played football, right?"

"I did."

"You see how crazy about the game that boy is."

"He definitely knows his stuff."

"He could use a guy to talk to about sports. What do you say?"

"Sounds like a plan."

Angela shifts her weight and rocks Katie a little. "You need to understand that if you're in, you have to be all in. These kids have enough pain in their lives. They certainly don't need you to come into their lives and then abandon them."

"I get it."

"See you tomorrow then?"

"You'll see me tomorrow."

Angela walks away. As she does, Katie opens her tiny little eyes no more than a sliver and waves at me. It's all I can do not to break down and cry right then and there.

I wheel myself back to the elevator as several nurses stare at me. A few minutes later, I'm back on the seventh floor and in my room. My sketchbook calls from the floor. It taunts me and calls me coward. Such a baby. Here I am whining about a busted leg and not being able to play football again, when a few floors up from me there's a boy who's never had a chance to play anything, and unless he has a miracle in his life, never will.

The disgust makes me sick.

I pick up my sketchbook, grab a pencil, and start drawing Andy and his friends. I want to capture the memories of the night the best I can. If nothing else, it'll be a reminder of how I feel right now.

Chapter Twenty-Two

"Is today the day you get that thing off?" The thing I like about Andy is he puts things as they are and says whatever he wants. There's no beating around the bush with him. He seems much older than his age.

"Yeah, I reckon so. About time ain't it?"

"Yep." He tiptoes back and forth. "Are you nervous?"

"About getting it off? No way."

"Not getting it off. Seeing what's underneath."

"Well, since I haven't seen my leg since the accident, I'm kinda ready."

"What if it's ugly? You said the doctor said it almost got ripped in half, right?"

I nod.

"Then it could look like Frankenstein's monster or something."

"Don't you mean Frankenstein?"

Andy laughs. "You don't read much do you?" Before I get a chance to say no, he continues. "Frankenstein is the doctor who created the monster."

"You sure?"

"Positive. My sister read it in her English class at college and told me all about it."

"Ha, so you didn't read it either, did you, smarty pants?" I tug on the bill of his UNC cap. I haven't seen him without it in the month since I've known him.

"It's a book for college kids, but when I get to college I'm going to read it."

"If you say so, smart guy." Andy's smart for a kid his age. Now that I think about it, he's smarter than most of the guys I know.

"Are you going to college, Slaughter?"

"I don't think so."

"Why not? My sister says it's so much fun." Andy talks about his sister all the time. I wonder if he even has a sister, since I've never seen her here. I've met his parents, but never her. I keep thinking the kid's got an imaginary friend or something.

"I'm not the kind of guy who goes to college, Andy. Not unless I'm playing football. And since I'm going to be lucky to walk again, I guess it's out of the picture."

"What are you talking about? You're a great guy." Andy looks confused. Under his breath I hear him say, "And you're my best friend."

"You're my best friend, too." His face lights up. Guess I'm the closest thing to a brother the kid has. At least I'm real. "I'm the kind of guy who goes to work instead of college."

"I don't understand."

"Even if I could get into college, there's no way I could pay for it. My family doesn't have a ton of money to pay for that sort of thing."

He stares at me for a long while. "I think you should go. I bet you'd love it even if you don't play football."

"Slaughter," a nurse interrupts Andy and me. "You have a visitor. Some girl is here to see you. Should I send her in?"

"I reckon."

Andy giggles like I used to when I was his age and someone mentioned a girl. "Slaughter has a girlfriend. Slaughter has a girlfriend." He repeats over and over in an annoying singsong way.

I snatch the pillow off my bed and toss it at him. Jenny Lee comes around the corner, and my stomach crashes to the floor."I don't have a girlfriend, buddy. Not anymore."

Andy notices her too. "Did she used to be your girlfriend?"

I nod. "But not anymore."

"Hey, Dusty." Jenny Lee says. "How's it goin'?"

"Andy, this is Jenny Lee. Jenny Lee, this is my best friend Andy."

"Nice to meet you, Andy," she says as she shakes his hand. She's always minding the rules of proper behavior, no matter who it's with. I roll my eyes.

"Jenny Lee is a girl I used to know. Back in my other life." Jenny Lee rolls her eyes this time. "Mind giving us a minute, buddy? I'll come get you after I get this thing off."

"Okay, Slaughter. See you soon." He walks past Jenny Lee then hesitates for a quick second. "Nice to meet you, ma'am."

"Whataya want, Jenny Lee? Been here goin' on two months and haven't heard hide nor hair from you or anyone else for that matter."

"I know, Dusty and I'm sorry. It's not easy for us, you know?"

"Give me a break, Jenny Lee."

"You don't understand, Dusty. When you left that night, I felt terrible. When I found out the next day what happened, I about died."

"Funny you should say that, because that's exactly what almost happened to me."

She whimpers and starts to cry. "Stop it, Dusty. That's not fair."

"Are you kidding me? Fair? You want to talk about fair?" Tears streak her cheek. "I walk in and find you making out with my best friend like he's a prized stallion, and I'm not being fair to you?"

"It's not like that. I swear."

"Then what's it like? Fill me in, please. I'd love to hear this one."

A nurse pokes her head through the door. "Is everything okay in here, Slaughter?"

"Yes, ma'am. I'm sorry for being so loud."

"Want me to close the door?"

"Please."

I keep my voice down the best I can, but every fiber in my body tenses with rage. Rage I haven't felt for some weeks now and didn't want to feel again. "Listen, Jenny Lee. You don't have to say a word. I get it. I'm here and you're there. You and Sully can make out every day now, and I won't know, because I'm stuck in this hospital trying to somehow figure out how to walk again."

"Stop it, Dusty. That's not fair."

"Don't use that word with me again. Life isn't fair. I know now how unfair it can be." Andy's smiling face pops into my mind. Talk about not being fair.

"It's just that, I've wanted to come sooner. I have, but the thought of you lying in this hospital depresses me."

It isn't even worth mentioning how depressing it is for me. I can see clearly now that no matter what I say, it's always going to be about her. I didn't recognize it when we were together, but I see it clear as day now.

"I'm sorry you're depressed, Jenny Lee."

She moves closer to me as I sit in my chair. "How's your leg? Coach told Sully and the guys what your doctor said. He said you can't play football and may not walk again. When does it come off?"

"Today."

"You should be excited, right?"

"I guess."

"Did you get the game DVDs yet? Sully said Coach sent them down to you."

"I did."

"They had a heck of a season, huh?"

"Don't know. I haven't watched it yet."

"They made it all the way to the semis. So close to going to state. Sully and Coach both said if you'd been there it would've been a no-brainer."

She mentions Sully's name too much for comfort. "Tell me something, Jenny Lee. And I want you to be honest with me."

"Sure. Anything, Dusty."

"Are you and Sully dating?"

Jenny Lee's face goes as white as my sketch paper. She stands with tears in her eyes. I already know the answer by her long pause and don't expect her to answer.

"Exactly what I thought," I say.

"Dusty, it's not what you think."

"What I think is the girl I fell in love with stabbed me in the back and broke my freaking heart. Am I close, Jenny Lee?"

She takes my hand in hers like she has hundreds of times before. "The night." She pauses and catches her breath. "The night when everything happened, Sully and I were both a little confused."

"That's your excuse?"

"I'm not giving an excuse. I'm just telling you what happened." I pull my hand free from hers and cross my arms. "Charlotte passed out, and Sully and I were messing around. Nothing more. Just messing around."

"Great word to use, Jenny Lee."

"We were just teasing with each other, and then he said he needed some water. He asked me if I wanted to go upstairs with him while he got some. It didn't seem like a big deal, so I went." She chokes back a sob, and I'm certain it's all for show. "When we got upstairs, he kissed me. He kissed me, Dusty. I didn't do anything."

"You kissed him back."

"Not at first. I pushed him away and told him to stop. I asked him what you and Charlotte would think."

"And?"

"He said what y'all don't know won't hurt anybody." She sits in the chair next to the wall. "Like I said, we were just talking and one thing led to another, and before either of us knew it, we were in his bedroom. It wasn't supposed to happen, Dusty. You have to believe me."

"I don't have to believe anything, except what I saw." I throw my head back and stare at the dotted ceiling tiles for what seems like forever. "So that was the only time?"

Through short bursts of crying she says, "No."

"Y'all are together?"

"Yes, but only for about the past month or so."

"And being together now makes it okay? You realize I'm alive and won't be back for months if at all. I'll never play football for sure, and there's a good chance I'll never walk again. So you drop me like a bad habit and fall into the loving arms of the guy who used to be my best friend. Cute."

"I'm sorry, Dusty. I am. I didn't mean for any of this to happen. The longer you were here, the harder it got." She squirms in her seat and does her best to lay her hand over mine. I push it away and fight back the urge to scream.

"Oh, I bet it got hard all right."

She grabs a tissue from her purse and dries her cheeks. Her bottom lip trembles in silence. "Stop it. Now you're just being mean."

My fists curl up into tight little balls. When I think about all of the time I spent on being what she wanted me to be, I shake with disgust. "I guess your dad hasn't threatened to bust his jaw, has he?"

She shakes her head.

"Didn't think so. Sully's like you."

"That's not fa…" She stops when she sees my eyes widen. "I cared about you. I still care about you, but things are different now."

"They sure are." My blood pressure soars so high I feel as if my head's about to burst. "I think you need to go, Jenny Lee."

"Please forgive me, Dusty."

"Time to go." I press the call button and a nurse shows up at my door. "Can you show her out, please?"

Jenny Lee gets up from the chair and walks over to me. She presses her warm lips against my cheek and then whispers "sorry" one last time before leaving.

Chapter Twenty-Three

After a couple of hours, I settle down and prepare for my visit with Dr. Riddell. It's been a couple of days since I've seen him because I spend most of my time with my physical therapist. She says my drawing has gotten me back on track with healing my hand. My right arm is much better, and now I have full rotation in my shoulder.

My bruises faded long ago and the broken ribs are back to normal. The only visible sign besides the scar on my head and hand is the scar on my gut where Dr. Riddell opened me up to stop some internal bleeding. If he hadn't cut me open, Miss Bernice says she would have missed the opportunity to get to know one of the sweetest mountain boys she's ever known. She knows I hate it when she gets all sappy, but I'm glad she's able to say it.

"Ready to go down?" a nurse says as she enters my room.

"I've been ready to get this thing off for weeks."

"Looks like you had a bit of a rough day earlier." Obviously, she's referring to the blowout I had with Jenny Lee. I don't want to relive it, but I can't be mean to her. She's such a sweet lady.

"Yes, ma'am, but it's over for good. I don't want to think about my old life any more. Time to get ready for my new life. Whatever it is."

"Good for you, Dustin." Even though I've told her a dozen times to call me Slaughter, she refuses. Says my name is Dustin and Dustin is what she's going to call me, and I better just get used to it.

She wheels me into a room that's empty except for a bed. The contraption on my leg has metal rods in it, and the nurses told me they actually dig into my bones. The rods are there, but I don't feel anything pressing into my leg. It's only recently that I started to feel my toes. For the first few weeks, I couldn't feel or wiggle them, and it made the doctors nervous. They were afraid the leg didn't reconnect properly or something. I overheard them talking one time about having to go back in and amputate it if it didn't start showing signs of life soon. Thank goodness it did.

"Andy wants you to come see him when you're done," the nurse says. "He told me to tell you he wants to see what the monster looks like. I'm not sure what he's talking about, but I figured you would."

"I do." That kid makes me smile. I thought I was tough, but that was before I met him. He's the toughest kid I know. "Any idea how long this'll last?"

"It's hard to say. Not long if it all goes well. They'll put you under, because it's going to hurt a little."

"A little?"

"Okay, a lot. But only if you're awake. That's why they knock you out when they remove the bolts from your leg."

The nurse clutches my hand and tells me it's all going to be okay. A weak smile crosses my face, and I tell her I know. One thing about these people is they are supportive. They seem to believe in me. They tell me every day I can walk again if I want. They say they've seen it hundreds of times over the years. I start to believe them.

When I wake up, I'm a little groggy, and Dr. Riddell is standing over me calling my name.

"Welcome back, Slaughter."

The room slides into focus. "It's over? It only feels like I've been out for a couple of minutes.

"Close to an hour," Dr. Riddell says. "Things look pretty good, but you've got some work cut out for you. Physical therapy will start in the morning."

"When can I see Andy?" Dr. Riddell tilts his head slightly. "I don't want to see my leg alone."

"The nurse will be back to get you in a few minutes and take you to your room. We need to monitor you for an hour or so to make sure there are no residual effects from the anesthesia. When you're given the all-clear, you can go show him everything."

"Perfect."

"Slaughter." Dr. Riddell's tone becomes more somber. "You've been doing great with your recovery."

"Thanks," I say, though I know he's not finished yet.

"When you see your leg, I want you to be prepared. I don't want you to slip back into the same pattern of behavior from when you first arrived. We've got professionals you can talk to if you want."

I'm not going to lie. I get seriously depressed sometimes when I'm alone in my room. I think it's why I spend so much time with

Andy and the kids on the tenth floor. Those kids crack me up and help me forget all my problems.

"Frankenstein's monster. I'm good."

Dr. Riddell furrows his eyebrows. "Just prepare yourself."

****

As the medication wears off, my leg screams at me in pain. I click the call button. A few minutes later, I'm surprised in a good way when Miss Bernice glides through the door.

"What do you want now, baby?" Her laughter brings a smile to my face.

"It hurts, Miss Bernice."

She reaches for the cord attached to my IV and some sort of numbing medication floods my bloodstream and eases the throbbing of my leg. "There you go, baby. Miss Bernice is here now."

The medicine does the trick and dulls the pain a little. She picks up the sheet and takes a look at my leg. "Don't say anything. I don't want to see it now."

"What's wrong, baby?" Miss Bernice drops the sheet and looks me in the eye. "You worried about what it looks like?"

"Nope. I don't care what it looks like." Most of what I said is true. I do care a little, but I'm learning to accept whatever's under the sheet. "I want Andy to see it with me." Miss Bernice knows all about Andy. Sometimes she comes to my room and I'm not here. She's used to finding me on the tenth floor now.

"You love that little boy." Her big white teeth shine through puffy lips.

I've never thought about it before. "I reckon I do." I think about Katie and the other kids I've grown attached to. "I think I love them all."

She slaps the side of her thick leg and flashes her beautiful white teeth. "You make me prouder and prouder every day, honey. Them kids is goin' to turn you into someone you never knew you could be."

"I reckon."

"Get a little rest, and I'll be by tomorrow to check on you."

"Yes, ma'am."

There's a slight twitch in my leg and my hip hurts more now than ever before. One of my regular nurses comes in to check on me. After a few minutes, she declares I'm A-Okay. At least as much as someone in my condition can be.

"I can get back in my chair?"

"I suppose so, but you may want to wait a bit longer. Dinner will be here soon."

"I'm not hungry."

I pull my chair closer but struggle to get in. I'm careful to keep the sheet on my leg, so the surprise isn't ruined when I get to Andy's room. The nurse tries to help me, but I refuse to let her. If I'm going to have to be the one struggling to walk, I need to get used to doing things for myself. I can't have a nurse with me all my life.

Once on Andy's floor, I look for him. I search the TV room and find some of his friends, but he's nowhere to be found. I wheel myself to the library he's so fond of, but it's empty, too. His nurse, Angela, is walking down the hall, so I stop her and ask where he is.

"You haven't heard?"

"Heard what?"

Angela cuts her eyes back to his room. "Andy isn't feeling so well today. It's been a rough afternoon."

"That doesn't makes sense. He was fine this morning."

"He was. And now he has taken a turn for the worse. It happens when their bodies get stressed out."

"Can I see him?"

"I don't see why not."

I get to Andy's room and his mom and dad are sitting by his side. "Sorry, I didn't mean to interrupt."

His parents look at me as if I just interrupted a secret meeting. I back my chair up and push the door closed when I hear a weakened voice say, "Slaughter?"

I pull the door open and roll slowly into the room. His parents stare at me for a brief moment but then invite me in.

"He talks about you all the time," Mr. Thacker says.

"Come on in, Dusty." Mrs. Thacker gets up from her chair and pushes it to the side so I can wheel in closer to him. "Anderson's been wondering when you were going to show up." She's wearing an expensive dress, which screams money. His dad wears a blue pinstriped suit. I think Andy told me he's a lawyer or something.

"Yes, ma'am."

Andy's face is pale, and his movements are slow. I've never seen him like this, and I don't like it. "Hey, Frankenstein," I say. Mr. and Mrs. Thacker raise their eyebrows about a foot.

"Hey, monster." Andy lifts his head, which is covered by his Tar Heel hat. "How'd it go? What's it look like?"

"Don't know. I wanted to wait for you before I took a peek."

His parents are a bit confused. "Slaughter…got his…leg contraption off today." His voice is weak. "I told him it was going to look like Frankenstein's monster."

"Oh," Mr. Thacker says. "That makes more sense."

"It hurts like crazy when the pain medicine wears off," I say.

Always the proper lady, Mrs. Thacker says, "I think we should wait until Anderson's feeling a little better before you show him." My guess is she doesn't want to see it. I can't say I blame her.

"Your mama's right, buddy. We can wait until tomorrow when you're feeling better."

"Promise?" It's clear Andy just wants to sleep.

"For sure."

Mr. Thacker follows me out of the room. "Dusty, have you got a second?"

"Sure. What's up?"

"When Anderson first told us about you, his mother and I weren't too sure what to think. Now that we've gotten a chance to get to know you a little, we've both decided you're exactly what Anderson needs. He looks up to you, you know?"

"I know." What they don't know is I look up to him just as much or more than he looks up to me. It breaks my heart to see the little guy in bed at six o'clock in the afternoon.

"His doctor tells us he's taken a serious turn for the worse in the past few hours." Mr. Thacker chokes up a little. "Don't get me wrong, we've been here before, but something about this time feels much different."

Mr. Thacker takes a long pause and chokes back his emotion.

"Can you do me a favor?"

"Anything. What is it?"

"Will you promise me you'll come check on him every morning?" Now there are tears welling up in Mr. Thacker's eyes.

His request confuses me, because Andy and I hang out with each other every day. "For sure."

"His doctor told us it's the medication, and he'll be back on his feet tomorrow once he gets a little rest, but his mother and I worry so much about him and don't want him to be alone." Despite the quiver in his lip, Mr. Thacker reins in his sadness and returns to the no-nonsense attorney I know him to be. "We are just so thankful he has you."

Tears well up in my eyes. "He's a great kid. He's helped me more than you can imagine. I just know he's going to be up and running around tomorrow, and when he is, he and I are going to take a peek under this here sheet and see how bad my leg is."

Mr. Thacker chuckles. "Thanks, Dusty." He reaches out his hand and shakes mine.

"Don't even worry about it."

Chapter Twenty-Four

The next morning, Andy wakes me up earlier than I'm used to. "So let's see it." His voice is full of excitement.

"You must be feeling better, huh?"

"Yeah, the new medicine kicked my butt, but my doctor told me it'll help me feel better. He said it may even help me get well enough to go back home."

As I work my way off the bed and into my wheelchair, I'm careful not to let the sheet slip off my leg. Andy helps me the best he can. "I'm glad, buddy. I'm sure you're ready to go home soon."

"I am, but I'm going to have Mom and Dad bring me to visit you if you're still here."

I slap my leg, forgetting the contraption is gone, and tense in pain. "I think this thing'll keep me here for a few more months at least. But I'd love a visit."

It makes me smile to know Andy may have a new medication that can put his cancer in remission. I wonder if he'll still wear his ball cap even after his hair grows back, but I don't ask.

"Let me brush my teeth and wash up a little bit, then we can take a look at the monster under the sheet."

He sits in my chair and folds his hands in his lap like he's at church. "You haven't peeked, have you?"

"No, sir," I say, with a mouth full of toothpaste. "I told you I'd wait for you, and that's what I meant." I spit the toothpaste into the sink and rinse my mouth out. I stand on one leg, still unable to support myself on the bad one.

"The way you have your sheet wrapped around you makes it look like you're wearing a dress." Andy laughs and points.

"Yeah, yeah." I fill my hand with a little water and splash it at Andy. He jumps away with a shriek. "Where to?" I ask as I sit back in my chair.

"The TV room on my floor? They've got the good couches."

He's right about that. I'm up there every night with Andy and the others watching TV. We haven't missed a Tar Heel game yet. It's early October, so we make our bowl predictions now. He thinks they'll get the Independence Bowl, but I say the Peach Bowl.

"Let's do it." I wheel out the door and he pushes me along.

When we get there, Katie is sitting on the carpeted floor playing with some dolls. A new little girl about the same age who I've never seen before is playing with her.

"Hey, Katie bug." She looks up and realizes it's me.

"Slaughter." She squeals my name every time she sees me like we haven't seen each other in years. She jumps into my lap and catches my leg. I wince in pain. "I missed you," she says as she kisses my cheek. Her new friend looks at her like she's lost her mind, but she doesn't say anything. Instead, Katie looks down at her and says, "This is Slaughter. He's my friend."

The new girl lays the doll on the floor and stands up. With such a serious voice, she looks at me and says, "You have a funny name."

I laugh. "I do, don't I?"

"It's not funny." Katie defends me. "It's a cool name."

"What's your name?" I ask the little girl.

She pushes up beside me and rests her hands on my wheelchair. She still has all of her hair. "I'm Megan. I'm five."

"Wow, you're a big girl, Megan. I'm so happy to meet you."

"I'm six, Slaughter. I'm bigger." Katie cracks me up. She hops down and goes to Megan. "Megan is my new friend, too."

"That's great, sweetie."

Within seconds, the two are back at play, dressing up dolls.

I climb onto the cushiony leather couch. It's much easier without the massive contraption on my leg. "Ready, Andy?"

"Yep."

I pull the sheet off my leg and Andy leans in close. He's like a little investigator as he moves up and down it slowly. It fascinates him, but it sickens me.

"It's pretty chewed up," I say.

Andy continues to move up and down the leg with his eyes. Katie and Megan stop playing and move near to get a good look. "Ooohh…gross," Megan says.

"It is pretty gross." It looks like someone else's leg. I almost don't even recognize it.

Andy stops inspecting the leg and speaks for the first time. "I think it's pretty cool." Andy's the kind of kid who doesn't miss much. He picks up on just about everything, including how I'm feeling. "Are you okay, Slaughter?"

I'm not ready to cover up the scarred, mangled mess of what used to be my leg just yet, but it disgusts me to look at it. It's like I can't pull my eyes away from it. I'm not sure if I'm trying to will it back to normal or something.

"Yeah, buddy, I'm okay," I lie.

"You don't seem like you're okay." Andy doesn't let it go. "Can I show you something?"

"Of course you can."

"You have to come back to my room, though, because it's a secret."

I fall back into my wheelchair and follow him to his room. It's not the first time he's invited me to his room, but I'm always surprised how much like home it feels. "Looks like your parents have decorated it for you some more."

"They brought some things from my room at home," he says as he reaches into a drawer.

There are sports posters of all kinds hanging on his wall. A giant baseball with Anderson painted in red. He even has Carolina Panthers sheets. A boy's dream.

"Whatcha got there?"

He tosses a notebook to me. "It's a composition book."

"A what kind of book?"

"Composition book. My sister gets them from college."

I shake my head. "You're too darned smart for me, Andy."

"Not true. You're smart too. You just don't know it."

This eight-year-old boy is staring into the face of death, yet he has the wisdom and confidence of someone ten times his age. Amazing.

With the notebook open, I see pages filled with words and drawings. Mostly words though. Words like *Believe, Strength,* and *Cancer* with a line through it glare back at me. Other pages are what look like something from a diary.

"What is this?"

Andy plops down on his bed. "I call it Excalibur."

"What're you talking about now?"

"Please tell me you know who King Arthur is." He opens his mouth and widens his eyes at me with a duh kind of look on his face.

"I know who King Arthur is. He's a basketball player that plays for that one team."

Andy throws his hand over his forehead and huffs. "Oh, brother."

"I'm kidding," I say as he slugs me in the arm. "He's the king in England who had a girl, what's her name."

"Guinevere."

"Yeah, her. And he got a sword from a rock or something." I'm feeling pretty smart all of a sudden. It seems I learned something in my British lit class after all.

"The Sword in the Stone. He's the guy."

"So why do you call your notebook Excalibur?"

"Because it's the name of his sword."

I hold the book in my hand and wave it around like I'm sword fighting to mess with the kid. "I don't think you're going to kill any dragons with this thing, buddy."

He huffs again and shakes his head.

"I'm going to kill mental dragons." Andy pulls the book out of my hand. "It's what I use to give me strength. Just like King Arthur's sword did for him."

"I'm not sure I'm following you, buddy."

"I get sad sometimes."

I've known the kid a little over a month, and I've never once seen him upset about anything, even when he's feeling like crap. "And how does this help?"

"Because I write in it. All the thoughts in my head. All of the things that make me happy. Anything that pops in my head or makes me mad. It's great because it helps me figure out how to handle the things that bug me."

"And you're telling me about your personal diary for what reason?"

"It's not a diary," he scolds me. "Girls use diaries. This is a journal. This is Excalibur."

"Sorry. How does *Excalibur* have anything to do with me?"

"To help you when you get sad and lonely." He waits for me to say something but I don't. "I know you're tough, Slaughter. Heck, you're the toughest guy I've ever known. But I see you sad sometimes. Like today."

"What do you mean, like today?"

"You got sad when you saw your leg."

"Maybe a little."

"But it's not the only time you get sad."

"Nope."

"I just think if you have your own Excalibur, it might help you."

"Maybe."

Before I'm able to think it over good, a nurse comes into Andy's room. "Slaughter," she says. "They're looking for you. Time for your physical therapy to begin."

"Great," I grumble. "Tell them I'm on my way."

She leaves without speaking.

"What're you doing later, Andy?"

"Same thing I do every night. Hanging out with you."

"I've got an idea. Something you might think is cool."

"What is it?" Andy jumps from his bed with wide eyes.

"Uh-uh, you have to wait because it's a surprise." I wave my finger at him. "It's for me to know and you to find out."

"Whatever."

"See ya', buddy."

"Okay."

Chapter Twenty-Five

Physical therapy doesn't work out as well as I hope it will. They strap me into some sort of walking machine that locks me in at the waist. There are bars like arm rests for me to lean on. I work hard to get my leg to work, but it's just dead weight that drags along the ground more than anything else. Can't even bend it.

My therapist reassures me that I'll eventually get it, and I don't need to put so much pressure on myself. After all, she says, "It's only the first day."

Back in my room, I take a shower and clean up. My room has a modified shower where I can wheel my chair in and sit on a bench inside the shower room. Now that my leg is free from captivity, I decide to stand up. All of my weight is on my good leg, and keeping my balance is a challenge.

Once I towel off and dress, I'm ready to head upstairs to hang out with the kids on the tenth floor.

Rolling out the door, something catches my eye and I remember the surprise for Andy. The game film Coach sent over stares at me and begs to be watched. "Andy is going to love watching these," I say out loud. I spin around, grab the backpack the nurses gave me, shove the DVDs inside and sling it over the back of the chair.

"What's going on, y'all?" There are seven kids playing games, and, of course, Katie and Megan are playing with dolls.

"Slaughter!" a few of the boys shout in near unison.

Andy walks over to me. "How was your first day?"

"Horrible." I answer Andy honestly. If there's one thing I notice about Andy and these kids is they are honest about everything. Even dying. So I decided that I have to be honest with them.

"But you did great, I'll bet."

"I really didn't, buddy. I walked with one leg and dragged the other behind me."

"It's okay," he says. "There's always tomorrow." He screws a strange look to his young face. "That's not true, actually."

He doesn't say anything more. My heart crumbles just a little bit more.

"I've got a surprise for you." It's a good way to change the subject and take his mind off his situation.

His eyes light back up. "How funny. I've got a surprise for you too."

"Oh yeah?"

"Yeah. You first."

I pull the backpack off the chair and unzip it. I toss it to him, and he eyes the DVDs inside. "Movies?"

"Kinda, but not exactly."

Andy pulls out a few of the DVDs and reads the labels. "Coosa County Eagles?" Andy rifles through more DVDs. "Is this the team you played on?"

I nod.

"But the dates on here are from the past few weeks. You were here."

"I played a few games early in the season, but those are the ones Coach sent me to watch to see how the team did after my wreck."

"Where are the others? The ones you played in? I want to see those."

"They're in my room. I didn't bring them."

"Why not?"

I shrug a shoulder, not sure of the right answer. "Guess I don't want to see me doing something I'll never get to do again."

"But I do." Andy shoves the DVDs back in the backpack and zips it up. He hangs it back on my wheelchair. "Can we watch them, Slaughter? I want to see you play."

How can I tell the kid no? "I reckon."

"Let's go." Andy grabs the handles of my wheelchair and starts pushing.

"I can do it myself."

"Not as fast as I can push you."

We get a little speed and the attention of the evening receptionist. "Slow it down, you two."

"Yes, ma'am."

"Yes, ma'am," Andy repeats.

"One of these days, we're going to have to have us a race."

Andy laughs. "I'll win."

We get back upstairs and put in the DVDs of my games. Katie climbs up in my lap like she normally does when we watch a movie. Usually we watch a Disney film about a princess and a prince. Or some of those popular kids' shows they all like.

"I missed you," Katie says as she gives me a peck on the cheek.

"I missed you, too, Katie bug." We have the same conversation every night.

We start with game one. Andy watches like his eyes are glued to the TV. We spend the next couple of hours watching Sully throw and hand the ball off to me. It's the first time I've watched myself in a game.

"You're good," Andy says on the final touchdown of the game. "The best."

"I reckon." I remember that game like yesterday. Watching myself is pretty cool, but it reminds me that I'm never going to be that guy again. I'm this guy. The guy with a busted leg stuck in a wheelchair.

"Can we watch another?" Katie asks through a stifled yawn.

"I think it's time for bed, Katie bug," I say.

"Noooo." All of the kids in the room cry.

"I'll be right back." Andy leaves the room.

The nurses come into the room and gather up all the kids to get them ready for bed. Angela takes Katie in her arms. Just like every night she leaves, Katie looks back over Angela's shoulder with sleepy eyes and waves goodbye.

"Here you go," Andy says upon his arrival. He hands me a composition notebook.

"Your book?"

"Nope." A devilish grin spreads on Andy's face. "It's yours."

I flip through the pages and realize it's brand new. "You got this for me? How?"

"My sister brought it for me today. I called her and told her I need one for my best friend."

"Thanks, buddy."

"You're welcome. Now you can start writing in your own book."

"Can I call it Excalibur like yours?"

Andy thinks about it for a second. "I reckon." His answer surprises me, because Andy never uses that word. "Goodnight," he says as he reaches up and kisses my cheek for the first time.

"Night, buddy."

I wheel myself to the elevator. Angela interrupts me as I wait for the doors to open. "I'm proud of you, Slaughter."

"For what?'

"I wasn't sure about you hanging out with the kids at first, but I have to say you've been the best thing for them over the past few weeks. You're all they talk about, especially Anderson. That little boy adores you."

"He's a great kid." I tell her. "They all are." My Excalibur rests in my lap. I drop a hand on it and realize how great Andy really is.

"I see he gave you the notebook." Angela points at the notebook in my lap. "He's been so excited all day to give it to you."

"I reckon I better start putting some words in it then."

Angela breaks into a smile. "You better if you know what's good for you."

"May I ask you something about Andy?"

She puts down the pen she's writing with and walks around the counter. "Sure. What is it?"

"How bad is he?" Angela looks at me with squinted eyes, deep in thought. I'm afraid she's not going to tell me anything because of all that confidentiality crap, so I rephrase my question. "I mean how bad is his cancer?"

"All cancer is bad," she says. Her smile dissipates.

I interrupt her and say, "Stupid question. I didn't mean it like that."

"I know what you mean." Angela taps her finger on her lip. "Anderson has leukemia. Chronic Lymphocytic Leukemia to be exact."

The elevator door opens, but I ignore it.

"I don't know what that means."

"It's a slower form of leukemia which affects the white blood cells." She must realize what she's saying goes right over my head. "What it means is he didn't know he had it for a few years before he was diagnosed because it spreads more slowly and the symptoms are harder to spot at first."

"Oh. That's a good thing. I mean, that it spreads slower."

"Yes, I suppose so, but the truth of the matter is he will die. They all will."

"So how long does Andy have?"

"It's hard to say. The kind of cancer Anderson has can turn on a dime and become aggressive."

"But things are going good for him now?"

"Yes. It looks like he may go back home in a few weeks. The new medication seems to be slowing it down."

"That's good."

Angela notices my sadness. "Don't worry, Slaughter, he'll come visit you."

I feel like an idiot for feeling sad about Andy going home. It's a good thing if he gets better. "I know."

Once back in my room, I grab a pen and write Excalibur on the front cover in black ink. I open it to the first page and write. At first, I'm not sure what to write about, so I just go for it. I make a list of things that piss me off about my wreck. It's easy to do. Then I write a list of all the good things I can think of that's happened since my wreck. Andy, Miss Bernice, and Katie bug top the list.

After the list is complete, I close the journal and stare at the words I wrote on front. I tap my pen against the hard cover for a few minutes, then put the book down and wheel back to Andy's floor.

"What's wrong?" Angela asks as I come through the door. "Did you forget something?"

"Do you mind if I look at the books in the library?"

"Help yourself."

After I wheel up to the shelves and search through all of the books, I spot the one I'm looking for on the top shelf. I push myself up onto my good leg and snatch it off before falling back into my chair.

"Can I borrow this for a little while?" I ask Angela as I roll back up front.

"Which one is it?" I hold the book up for her to see. "*The Once and Future King*, huh?"

"Yes, ma'am."

I assure her I'll take care of it and get it back on the shelf before Andy comes looking for it.

It's still early, so once I'm in my room, I start reading the section called *The Sword in the Stone*.

Chapter Twenty-Six

We watch a game a night for three nights. The third game of the season is the night the scouts are there. It amazes me almost as much as it does Andy when I dive over the linemen, spin around with my head inches from scraping the ground, get back to my feet, and score.

"You're like Superman," he squeals. "You should've been down."

I put my hands to my chest and fake open my shirt as if I'm revealing my Superman clothes underneath. "I kinda got lucky."

"What you're doing isn't luck, Slaughter. If there's one thing I know, it's football." The kid isn't kidding at all. No matter if we watch UNC or the Carolina Panthers, Andy knows his stuff. I know he can never play football, but he sure could make a great coach if he ever had the chance.

"I reckon."

The fourth night is the night we watch the last game before my tryouts with the Tar Heels. It's a good game, and Andy knows the scouts came to the game the week before, because I make sure to point them out.

When we watch the last game of my life, both pain and pride battle inside me like confused lions. I write in Excalibur every night before going to bed, and I think tonight will be a night that will take several pages.

As we're getting close to halftime, a girl about my age bounds through the door. Long curly brown hair pulled back in a loose ponytail. She's wearing jeans and a zipped up jacket. She's carrying a couple of pizzas.

"Hey, Anderson," she says as she leans in for a kiss and hug.

Andy gives her both. "Collins, I didn't know you were coming tonight."

"It's a surprise."

"What's the pizza for?"

"That's part of the surprise." Collins puts the pizza on a table. "I brought it for you and your friends."

"Awesome," Andy says. The smell of melted cheese and pepperoni lures a few of the kids away from the TV.

Then, as if I just happen to blink into existence, Collins jerks her head up and looks straight at me. Her big brown eyes are full of life. "Oh, sorry, I didn't mean to interrupt."

"Slaughter, this is my sister I've been telling you about."

With a suspended hand in the air I say, "Hey there. Nice to meet you."

She hesitates to shake my hand but does so to be nice. "This is…" She pauses and cocks her head sideways. "I mean…wait…this is your new friend? The one you talk about all the time?"

"In the flesh." Andy chuckles when he realizes the same thing occurs to me. "You thought he's a little kid like me."

"Uhhh…yeah, why wouldn't I? Mom and Dad didn't mention he's…"

Before she finishes her thoughts Andy blurts out, "Your age."

"They said you had a new friend. I just figured he was your age."

"What's your real name?"

Andy pipes up before I can. "Slaughter is his real name."

She looks me in the eye and waits for an answer. "Dusty Slaughter. It's actually Dustin, but nobody calls me that. Most people call me Slaughter, but a few call me Dusty."

"Nice to meet you, Dustin." She peels back the lid on the pizza box. "So who is ready for some pizza?" Every kid in the room gets excited.

"Can I have some, too?" Katie bug slides from the couch in anticipation.

"Of course you can." Collins realizes she doesn't have any plates. "I'll be back in a sec." She races out of the room and returns in less than a minute with paper plates and napkins. A couple of the nurses return with her to help hand out the pizza.

"Where are you from?" She continues to hand out pizza and talk without laying an eye on me.

"Flatbush."

"I've never heard of Flatbush."

"Most people haven't. It's way up in the mountains."

"So why are you here?" Collins stops handing out pizza and all the kids start eating. The nurse is filling their cups with soda. She's totally confused and looks to Andy for a little help. He throws her a lifeline. The way my leg stretches out on the couch and my sweats hide the junked up mess underneath, I bet she thinks I'm just relaxing. "He's from the seventh floor."

It slowly sinks in. "You're a patient?"

Careful to make sure none of the other kids see my chewed up leg, I pull the sweats up slightly. Her eyes go wide. "Yep."

"He was in a bad car wreck. Almost died." Like I say, Andy's honest.

"Mom and Dad left that part out too. Sorry about your accident. I hope you feel better."

"Thanks."

"Have some pizza." She motions to Andy. "Want to sit over there with me, Anderson?"

Andy takes a breath. "I reckon."

"You what?" Collins asks.

"It mean—" Andy starts to answer but is cut off by his sister.

"I know what it means. What I don't understand is why you're saying it."

"Because he does." Andy points at me.

"Don't blame me, buddy. I'm not getting in trouble by your sister. She's a tough one."

Collins cradles his hand in hers. "Well, just because he says it doesn't mean you can too."

Andy and Collins walk over to a table in the corner of the room to eat and chat. Andy laughs and smiles as his big sister talks. He grabs a gooey piece of cheese and dangles it above his mouth. Collins tells him to use better manners, but Andy doesn't listen. He fiddles with the pizza and his sister talks and talks.

The temptation forces me to shove a slice of piping hot pepperoni in my mouth, inhaling it all in one bite. Sauce drips down the side of my face. I'm so used to the hospital food because I have been eating it for so long I almost forgot what real food tastes like. The last time I ate pizza is the night the scouts came out to watch our game. It seems like years ago. I snatch another slice and chomp down.

I catch myself staring at Collins a little too long. She lifts her head and sees me, so I jerk my eyes away and stare at Katie. I think I see Collins smile.

After everyone finishes eating, Collins picks up all of the trash and puts it in a large trashcan one of the nurses brought in for us. Andy jumps on the couch beside me.

"Collins." He waits for her to answer. The best he gets is a look. "Slaughter is a football player. He's the guy on the TV."

Collins looks to the screen but doesn't seem all that interested. "For real?" She sits on the other side of Andy.

"I played football. I don't do much of anything now."

"You will again one day, Slaughter. I know it."

"Thanks, buddy. When I do, you can be my coach."

"He's the best player in the entire state." Andy hops down from the couch and puts a finger on the TV while the game is paused. "That's him right there. He's so good. He was going to play for the Tar Heels before he got into the wreck."

Collins unzips her jacket to reveal a baby blue Tar Heel shirt. "I go to school there." What I pay attention to the most is the way her shirt clings to her.

"I know. Andy talks about you all the time." I keep my eyes on her shirt a little too long. "He's told me everything about you."

"Yeah, he told me a few things about you too. Obviously not everything."

"Go ahead and hit the play button, and we'll finish the game."

Andy pushes the button and hops back on the couch between his sister and me. Thank goodness I had a heck of a game that night. Actually, an amazing second half. I rang up close to a hundred and fifty yards and got three touchdowns. One through the air and the other two hard and heavy up the middle.

Watching the game is strange. I've never seen myself playing the game before this. Sure, Coach shows us game film all the time, but they're only short clips at a time. It's almost like I'm up in the stands watching it. As I watch myself and my teammates sweat our tails off in the cool air, I'm a little proud and a lot sad. I live for football, and now it's gone.

The final seconds tick off the game clock and the buzzer sounds. "Game over," I say.

Collins looks at her watch. "Time for bed."

"Already?" Andy looks to me for rescue. I know better than to get mixed up in their mess.

"What if I take you to your room and read you a bedtime story?"

Andy crinkles his face and whispers in Collins' ear, still loud enough for me to hear. "Don't say that. Slaughter will think I'm a baby."

"No way, buddy. You're the toughest guy I know. Way tougher than me." What he doesn't realize is I'm completely serious. I wish I had half his courage. "I've been reading myself."

"You have?"

"Yep."

Andy perks back up. "Slaughter doesn't read. He didn't even know about Dr. Frankenstein's monster."

"You didn't either until I told you," Collins reminds him.

"But I'm going to read it when I'm old enough." Andy lets out a slight yawn and looks at me. "What did you read?"

"Last night I read one of your all-time favorites. I read *The Sword in the Stone*."

"I love that book, don't I Collins?"

"Yep. Do you still keep Excalibur?" Collins doesn't wait for Andy to answer the first question before asking another. "Is that why you wanted me to bring you the notebook yesterday? To give to Dustin?"

"Uh huh."

"I've named mine Excalibur, too. I've been writing in it every night."

"My sister told me about writing things down. She got the idea from her English class. She said it will help me and be neat to read years from now when I'm all better."

"I think your sister's a smart girl."

"Of course she is. She goes to UNC."

"I'm right here, y'all. You two don't have to talk like I'm not in the room." Collins stands up and tugs on Andy's robe. "Let's go, squirt. We need to let Dustin get some peace and quiet."

Collins and Andy head toward the door, but Andy stops and runs back to me. He leans up and gives me a quick kiss on the cheek and says, "Love you."

"Love you back."

He catches back up to Collins. As she leaves, she mouths the words, "Thank you."

When I get back to my room, I think about what Collins said about getting some peace and quiet. Peace and quiet is a funny thing. When I'm alone in my room, I have all the quiet I can stand. It's scary sometimes how deafening the silence can be. The one thing I never have when I'm alone is peace. The only peace I have these days is when I'm with the kids on the tenth floor.

I pull Excalibur off the table and start writing.

Chapter Twenty-Seven

The next morning is completely boring. I go to find Andy, but he's gone home for the weekend. Which means he's getting closer to going home for good.

I circle the hospital in my wheelchair, trying to think of something to do. I'm hanging out in the indoor garden when Miss Bernice comes in and scares the living daylights out of me. She laughs and I about jump clean out of my skin.

"What's wrong with you, Miss Bernice?"

"Nothin' baby. I just wanted to check on you."

"By scaring the puddin' out of me?"

"Yep."

"I know there has to be some kind of rule against nurses going around and scaring patients."

"They're probably is. You goin' to go report me?"

"Nah."

"So why you mopin' 'round this hospital all day long?"

"I'm not moping."

"Whatchu call it then?"

"Boredom."

"The nurses on the tenth floor told me you came lookin' for yo' friend, Andy, first thing this mornin'."

"I did."

"You know he'll be back in a coupla days, right?"

"Yes, ma'am."

"Then what else is buggin' ya', baby?"

"Nothing."

"I was also told you and that little boy's sister got along quite nicely last night. Hear she's real pretty, too." Miss Bernice's drops a knowing wink my way.

"She's all right. She's nice."

"You sure that ain't what's got you all down?"

"Yep." The truth is I'm not sure. I only met Collins last night, but her face and her tight blue Tar Heel shirt keep flashing through my mind.

"Well, baby, the way I see it, you can keep on doin' laps in that chair of yours the rest of the weekend, or you can go find yourself somethin' productive to do."

"Like what?"

"You still have the sketch book I gave you?"

"Yes, ma'am."

"That's a start." She throws a hand on her wide hip and spins like Miss America. "You can always go draw another picture of yours truly."

"I s'pose."

"Listen, baby." She gets right down in my face and I smell mint on her breath. "Find you somethin' to keep your mind active. Ain't nothin' better than an active mind. Imagination can go a long way, baby."

"Yes, ma'am."

"Now, I've got to get back upstairs and do my rounds, but don't forget that Miss Bernice takes care of all her babies. Don't matter how old they is." She walks away, but tosses one last comment and a laugh my direction. "You could draw a picture of that pretty little girl who's got your head all up in knots."

"Yeah, yeah," I say, but she's too far away to hear.

What she said gnaws at me for a little while, and then it gives me an idea. I wheel back to my room and grab the sketchpad and notebook. I head back down to the indoor garden and get to work.

After a few hours of writing and drawing, I need a break. This is the most work I have ever put into something. Something other than football.

I'm hungry, so I go upstairs to the cafeteria. Now that I'm moving about on my own, I don't have to wait for the nurses to bring me lunch. I can do it all on my own. Get my food, tell them my room number, and eat. Such a great system. Plus the food's better in the cafeteria.

"In a little late this evening," the lady at the counter says. We talk all the time, but I don't even know her name.

"Yeah. Been doing other things." Normally, I eat early and then head down to hang out with Andy and the gang. Since he's gone and the weekends are full of family and friends visiting, I'm not much in the mood to do anything.

"Hang in there. Pretty soon you won't even need that thing." She didn't say it, but I know she means my chair.

Here is a lady who only knows me from coming through her line to get food, and she acts like she cares about me like I'm her own son. Talking to her makes me think about Mama and wonder how she's doing. It's been several weeks since I've heard from Coach or anyone. The holidays are getting close and I'm isolated hours from Flatbush with strangers who care about me more than my own people.

The cold must've set in up in Flatbush for the winter. I worry about Mama and hope someone is getting some wood for her to heat the house. For all I know, she may be dead from the junk in her veins, rotting away. I miss Mama.

Jenny Lee's face flashes through my memory. Every time I think of her, I think of Sully. The memories are hard to swallow, but I still don't remember the accident. Bits and pieces filter through my brain every now and again, but the accident is as foreign to me as my new leg. I wonder why my brain didn't block out the memory of what caused the accident in the first place. Why do I have to remember walking in and finding Jenny Lee making out with my best friend? Why do I have to know the rest of my life that Sully betrayed me like I never thought he would?

I wheel up to the table, settle in to eat, and flip open my sketchbook to look over the images I've created. Since Miss Bernice gave me the art stuff, I feel like I'm someone else. I never knew I could draw. It's not the greatest artwork, and it will never make it into a museum, but it's good enough for me. The images of Andy and his friends stare back at me, allowing happiness to wash over me like healing waters.

I chug some sweet tea as I flip pages and marvel at what I see. It's still hours before bedtime, and I'm super bored. Then it hits me. Andy's got a birthday coming up soon.

If anyone can help me get what I need, it's Miss Bernice. I find her in the break room with some other nurses laughing and cutting up.

"Baby, whatchu doin' in here?" The other ladies stop their laughter immediately. "Who let you back here?"

"Nobody," I say. "I asked where you were, and some lady said you were on break. I did the rest."

"This is the boy you're always talking about?" Another nurse asks Miss Bernice.

"Mmm hmmm." Miss Bernice doesn't even open her mouth.

"You are more handsome than Miss Bernice said," the other nurse says.

Another lady pipes up. "That's the truth, Brenda." She looks back at me. "Do you have a girlfriend?"

"Touchy subject for Dusty," Miss Bernice warns.

"It's okay." I say. And the truth is it is okay. I feel good about being me and realize I don't need Jenny Lee or anyone else for that matter to feel good about who I am now. I only need me. "No, ma'am, I don't have a girlfriend."

"Want one?"

I scratch my head and laugh. "Not sure I need one. Why? Are you looking for a new boyfriend?"

All of the ladies break into laughter. "Yeah, Alice," Miss Bernice says, "you lookin' to get you a man?"

"Very funny, ladies." Alice holds her hand up to silence the other two. "I have a granddaughter I think you might just love. She's a student at UNC."

Collins springs to mind. There is no way she's Alice's granddaughter. Andy and Collins seem like the kind of people who come from money. Not the kind of money Sully and Jenny Lee come from. They seem like the kind of money that gets passed down from their grandparents. It's the way Mr. and Mrs. Thacker dress and talk. Not quite snobby, but definitely a bit on the snooty side. I'll bet if my leg was good and I could walk, those two would look down their noses at me. Not Andy though. He doesn't care that I'm piss poor.

"Oh yeah?" I ask.

"My Talon is a real pretty girl. She's studying to be a nurse, too."

"The boy don't need a nurse," Miss Bernice barks. "He's got him plenty of those."

Alice holds her hand up again. "I know he doesn't need another nurse," she says to Miss Bernice before turning back to me. "She needs her a handsome young boy like you."

"I appreciate the offer, but I don't think I'm in any condition to be dating. The best I can offer is dinner at the third floor cafeteria."

The ladies laugh. "The next time she's here," Alice says, "I'll bring her by to meet you."

"Sounds good."

"Now, baby, I done asked you once. Whatchu want?"

"I need you to do me a favor."

"Anything. What is it, baby?" I glance at the other two ladies and Miss Bernice notices. "You can tell me in front of the girls. I'm goin' to tell them eventually anyhow."

"I need some art supplies. I want another book, and I need some colors."

"My baby's an artist," Miss Bernice tells the other two. "Draws real good, don't ya'?" I shrug my shoulders. "Show them the picture of the beautiful lady you first drew."

I pull out the pad and open to the picture of Miss Bernice.

"Oh my," Brenda says. "You are a talented artist if you can make her this beautiful."

"Don't be hatin' 'cause I'm so gorgeous," Miss Bernice says. "Ain't that right, baby?"

"For sure."

"Thank ya', baby." Miss Bernice tosses her trash in the can. "I'll have them for you soon."

"Thanks." I back my chair to the door. "Y'all stay outta trouble."

"Never," Alice says.

Chapter Twenty-Eight

Miss Bernice is true to her word, and less than an hour later I have everything I need to start working on Andy's birthday present. To get it done in the few weeks I have left, I have to work on it for hours at a time. This weekend is a good start.

Sunday night rolls around and I'm busy working on his present in the indoor garden. I focus completely on the work and totally miss Collins walk in. It isn't until her voice reaches my ears that I look up and see her standing right in front of me. I slam the book closed.

"What are you doing?" Her eyes focus on the closed book.

"Just drawing," I say.

"Can I see it?"

I don't want to sound like a jerk by telling her no, but I have no choice. I want it to be a surprise. "It's secret."

She dismisses it quickly. "How's it going?" Her curly hair hangs loose around the front of her face. She's wearing blue sweat pants and a long sleeve Under Armor shirt with a fleece jacket.

"Fine." I'm still surprised she's here. "What are you doing here?"

She tucks her hands into her jacket pockets and rocks back and forth on her heels. "My brother's a patient here, remember?"

"Yes, I remember." There's no way I could forget why she comes here. "What are you doing here? Right here with me? Shouldn't you be with Andy?"

"I've been with *Anderson* all weekend. Mom and Dad are getting him ready for bed. It's always hard on him when he has to come back to the hospital after being home."

I drop my head a little and think about the pictures in my notebook. Thinking about all he has to go through forces a shiver down my spine. "I'm sure it must be hard on the little guy."

"You don't know the half of it." She taps the leather seat across from me. "Care if I sit for a few minutes?"

She doesn't have to ask permission to sit, so I'm slightly confused when she does. "Sure. Go ahead."

She plops down onto the leather cushions. "You know, he talked about you the whole time he was at home."

"He did?"

"It was Slaughter this and Slaughter that. Everything that came out of my brother's mouth was about you. He has grown attached to you." Her eyes bore into me like she's searching for an answer that may never come.

"I've grown pretty attached to him too." I hide the fact that his visit home left me with a hole I don't want to admit is there.

"Doctors say after the holidays, if he's still reacting to the medicine the way he is now, he can come back home permanently."

"That's great news," I say, though secretly I wish he'd stay here longer. It makes me mad at myself to be so selfish. His going home means he's getting better, and I'm being a jerk.

"Yeah, he's pretty excited, but it's going to crush him when he leaves. He's never been as happy during his hospital stays as he is now. And it's all because of you."

"I doubt it."

"I don't." Collins pulls her phone out when it vibrates. "My parents want me back in the room."

"No problem. Thanks for coming by to let me know. I appreciate it."

"I didn't come by to let you know about him." Her face reddens slightly. She hesitates to speak as she leans forward.

A lump gets caught in my throat. "You didn't?"

"I came by to see you, silly."

My jaw drops to the floor when she says she came to see me. I freeze and don't know how to respond. I hear my heart beat in my chest like a hammer against a steel drum and worry she can hear it, too.

Collins waves a hand in front of my face like she's trying to get my attention. "Are you okay?"

I'm a bit lost and stare into space, doing my best to comprehend her words. "Yeah, sorry. Yeah, I'm fine. Surprised is all."

"Why does it surprise you?"

"I don't know. I just didn't expect it is all."

Her smile slackens into a straight line and her forehead crinkles between her eyes. "Is it okay?"

I don't want to seem too excited, and even though I'm bursting on the inside, all I can manage to say is, "I reckon."

"That's another thing we need to talk about." She squints one eye like she's a teacher getting onto a student. "You have my brother saying that awful word all the time."

"Awful?"

"The first time my dad heard him say it, he about lost his mind. He told Andy he's a Thacker and Thackers don't talk like that."

I've heard this song and dance before with Jenny Lee's dad, so I know where it's going before she says another word. "Yeah, I thought y'all were the fancy kind. I'm used to it. Sorry for corrupting Andy with my hillbilly talk."

"Let me finish. Geez, what is it with you boys always talking and interrupting?"

I wave my hand in the air like a magician as a cue for her to keep talking.

"Anyhow, he told Anderson we don't talk that way, and Anderson told him he hears you say it all the time."

She opened the door for me to poke at her a little bit. "I reckon I do."

"Funny guy." Collins purses her lips then continues. "When Dad found out he's copying you, he gave Anderson permission to say it."

"For real?"

"My Dad is a tough man and values who he is and where he comes from. He's the country club type. I'm sure you've seen them."

"I have. From a distance." I smile a half smile then say, "I'm just the country type, I s'pose."

"Wow!" Collins raises her voice then brushes her hand against my arm. Chills run up my spine. "You're on fire. Did I miss it? Are we in a comedy club for open mic night?"

"Yeah, yeah."

"Back to Dad. He's tough, but he's fair. He judges people for sure. It's the way he was raised. But Dad gives everybody a chance to prove themselves."

I'm not sure if I should be offended or happy. "What a guy."

"I have to tell you, he likes you."

"I've only talked to him a couple of times. He doesn't know me at all."

"He doesn't have to. He's seen the impact you've had on Anderson. I overheard him tell Mom Anderson's never seemed happier in his life."

"I don't know if he is or not, but I do know he's a great kid."

Collins' phone vibrates again. She doesn't even bother looking at it. "I have to go. They're dropping me and a load of clean clothes off at school."

"I thought you drove."

"I do. They picked me up since they were already in the city."

"Better go then."

"Yeah, I..." she stops and looks at me. "What is it you say? S'pose?"

"I s'pose," I say.

"Then I s'pose I better go." She doesn't have the same drawl and it comes out unnatural, but it makes me happy she tries.

"I reckon," I say with a wink.

She looks at her phone once more and rushes to the elevator. My eyes follow her all the way. She waves just as the door closes.

Chapter Twenty-Nine

Three days pass and all I think about is her. Collins consumes my thoughts day and night. Something about the way she wears a smile on her face.

Physical therapy is difficult and I'm getting nowhere. I can twitch my foot a little bit but still can't do anything more than drag it behind me as I slave away on the treadmill torture device they strap me into.

Brooke, my physical therapist, is nice and encouraging, but no matter how much encouragement I get, I'm afraid my leg is a dead piece of meat destined to weigh me down the rest of my life. Maybe amputating it the night of the accident instead of saving it like Dr. Riddell did would've been better considering the way things are now. She tells me I'm being ridiculous, and she's determined I will walk again in the next few months. According to her, when my brain and muscles get back in sync, I'll be on my feet. Never back to normal. I realize those days are over, and I need to find a new normal. Embrace it. And move on.

Andy, Katie bug, and the others are the ones who get me through the day. After hours of grueling work with Brooke, all I want to do is head up to see them. They keep me going. Tonight is no different.

"How did it go?" Andy waits for me at the elevator like he always does at six-thirty.

He grabs the handles on my chair and pushes. He likes pushing me for some reason, and I don't mind. "Toughest one yet, buddy."

"Did you walk?"

"No."

He asks me the same question every day, and gets the same answer every day. And every day he sighs like it's the worst news he's heard in his entire life. And every day he says, "Tomorrow you will."

There's a secret I haven't shared with him yet. I want to show him my new trick after things settle down, but I have to spend time with all of them first. Katie and I play dolls, because Megan got better and went home. Later, I kick back and play Xbox with Jake. He loves to whoop me in Madden Football. The way he romps me, he doesn't believe I ever played football. Andy is quick to my defense and tells him I used to be the best running back in the state. Sometimes I believe him.

We settle in and watch TV. Katie puts her dolls away and climbs up on the couch beside me. Most nights she sinks in next to me and I wrap my arm around her. It's chilly in the hospital, so I throw a little blanket over us. It's just the three of us. Me in the middle, with Andy and Katie on either side.

Right in the middle of watching some cartoons, Collins strolls in. My eyes pop out of my head, and I nudge Andy.

"Collins," he shrieks. "What are you doing here?"

"Can't I come see my brother?"

"Of course." Andy tosses the blanket to the side and jumps into his sister's arms. "It's just that Mom and Dad said you weren't coming until Saturday."

"I am coming Saturday, but I'm also here now. Is that okay?" She puts him down and Andy smiles. "My dorm isn't too far from here. I could come here every night if you didn't have to go to bed so early." She looks at me when she says it, and my mind runs wild.

"Sit with us. There's room." Andy sits on the far end and pats the space between him and me. "Slaughter doesn't care, do you Slaughter?"

Is he kidding? If he only knew how much I want her to sit with us it would blow his mind. My cheeks heat up as she waits for an answer. "No…it's fine with me, I s'pose."

A smile splits Collins's face in half. She sits beside me, and Andy snuggles up close to her. "Don't hog the blanket," she says.

I throw the blanket over her lap, and she stretches it over Andy. I'm in foreign territory and don't know what to do with her so close. She sits only inches from me, and the scent of her perfume invades my nose like fresh peaches on a summer day. Desperation to wrap my arm around her bubbles to the surface, but I fight back the urge. "How's it going?"

"Great. What are y'all watching?"

Katie looks across me to Collins with suspicion. "My favorite cartoon. You're not going to change the channel are you?"

"No, sweetheart, I'm not going to change the channel." Collins raises her eyebrows at me. "Looks like she's got you wrapped around her little finger."

"Fine by me."

"You know, I've got a finger." Collins swirls her pinky finger in the air.

"What are you talking about, Collins?"

"Nothing, Andy. Just messing with your big, strong football player friend here." This time she squeezes my muscle. Don't get me wrong, I know what flirting is when I see it, but Collins doesn't strike me as the kind of person to be flirting like this. Not in front of her brother.

I put my hand to my temple and make a circle like I'm asking him if she's crazy. She mouths the word, no.

"Y'all are acting weird." Andy doesn't know what's going on, and like me, he senses something isn't quite right.

"Sorry, Anderson. Tell me, how did therapy go today?"

"Same as every day. Slaughter didn't walk today, but he will tomorrow."

She tilts her head to one side. "Is it true?"

"I doubt I'm going to walk tomorrow or the next day, but I'm still working on it the best I can."

"I agree with Anderson. I think you'll walk soon."

I suddenly remember my little surprise for Andy. Since he brought it up, I figure I may as well show him now while Collins is here. Two birds and all.

"I do have a surprise for you," I say.

"What is it, Slaughter?" Andy asks.

Katie is curious, too. "Yeah, Slaughter, what surprise did you bring us?"

"I didn't bring anything, Katie bug," I say. "I learned to do something today. Something I haven't done in a long time."

Katie is now more interested in the cartoon than any surprise I have. Andy isn't. His eyes open wide. "Show us. Show us."

"Yeah, Dustin, show us," Collins says.

I pull the blanket off Katie and me, and when I do she whines because she's cold. I'm forced to scoot out to the edge of the couch and tell her to crawl behind me to Collins. She curls up in her arms, and all of a sudden I'm thinking I made a big mistake by losing my spot next to Collins because I want to be wrapped up in her arms like Katie bug.

I press on with my trick. "It isn't much, so don't get all disappointed."

"We won't," Andy assures me.

Within a minute or so, I'm up on my feet, standing all by myself. I can't move an inch, but I can stand on both legs, and like Brooke says, it's one heck of an accomplishment. Funny how perspective can change. Two hundred rushing yards in a game always seemed like a huge accomplishment, but today the simple act of standing on my own two feet is an accomplishment of gargantuan proportions.

"You're doing it, Slaughter! You're doing it!" Andy is on his feet and beside me in no time flat.

"It's a start, Dustin." Collins shifts her weight and Katie looks around me to see the TV.

"I reckon."

I maintain my balance for close to three minutes. Which is about two and a half minutes longer than I did this afternoon. My left leg feels wobbly and weak, so I lose my balance and fall onto the couch, nearly crushing Katie bug. Thankfully, she moves over just in time to see her show better. What actually happens is I land halfway on the couch and halfway in Collins' lap.

"Howdy, cowboy," she says with an embarrassed laugh.

I'm the one who should be embarrassed. "Sorry," I say as I move off her. "Still trying to figure all of this out."

"Don't be sorry," she says. "I didn't mind." Her face reddens.

"Slaughter, that's awesome. You're going to walk again. I just know it."

"Thanks, buddy. I'm taking it one day at a time." I struggle to get myself back on the couch even though I'd rather stay right where I am.

"Anderson, it's time for bed."

"Not yet." Andy looks at the clock on the wall. Five minutes to eight.

"Sorry, buddy," I say. "I'll be back tomorrow."

"I know." Andy looks to his sister. "Will you?"

She takes a moment to think about what she wants to say. "Maybe, if Dustin doesn't mind me crashing y'all's party."

Andy's face lights up like a candle. He looks to Collins and then to me. "He doesn't mind, do you, Slaughter?"

I welcome any chance I can get to spend time with Collins. "Not if you don't."

"Oh, yeah, I almost forgot." Collins stands up and throws the blanket onto my lap. "Mom and Dad want me to ask you what costume you want to wear for the Halloween party they're having for you guys next weekend. They're going to be out of town for business, so they want me to get it and bring it over."

Andy twists up his face like he's deep in thought, and then answers. "I want to be a mad scientist."

"Are you sure, Anderson?" Collins pulls her head back in shock. "You don't want to be a football player or Batman or something like that?"

"Nope. I want to be a mad scientist."

"I didn't see that one coming, buddy," I say, "but it's cool."

"You have to dress up, too, Slaughter." Andy is dead serious.

I haven't dressed up for Halloween in years. "I do?"

"Yep. We're going to be a team costume."

"You want me to be a mad scientist, too?"

"Nope. Even better." He gets the wicked little grin of his on his face like he does when something's brewing in that brain of his.

I'm totally clueless about what he's thinking. I search my brain for anything that may offer a clue, but have no luck. "What kind of crazy idea you got cooking up inside your head?'

"You know." He pauses. "Think about it." He points to my leg.

Just when I'm about to give up, it hits me. He has a mind like a steel trap. "Do you think your sister will get me a costume?"

"Uh-huh."

Collins doesn't seem to be as sure. "What are you two weirdos talking about?"

"He wants me to dress up like…" I wait so we can say it together. At the same time we say, "Frankenstein."

"You two are crazy. Y'all are like two half-cooked peas in the same pod." She tickles Andy's tummy, and he coos. "Are you sure you want to do that?" she asks me.

"I reckon."

"What about you, little man?"

Andy looks at his sister with a Cheshire cat grin on his face because he knows the next words he's about to say are going to bug the heck out of her. "I reckon."

She rolls her eyes and shakes her head. "See what you've done, Dustin. It looks like you should be the one wearing the mad scientist's costume, because you're the one who's created this monster."

We both laugh, but she just huffs.

"Night, buddy. Love you."

"Love you, too." He leans up and kisses me on the cheek like he does every night. I never had a brother, but I feel like Andy is my little brother. If I ever did have one, I would want him to be just like Andy.

"Let's go," Collins says to Andy. "I'll read you a story before bed." When he turns his eyes, she mouths to me. "Meet me in the garden."

Chapter Thirty

It feels like an eternity waiting on Collins to come downstairs. A half hour passes, and I think she's changed her mind. She didn't. She waves to me as she exits the elevator. It's eight forty-five in the evening and the hospital garden is empty.

"Miss me?"

If she only knew the half of it. I miss her every minute of every day when she's not with me. "I reckon."

"I think you just say that to get a rise out of me."

There's a little bit of truth in her words, but not much. "Nah, I've been saying it my whole life. It's a bad habit I picked up in Flatbush."

"You've mentioned Flatbush a couple of times. Tell me about it."

"What's to tell?"

"Lots of things, I'd imagine."

"What do you want to know?"

"Well, tell me about your family for starters." She pushes up next to me on the couch. "I've never heard you mention your mom or dad."

"Want the short version or the truth?"

"The truth."

"Why? What's it matter?'

"Because I want to know who Dustin Slaughter is. I've been hearing about you for weeks now, and now that I've met you, I'm thinking I'd kinda like to get to know you a little better."

Talk about pressure. Here's a beautiful girl who wants to get to know me for some reason. A crippled ex-football player from Nowhere, North Carolina. It makes no sense.

"Short version is I've never known my dad. Not really. And Mama is sick."

"Great start." She presses a finger into my chest. "Now the truth."

Since I don't have anything to lose, I tell her everything about Mama and Daddy and let her know about Daddy, the preacher's wife, and all about how Mama is an addict. It doesn't seem to faze her one bit. She just listens as I talk and takes it all in without even flinching. At one particularly hard part of my glorious tale, a tear wells up in my eye. I fight to press it back but not before she reaches for my hand and holds it between both of hers.

When I finish telling her all about my childhood and life on the mountain, she sits there for a few stunned moments. I'm pretty sure she's trying to figure out an easy way to leave without looking like a snob.

It surprises me when she doesn't. "I'm so sorry, Dustin. No kid should ever have to grow up like that."

She's right and I know it, but at least my childhood wasn't spent in a hospital. "What's sad to me is Andy has to put up with all of the cancer stuff."

"It's been hard on all of us, but especially him." Now Collins fights back a tear or two. "Anderson is the most wonderful brother anyone could ever hope for."

"Believe me, I know."

"When we found out he had cancer and only had a couple of years to live, we were devastated. I was close to graduating high school and he was so excited I was going to college. Once he found out I was accepted to UNC, he almost peed his pants. It's his dream school, you know."

"Yep, I know."

"It isn't mine, though."

"No?"

"I wanted to go to UCLA in California."

"I know where UCLA is."

"I'm sorry, that's not what I meant." She lets go of my hand to dry her eyes. "When I found out about Anderson's diagnosis, there was no way on earth I was leaving him."

"That's sweet of you."

"What choice did I have?"

"We all have choices," I say. "My mama chooses to swill alcohol and pop pills, and I chose to drive like a madman the night of my accident.

"Anderson doesn't."

When she mentions Andy, it feels like a punch right to my gut. I can't believe I still focus on all the crap in my life when my best friend is up there fighting for a miracle. "I shouldn't have said that."

"It's okay. I know what you mean. Life sucks sometimes, and we just have to deal with it."

"Ain't that the truth!"

"Tell me something else about Flatbush."

"Flatbush is the place where dreams go to die. My only chance out of there was football, and now that's down the toilet. Which means my fate will be a job at the local plant cleaning toilets or working an assembly line for the rest of my life. If I don't ever walk again, who knows what I'll be qualified to do."

"You do know there's more to life than football, don't you?'

"Not in Flatbush. Not for me."

"Then get out of Flatbush."

"It's all I know."

"Then learn something new."

We sit in silence for a moment or two, and I let her words rattle around inside my head. "Like what?"

"For starters, learn to walk."

What's with all these people wanting me to just learn to walk? If I could, don't they think I would? "It's not quite that simple. My body won't work right."

"It will if you give it time and fight for it like you did on the football field." Before I have a chance to say anything else she asks, "What's your girlfriend's name?"

"I don't have a girlfriend," I say.

"Maybe not now." The same devious smile I've seen Andy wear flashes across her face. "But you did. What's her name?"

She doesn't know how badly I don't want to say her name. It worries me that if we keep talking about her, she'll want to know the whole story. I take my chances. "Jenny Lee."

"Hmmm…it sounds like the perfect name for a southern girl." Collins crinkles her nose like someone does when something stinks. I can't tell if it's curiosity or jealousy. I'm hoping for jealousy. "Tell me about her."

After beating around the bush for a few minutes, I close my eyes and take a deep breath. I tell her she's the only girl I've ever dated, and when she asks me if I love her, I tell her that I thought I did, but I definitely don't now, and now that so much time has passed, I'm not even sure I ever did.

She presses me to tell her what she looks like, so I admit that she's pretty. One of the prettiest girls in school. She crinkles her nose again when I tell her she has long blonde hair. She asks if I like blondes, and I tell her that I don't necessarily like blondes. I just liked her.

She shifts on the couch and moves a little closer to me. My pulse quickens. When she asks why we broke up, it goes into overload.

We share the couch until close to midnight. I tell her everything about the night of my accident. The parts I remember anyhow. I tell her about Sully and Coach and the scouts. I tell her about UNC and my dreams and how the dreams all got smashed to bits when my car went off the side of the mountain.

Collins never says a word the whole time I talk. She just listens to everything I say like she cares. Like she's been waiting to hear my story her whole life. I'm surprised she doesn't even make a big deal when I lose it and bawl like a baby about walking in on Sully and Jenny Lee. I thought I was past all of the crying and hurt, but when I talk about it again, it's like ripping a Band-Aid off of a fresh wound and the blood oozes out all over again. Collins doesn't freak out about any of it. What I don't realize until I stop talking is she has her arm around me.

All she says after everything is, "Life's going to go your way one of these days, Dustin."

"I hope so."

"Hope's all we have, isn't it?"

"I reckon." Collins pulls her arm from around me and slugs me in the arm.

"Now, baby, what're you doin' down here?" Miss Bernice walks up and interrupts us. "They're lookin' all over this hospital for you."

"They are?"

"You were supposed to be in bed an hour ago." Miss Bernice eyes Collins like a protective grandmother. "You need to get on upstairs before they have a fit."

"Yes, ma'am."

"I guess I need to be going," Collins says.

"Who's your lady friend, baby?"

"This is Andy's sister, Collins."

"Mmm hmmm. So you're the sister of the sweet boy Dusty's so crazy about."

"Yes, ma'am, I am." Collins stands and shakes Miss Bernice's hand. "Nice to meet you."

"Nice to meet you too, honey, but you best be goin'. Dusty needs to get upstairs and get his beauty rest. He's got therapy all day tomorrow."

"I understand." Collins reaches down to give me a hug. "See you soon."

"Don't forget our costumes for the party," I remind her.

"I won't."

Miss Bernice watches her leave the hospital, and then whips around with arms crossed. I get in my chair and start rolling, hoping not to hear another word, though I know Miss Bernice isn't going to let it go.

"Looks like ol' Romeo got himself a Juliet."

"She's Andy's sister. That's all."

"Mmmm hmmmm."

Chapter Thirty-One

A week passes and we're only a day away from the Halloween party. Collins comes by the hospital just about every night. Most nights she arrives after Andy is in bed. I feel bad for the little guy because his sister comes to see me, and he doesn't get a chance to see her. It's okay, I guess. For now.

My day is the same old routine. Therapy steals most of my waking hours. It's exhausting and pisses me off. Brooke pushes me harder than Coach ever did. Ever. She barks at me and expects me to do whatever she says, whenever she says. She refuses to listen to my *excuses,* as she puts it. Says she works with girls half my size who are much tougher than me. I don't know if she's telling the truth or not, but I hate when she challenges me, so I bust my butt to make sure I don't have to listen to her.

I spend time with Andy and Katie bug like always. That part of my schedule doesn't change. Every night I go up and hang. Angela tells me Katie bug will go home before Christmas. Her cancer is in remission. Angela says she still cries for her parents every night. I notice the hair on her head sprouting in fine little pieces of white. She's a pretty little girl, with or without hair. I pray every night she, and all the other kids, can grow up, but I know most of them will not live even a few more years.

Andy and I wait for Collins to arrive with our costumes. "Do you think she'll be here soon?"

"For sure, buddy."

"She told me last night she would be here by dinner." He slumps in his chair. "It's past dinner. The party is tomorrow."

"I bet she's just running late from class." It isn't like her to be late, and I don't want Andy to worry, so I think about something we can do to take our minds off Collins. It's more for me than him. "How about we do something fun?"

"Like what?"

There's an unused wheelchair in the corner of the room. "Over there."

"What are you talking about?"

"The wheelchair. Let's have a wheelchair race."

"They won't let us."

"We're not going to ask permission." I wheel over to it and pull it out of the corner and shove it to Andy. It rolls half-heartedly toward him and stops about ten feet from where he's sitting.

"Are you sure?" He looks stressed. "We're going to get in trouble."

"I heard something a long time ago I like to say. Want to hear it?"

"I reckon," he says.

"It's better to ask forgiveness than permission."

"What does that mean?"

"It means when a moment like this, like the first ever wheelchair race, stares us in the face, we need to hop all over it. If we ask, what will they say?"

He pulls himself out of the chair he's sitting in and stares at the empty wheelchair. He hesitates to get in it. "No."

I roll closer to the empty wheelchair, hoping he'll do the same. "Exactly. So if we don't ask and do it, what'll happen?"

He raises his hand to his chin and rubs it like he's deep in thought. "We'll get in trouble."

"Maybe a little bit, but it'll be so worth it, don't you think?"

"Yeah." His eyes widen as he sits in the seat of the wheelchair.

"And when we do, we'll simply ask them to forgive us."

He wraps his little fingers around the wheels and gives them a slight shove. His chair rolls a few inches before he stops it. "Will it work?"

"Are you kidding? Who's not going to be able to forgive the two best looking dudes in the entire hospital?"

He laughs and clumsily rolls over to me. "Let's do it."

"The course is simple," I say. "We'll start here and finish here." Andy's floor is a giant rectangle, two long halls with two connecting halls at each end. An open area swallows up the center where the doctors and nurses congregate. There's no doubt we'll pass them at least twice. "We will go this way down the hall, hang a left, down the other hall, hang another left, and back here."

A smile replaces the frown of concern he's been wearing. "Just like NASCAR," he says.

"Exactly. I didn't know you like NASCAR."

"It's not my favorite, but the cars fly. Dad took me to Charlotte Motor Speedway once. Have you ever been?"

I spin my wheelchair in a circle and make racecar noises. "Nope."

"Man, they are so fast and loud. So loud Dad had to buy earplugs for us."

"Cool. Maybe one day you and I'll go."

"That'll be awesome." Andy holds up a tiny little hand for me to high five. I reach over and press mine against his.

"Ready to roll?"

"I reckon." Andy cracks me up when he copies me, because Collins hates it, though she lets him get away with it now.

"The first time we pass the nurses' station, they won't realize what's going on, but when we double back, they'll be on to us. We'll be busted, but keep going until you reach the finish line."

"Okay."

I line up right next to Andy and pat him on the back. "You do the countdown."

He's eager to start. "Gentlemen, start your engines." Andy makes rumbling car noises. I do the same. "On your mark. Get set." Andy starts rolling down the hall. "Go!" He yells back at me over his shoulder.

"No fair," I shout.

"Life's not fair. Get used to it." He's right about that, but I don't think I'll ever get used to it.

The little guy burns down the hall faster than I thought he would. "Slow down, speed racer."

"Never," he shouts. "Better go faster if you want to catch me."

I figure since I've been in this thing for close to two months, I'd be faster than Andy. I'm wrong. The little guy cuts hard left, and I follow close behind. I cut too sharp and almost flip the chair over on its side. He gives me a quick glance, laughs, and keeps on moving. None of the nurses we pass say anything to us. At least not yet.

We scream down the other long hallway and enter the central nurses' station for the second time. To my surprise, they're all standing to the side holding pieces of paper with *Go Anderson* written on them. As we pass, they and some other kids cheer Andy on. This energizes the little guy and his arms start pumping like engine pistons. It's all I can do to stay close to him. Before the race, I planned to let him win, but at this point, I do my best to beat him.

He takes the last two corners without any trouble. I'm not as lucky. I slow down to avoid another near crash and lose momentum as a result. The kids, doctors, and nurses stand near the finish line and cheer him on. Andy crosses the finish line as his adoring fans clap and whistle. He slams on the brakes and spins around just in time to watch me cross the finish line, sweat beading up on my forehead.

"I won! I won!" he shouts. Everyone rushes to him. The guys high five or knuckle bump him and the ladies are quick with hugs and kisses.

Collins walks in on the celebration, carrying bags. She worms her way through Andy's cheering section. "What's going on here, Anderson?"

"I just blew Slaughter out of the water in the first ever wheelchair five-hundred. It was awesome!"

Most of the hospital staff walks away, leaving Andy and me alone with Collins. She doesn't seem too happy with our little stunt.

"Was this your idea?" Collins puts a hand on her hip; the bags dangle from her wrist.

"Yeah, well…" I pause. She's kind of scary when she's serious. "We were bored waiting on you."

"Don't blame this on me, mister."

"What's the big deal, Collins? Relax. It was fun."

"I guess they didn't mind." She motions to the nurses. Then glares at Andy. "But what if you wrecked? You could've gotten hurt."

"But he didn't." It becomes immediately clear she doesn't want my input. I take my life in my own hands and continue. "It was fun and nobody got hurt."

Collins takes a long moment to think things over. With a sigh of resignation, she's over it. "So you beat him?"

"Blew him out of the water."

"You got a head start." My excuse sounds more like the words of a poor loser. "But you're right. You kicked my butt."

"That's my brother," Collins says as she high fives him. "He's a Thacker. Thackers kick butt and take names."

Andy gets out of the chair and rolls it back to where we got it. "Did you let me win, Slaughter?"

"No way, dude. I never let anyone win. They have to beat me outright, and that's what you did."

"Thanks," Andy says.

"You're the man. Now let's go try on your costume," Collins tells him.

Minutes later, she comes back out. "Will you do something for me?" I ask.

Collins shoots me a skeptical look. "Depends on what it is."

I look past her to make sure Andy is nowhere around. "Will you shave my head to match his?"

My request catches her by surprise, and she slaps her hand over her mouth. "I'd love to."

Chapter Thirty-Two

The night of the Halloween party arrives, and Andy and I look spectacular. His mad scientist get-up is perfect. He has a big head of wild, grey hair, crazy glasses, and a lab coat spotted in what looks like real blood.

Since most of the kids have seen my leg already, I cut the left leg off of the old suit pants Collins got for me from Goodwill and let the scarred mess speak for itself. A torn t-shirt under a suit jacket, which is at least two sizes too large, the Frankenstein monster mask, and I'm set for the night. I take the mask off for the first time in front of Andy.

"What happened to your hair?" Andy rubs my bald head.

"Shaved it off to match you."

Andy walks around in a circle investigating my head. "Looks perfect. Collins may not like it, though. Just saying."

"Who do you think shaved it for me?"

"Seriously?"

"Yep. When do you think she'll be here?" I ask Andy.

He shrugs his shoulder. "You like her, don't you?"

His question surprises me. "She's your sister, so duh, yeah I like her."

"I don't mean that kind of like. I mean, you *like her* like her."
Another sly grin.

The kid's too smart for his own good. Collins visits me every night, and most nights she stops in to see Andy and reads him a story. We spend the evening talking and laughing about anything and everything. She tells me mostly about her day at school. About the classes she likes, and the ones she hates. She's smart, and I like that. I'm an okay student, but only because I busted my butt studying so I could get a football scholarship. Football will get me in the door. Grades will keep me there. That was my motto. Now, things are different, since I don't have football to fall back on.

I'm doing all right with the homework and assignments the lady from back home brings down for me to do. And I pass most of my tests and quizzes with A's. I've gotten a few B's, though. My essays aren't anything to write home about, but I'm passing English with an A somehow. I'm pretty sure it's because Collins helps me with my writing. She doesn't do it for me, but she definitely helps. I like spending time with her, and if it means doing homework together, then I'm all for it.

"She's all right," I tell Andy, but he doesn't buy it.

"She likes you."

My eyes widen and my heart skips a beat. All of a sudden I feel like I'm back in third grade. "She does? How do you know? Did she tell you?"

"Nope. Just made it up to see what you'd say." He makes a goofy little *I told you so* face.

"Very funny, buddy." I'm busted, so I admit it to Andy. "You got me. Yeah, she's pretty cool. For a girl."

"She's pretty, too," Andy says. "All the boys want to go out with her, you know!"

"They do?" A tinge of jealousy sweeps over me. I don't know why, because it's not like Collins and I are dating.

"They always have for as long as I can remember. In high school, she had three boys wanting to take her to prom. She liked all three of them but couldn't go with all of them."

"What'd she do?"

Andy says that instead of breaking their hearts, she decided to go with her friends. He says that she did it to be nice. I ask him if he thought I had a chance. Whether or not she'd ever go for a guy like me. He gives me one of those "are you crazy" kind of looks. Andy pulls his head back with a jolt and twists up his face. "What are you talking about? You're awesome."

"You know what I mean." I look at my leg.

"Collins isn't like that, Slaughter. She doesn't worry about looks. Her last boyfriend was what Mom called a mutt."

A snort of laughter escapes. "Sorry, that's mean."

"But funny." Andy adjusts his scientist's wig. "Mom tells it like it is."

"You don't think a cripple like me bothers her, do you?"

"Nope. She does like you, because she always asks me about you when she calls. You should ask her out. When you get out of the hospital and all"

"Maybe."

Collins sneaks up on us all the time. "What are you two talking about?"

"Uhhh…nothing," I lie.

"Slaughter was just asking…" Andy pauses long enough to get me to squirm. "when you were going to get here."

"I'm here." Collins pulls off her long coat, and underneath she's wearing an outfit similar to mine, but much, much better. She's wearing a woman's suit jacket and a tight, black top that looks good on her. Her pants are those skin-tight black leggings. Sadly, the jacket hangs too low to get a good look at her. She pulls out another wig and some makeup. "I'm going to be the Bride of Frankenstein."

"I told you." Andy slaps me on the shoulder.

"You told him what?" Collins looks back and forth at both of us trying to figure out what's going on.

"He said you'd dress up." My second lie.

"Whatever," Collins says and walks away.

"Looks like she's mad, buddy."

"Nah, she always does that when she doesn't get her way." Andy straightens his jacket. "Put on your mask and let's go."

We make our way to the playroom. They've had it closed all day long. Andy and I wait outside, along with the other kids and their families, for them to open it.

One of the doctors gets everyone's attention. "Before we have the party, our staff decided it would be fun to do something a little different this year." He's wearing a cop's uniform, and it makes me wonder if he wanted to be a cop instead of a doctor. "What we decided to do is have you all celebrate in the trick-or-treat fun of the holiday. We talked to a couple of the other floors just below us, and they agreed to set it up for you all to go door-to-door, so to speak, and get some candy."

"Yay," a few kids say.

"We've even brought you Halloween baskets," he says. A few of the nurses come around the corner with plastic pumpkins for all of the kids.

"Are you going with us, too, Slaughter?"

"For sure."

"Good," Collins says.

"What do you think?" Andy dangles his plastic pumpkin in front of me.

"It looks like you'll have candy for weeks with such a big pumpkin. Should last you till Thanksgiving."

"You obviously don't know Anderson as well as you think you do. He loves candy."

"But I never get any."

"True," Collins says. "Mom and Dad never let us have it."

"That stinks, buddy." I thump the pumpkin. "They're not here now, are they?"

"Nope. Ask forgiveness, right?"

"Yep."

"What are you two talking about now?" Collins asks.

"Just something between us." Andy pushes his glasses up on his nose again.

"Whatever," Collins says. "Ready to go get some candy?"

"I reckon," Andy says and receives an instant glare from his sister. I can't tell if she is pissed or just pretending.

We follow the crowd to the elevators. There isn't enough room to get us all on at once, so we wait our turn. We're toward the back, and fifteen minutes pass before we slip inside. We go down two floors and start. It's a pretty cool thing they do. They have the kids going room to room with doctors and nurses waiting with candy. Most of them are dressed up in crazy costumes, holding candy bags. The kids have to go in and say trick-or-treat to get the candy. Most of the kids have no trouble at all, but a few are a little scared by some of the costumes. Understandable, I guess. Adults can be a little creepy sometimes.

Everyone seems to be enjoying themselves. The nurses and doctors get a kick out of it, too. Some keep talking on and on about how cute the kids are as they toss candy into their buckets. Others get lost in stories of their own childhood.

We move to each room as fast as we can, talking to the doctors and nurses a little bit here and there. By the time we get back to Andy's floor, the kid has filled his pumpkin up to the brim. The good stuff, too.

"I'm thinking Christmas," I say. Andy and Collins look at me with confusion plastered on their faces. "That's how long his candy'll last."

"I don't think so." Andy licks his lips and rubs his belly. "Want a piece?"

"Nah, I think you should put it in your room and we should go to the party now."

"Great idea." Collins takes Andy's pumpkin and disappears.

"What do you think they did to the room?"

"No idea. Made it scary, I guess."

Collins returns and we go to the party. We're one of the first to arrive and I find an out of the way place in the corner to park my chair.

"It's so cool," Andy says as he looks around.

The lights are off, and black lights create a spooky glow. The speakers blast out scary Halloween music. They brought all sorts of creepy things like ghosts and monsters. Spider webs and giant spiders hang from the ceiling. They even have a machine blowing fog into the room. They went all out putting it together.

"They must've spent all day on this thing." I tug on Andy's lab coat. "Check it out. You're glowing."

"Totally awesome." A few of Andy's friends come in with their parents and he disappears into the fog.

"Just you and me now," Collins says.

"I reckon."

"You're not scared are you?"

"Only a little," I tease. "But you'll keep me safe, won't you?"

"You're the monster tonight. Not me." She laughs and pulls a metal folding chair up beside me.

"He's doing great, huh!" I watch Andy with his friends and he seems so happy.

"He is, but his health changes all the time." Collins crosses her fingers. "His doctor says he may be able to come home even sooner than they originally thought."

"Before Christmas?"

"Yes. Maybe even before Thanksgiving, but they're not sure."

The news hits me hard. I hadn't thought about spending Thanksgiving and Christmas in a hospital before, but now that I have to, I never thought about spending it alone. "That's great. I'm sure your mom and dad will be thrilled."

"We all will." Collins puts her hand on mine. "It doesn't mean I can't still come visit you, though."

Her hand is warm and soft. "You still want to come visit me even after he's back home?"

"Yes, silly. My dorm is right around the corner, so it's easy. I'm off the whole week of Thanksgiving, so I won't have classes. And then I'm done in early December for the semester."

"I'd like you to visit."

She squeezes my hand a little harder. "I like you, Dustin. You're different than most of the guys I know. Plus, I see how great you are with Anderson. You've got a big heart and that's important to me."

"Thanks, but that's about all I have now."

"Not true at all. You have so much more in front of you."

"Football is all I had. What's left of me other than a former running back who can't run?"

"Only those without a future continue to live in the past, Dustin." Collins puts her finger on my chest and pokes. "It's time for you to find yourself a new future."

I sit in weakened silence for a few long moments. She's right and I know it. I need to let everything go and focus on something else, but what that something else is remains a mystery.

Collins stares at Andy as he fills a cup with punch.

"My parents and I aren't idiots. We know it's unlikely Anderson will live as long as the rest of us." A tear rolls down the side of her face, smearing her makeup. "We just pray he can beat this thing, but if he doesn't, we want him to have the best life possible. Things look good right now, and we're hoping he'll be with us for a few more years, but we've all readied ourselves for when he can't fight any longer."

The quiver in her voice causes my heart to ache. She wipes the tear with the back of her hand and straightens herself. My hand is cold without her hand on mine.

"He's the best friend I've ever had, Collins. It breaks my heart every night when I have to leave him and Katie bug and go back to my room knowing any day now they could be gone. I hate to think about it and try not to, but there are some nights I write in Excalibur for hours." Now it's my turn to fight the tears. Fortunately for me, they're behind a mask. "Do you think he'll be here until his birthday?"

"Yes. It's in two weeks. The earliest he'd go home is Thanksgiving week. Why?"

"I've been doing something for his present."

"You don't have to get him a present," Collins says.

"I didn't get him anything. I'm making him something."

"What is it?" Collins asks.

"It's a surprise, and it's not finished yet."

"Okay, be that way."

They switch the music from the spooky sounds to regular dance music. The kids get out on the floor and start acting goofy and having a ball.

Collins stands up and reaches out her hand. "Want to dance?"

I'm not much of a dancer and never have been, but dancing in a wheelchair isn't as easy as it looks. I mostly shake my arms and move my body while Collins dances. She looks beautiful in the glow of the light. Her eyes sparkle in the darkness. Even though I roll over her toe every now and then, she doesn't complain. She just keeps on dancing.

Eventually, Andy dumps his friends and comes over to us. "Want to dance with me, Collins?"

"For sure," she says as she winks at me.

I watch the two of them dancing their butts off. Andy is having a great time. All of the kids are having a blast. They shake and move, some slower than others. A few are stuck in wheelchairs like me, but they all have smiles on their faces.

Collins eventually returns, and stands in front of me.

"Are you asking me to dance?'

She pulls my monster mask off of my face. "Nope," she says as she leans over and grabs my face with both hands. "I came to do this." She leans in close and puts her soft lips on mine. My body tingles all over. My mouth opens in slow motion and her tongue slides in. I reach out to hold her and do the best I can. Her body is warm and soft. Heated breath lies heavy on my face and I wonder if it's from the dancing or this moment. My eyes seal shut and I forget I'm in a hospital surrounded by ghosts and goblins and kids with cancer. At this moment, I'm happier than I've ever been in my life.

Chapter Thirty-Three

The days pass one after the other. Collins comes by every day. When she's here the time flies by so fast, and drags on and on, hour after hour when she's away.

I'm learning to use my leg again. It's slow and painful, but the therapy is working. I can move myself on my own and keep my balance at the same time. It about kills me, but it's all right because the next time I have a chance to dance with Collins, it's going to be on my own two feet.

Brooke tells me I'm progressing faster than anyone else she's worked with who has an injury like mine. I think she's lying to me to keep me pumped, but I don't say anything. Even if she is lying, it's fine by me because now more than ever I have a reason to walk.

Once I finish Andy's birthday present, I look it over and think it's pretty good. I don't show it to anyone before I give it to him, so I don't know if he'll like it or not. Collins tries to get the secret out of me every day. Some days she almost succeeds. It's hard to say no when she's kissing me.

I'm only hours away from the big reveal. His parents and Collins are spending some time with him alone first. Then they're throwing a party for him in the TV room. Collins says they're going all out for this birthday party for him. She says they do it every year. This one is different, though, because it's the first one he's spent in a hospital. I think it's why they're so eager to get him home before Thanksgiving.

A few of the guys from the team have come down to visit me in the past couple of weeks. It's good to catch up and find out what all's going on with them. Even though it's been about two months since I've seen them, it feels like it's been years. Sully and Jenny Lee are still going at it hard and heavy one of the guys tells me. He also tells me most of the guys don't talk to Sully too much anymore, and after what happened the night of the accident, they don't want anything to do with him other than what they have to do on the field for Coach and the team.

I congratulate them for having a great season, and they say it wasn't great because I wasn't with them. Bean tells me they dedicated every game to me, and it's what got them as far as they got. He tells me that if I had played with them, the team would be state champions. I don't know if it's true or not, and, honestly, now I don't care. Like Collins says, I have to find a new future and stop living in my past. The old me is dead.

It's time for the party, so I grab his present and wheel myself to the elevator. Miss Bernice is in on part of my surprise, so she's already made arrangements with the people on Andy's floor.

"Good luck, Slaughter," another nurse says. "I'm proud of you."

"Thanks a bunch."

My nerves twist up inside me so tight I feel I'm about to burst into a million pieces. The bell dings and I get in and push the button.

Collins asked me to get there at six on the dot, so she's waiting for me when the door opens.

"Hey, sweetie," she says. The first thing she called me was babe, and since it reminded me of Jenny Lee, I asked her to think of something better. She understands and has never called me babe since.

"Hey, beautiful. Miss me?"

"Every minute of my life when you're not with me."

"Me, too." I reach my head up, and she plants a kiss on my lips. "Did he have fun with the family?"

"A blast. Dad somehow managed to get him a Panthers signed jersey."

"Awesome." When you have money, you can pretty much get whatever you want.

"So what did you get him? Is it in your backpack?"

"You'll have to wait, and yes, it is."

"Man, you're good at keeping secrets."

"It's not a secret. It's a surprise." We work our way to the TV room. "I've kinda got a surprise for you, too."

"Oh no you don't. You can't do that to me and not tell me. Besides, it's not my birthday."

"I can, and I did."

She fake punches me in the arm. Then she follows it up with a quick peck on my cheek.

When we enter, Andy's sitting on the couch. He's wearing a pair of slacks with a shirt and tie. "What's with the get up?"

He huffs and tugs at the collar of his shirt. "Mom and Dad make me wear it for my birthday every year."

"Bummer, dude." The jeans and shirt I'm wearing suddenly make me feel underdressed for a nine-year-old's birthday party. "If it makes you feel any better, you look great."

"It doesn't."

"Good evening, Slaughter," Mr. Thacker says as he and his wife enter the room. He shakes my hand. "Great to see you again."

"Nice to see you, too, sir."

"Mrs. Thacker, you look lovely as always," I say, scoring more brownie points.

She pretends to be embarrassed and says, "Now, Dusty, you're going to make Mr. Thacker jealous."

It no longer surprises me that they never refer to one another by their first names. Now that I think about it, I don't even know what their names are.

"Collins, why don't you get Slaughter something to drink?"

She goes to the table and pours me a Coke even though I'm not thirsty. Her parents are particular about how things are supposed to be. I take a sip and say, "Thanks, honey."

Mr. Thacker doesn't even bat an eye because Collins told him a week or so ago we're dating. Andy thinks it's the coolest thing ever. He says if we get married one day, it'll make me his brother-in-law and it's as close to a brother as I can be. Collins thinks it's funny but never says anything about it.

"Time to get the party started, son." Mr. Thacker leaves the room. Within seconds, kids flow through the door.

Angela brings a giant sheet cake in and puts it on the table. There are nine candles sticking out of the center of the cake and Mrs. Thacker lights them. "Time to make a wish."

If I were in Andy's spot, I know what I would wish for. He closes his eyes and thinks for a moment. When he's ready, he leans in close to the candles, takes a deep breath, and blows them out. The smoke from the burning candles floats into the air.

"Time to sing happy birthday," Collins says.

On the count of three she starts and all the kids join in. They sing loud enough to drown out my tone-deaf attempt at singing.

"Who wants cake?" Mrs. Thacker asks and receives lots of "I do's."

After the cake and ice cream are all gone, it's time for the presents. All of the kids made something for Andy since they can't go out and buy toys. This makes me feel much better since my gift is homemade, too.

There are lots of hand-drawn cards, a few arts and crafts projects that don't resemble anything I've ever seen before, but it's sweet. These kids love one another.

It's my turn. "Ready for my present, buddy?"

"I reckon." Mr. Thacker cracks into pieces when Andy answers me. He bites his tongue like he does every time Andy says it.

Collins hands me the bag and puts it in my lap. I unzip it and pull out the pad Miss Bernice bought me. It's inside a box and wrapped up. Miss Bernice helped me with that, too. Andy's eyes widen when I hand the wrapped box to him. He takes his time looking at the wrapping paper. It's sports wrapping paper with just about every kind of sports equipment on it. There's no telling how Miss Bernice found it, but she did, and it's about the most perfect wrapping paper for Andy.

"It's cool," he says. Mrs. Thacker leans in close and helps him remove it without ripping it up. He looks at me and says, "I'm going to save it."

"It's yours, buddy. You do whatever you want with it," I tell him.

He lifts the top off the box and pulls out the pad. On the front cover there's a giant picture of Andy in a football uniform. The lettering on top says, *Andy's Big Game*. He spins the book around to show Collins. She cups her hand over her mouth, and then cuts her eyes to me.

"Show it to us," Mr. Thacker says.

Andy shows it to them and they both start to tear up.

"Did you do this?" Mr. Thacker asks.

I nod a couple of times. By now, the three of them are leaning over Andy's shoulders and reading along with him. Andy flips the page to the second one, stares at the pictures for a minute, and then closes the book. He lays it on the table and starts to cry. The other kids look at him like he's crazy. Katie bug asks, "Why's he sad?" One of the nurses whispers in her ear something I can't hear.

The nurses and doctors gather around. I see Miss Bernice in the group. She smiles a big toothy smile and watches.

Andy gets up from his chair and stands in front of me. "Slaughter, it's awesome. Thank you."

"You're welcome, buddy. I know how much you love to read, so I figured what better gift could I give you than a book all about you?"

"You're my best friend in the whole world."

"You're mine, too, buddy."

Collins picks up the book and thumbs through the pages, checking it out. She passes it to her parents, and they stare at it in disbelief. They seem blown away by the fact that I wrote an entire book, complete with pictures of Andy as a football player and all the kids in the hospital as his teammates.

"That's not all I have for you, buddy."

"What else is there? Your bag is empty."

"It's kinda for you, too, Collins."

By now, tears stream down her face. Miss Bernice brings over the walker and puts it in front of me.

"Are you serious?" Andy asks.

I flip the feet holders on the chair out of the way and grab the grips on the walker. I've practiced doing it for days now. It's difficult to scoot to the edge of the chair, but with all the strength I can muster, I pull myself to my feet. Everyone backs away and gives me some room. One foot after the other, I shuffle a few inches at a time.

"You've got to be kidding me," Collins says. "You can walk."

Nearly everyone tears up as I take step after step to Collins. "It's not much, but it's a start," I say.

"I'm so proud of you, baby," Miss Bernice chokes out.

When I stop in front of Collins, she stares at me through cloudy eyes. "I told myself the next time I get the chance to dance with you, it's going to be on my own two feet."

Collins just about knocks me over as she wraps her arms around me and starts kissing me. After a few seconds, she pulls away and I look at Andy. "This is all because of you, buddy. This is because you believe in me. You and your sister both do."

Andy slides his hand into mine. "Slaughter," he looks up at me. "Thank you for making this the best birthday ever. I love you." He wraps his skinny little arms around my waist.

"I love you, too, buddy."

Chapter Thirty-Four

Thanksgiving week arrives and Collins comes to see me every day. She comes to see Andy, too, because the medicine he's taking isn't working like it has been. The doctors say he can't go home now, and they're not sure whether or not he'll be able to by Christmas, either.

Andy carries the book I made with him everywhere he goes. He's read all thirty pages of it at least a half dozen times. When Collins reads to him at night, it's always from *Andy's Big Game*. She's read it three times.

"What're you doing tomorrow?" I ask her. Andy's gone to bed, and we're in the garden talking like we do every night.

"My family is having dinner at our house. Mom and Dad are coming to get Anderson for the day."

"That's cool."

"What about you?"

"I don't know for sure. They're having turkey and dressing for dinner tomorrow night in the cafeteria, so that'll be good."

"I may not get to see you tomorrow," she says. "Dad's picking Anderson up early and needs me at the house to help Mom get dinner ready."

"No biggie." Collins and I have been together every single day since Halloween, and my heart sinks when I think about a day passing that I don't get to see her beautiful face. "I understand."

She helps me to my feet and wraps her arms around me. I hold her, using her body to help me keep my balance. We kiss for a few minutes.

"I'm going to call you tomorrow."

She backs away and pushes my walker to me. I'm not much faster than I was the first time she saw me walk, but I manage to get places a little quicker than before. From snail to turtle. Not as fast as the wheelchair, but I'd rather have my legs than wheels any day of the week.

"Collins," I say.

"What is it, sweetie?"

"I love you."

She hesitates for a minute, and I feel like I've screwed up big time. She looks me in the eyes and says, "I love you more."

She kisses me one more time and then leaves. I watch her go, just like I do every night. Then I make my way to my room at a turtle's pace.

****

The next morning, a booming voice jolts me out of bed. "Get up, Slaughter. And get ready."

Mr. Thacker looms in the doorway with a suit and tie. He hangs it on the rack, along with a pair of black shoes and socks.

"What's going on, sir?"

"You're getting up from bed, putting on this suit I bought you, and meeting Anderson and me in the lobby in half an hour."

"I don't understand." At first I think I'm dreaming, but the chill in the air lets me know I'm not.

"I've pulled a few strings, and you're coming to my house for Thanksgiving."

Collins didn't mention anything about it last night. "Does Collins know?"

"She does not. It's kind of a surprise for her. And for Anderson because he doesn't know either." Mr. Thacker's serious tone never changes. "Now get ready and be in the lobby in thirty minutes."

"Yes, sir."

Thirty minutes are up and I'm waiting in the lobby. A few minutes later, I see Andy and Mr. Thacker walking toward me. Andy doesn't recognize me at first. Once he does, he lets go of Mr. Thacker's hand and runs to me. "What are you all dressed up for? Where are you going?"

"With you."

Andy looks at Mr. Thacker, who is now standing behind him. "Is he, Dad?"

"He is, Son. Slaughter is spending Thanksgiving with us."

"Yay!" Andy shrieks. "I can show you my room."

"For sure."

"Look, Slaughter." Andy points at me and then at himself. "We're wearing the same suit."

He's right. I didn't notice it at first, but he's absolutely right. Mr. Thacker got us identical navy blue suits, light blue polo shirts, and UNC ties. He even brought me a matching UNC hat just like the one Andy wears all the time. "We're twins, buddy."

Andy walks beside me as I make my way to the front door slower than a snail. Mr. Thacker doesn't rush us.

There's a black Mercedes with tinted windows parked out front. A driver jumps out and races to open the back door.

"Put his walker in the trunk, Thomas," Mr. Thacker says.

"Yes, Mr. Thacker."

Andy helps me slide into the big back seat. He slides in next to me, and Mr. Thacker gets in last. Thomas shuts the door, puts my walker in the trunk, and then drives away.

"You're going to love my house. It's awesome." Andy is more excited than I've ever seen him before.

"I'm sure I will, buddy."

"Slaughter," Mr. Thacker says. "Thank you for coming to our home for Thanksgiving. You mean so much to Anderson and Collins, and Mrs. Thacker and I want to show you how thankful we are for you."

I'm not sure what to say. "No problem, sir."

It's about an hour's drive to their house. Thomas slows the Mercedes and makes a right onto a long driveway that winds its way up to the biggest house I've ever seen in my life. It sits on top of a hill, and there are several horses grazing in the green grass surrounding it. There's a massive stable just off to the left.

"You like horses?" I ask.

"Nope. Mrs. Thacker does."

"And Collins," Andy chimes in.

"And Collins," Mr. Thacker repeats.

"Your house is beautiful, sir."

"Thank you, Slaughter."

Thomas loops around a giant fountain in the center of the circular driveway and stops at the front steps. He hops out and whips my walker around before I open the door. Mr. Thacker is halfway up the steps before Thomas brings my walker around to me.

It occurs to me that I've never walked up steps since my accident. My knee won't bend, and I wonder if I can even do it. There are only a few, but if I can't get my leg to work right, there might as well be a thousand of them.

Andy helps me around the car. Mr. Thacker comes back out with Collins by his side, and she looks annoyed until she sees me. Surprise registers on her face, and she races down the steps and wraps her arms around me tight. "What're you doing here?"

"Nice to see you too."

"You know what I mean." Collins takes a step back and looks at Andy and me. "You clean up nice. Looks like you two could be twins." She tugs on the bill of my cap and kisses me once more before picking Andy up and showering him with kisses.

"Careful, buddy. Those are my kisses."

Andy giggles.

"Y'all come on now," Mr. Thacker says. "Collins and Anderson, take him through the garage."

We walk toward the garage, and I'm glad not to have to try to climb the steps.

Once inside the house, Andy says, "Come see my room."

"Give him a second to get settled in, Anderson." Mrs. Thacker comes over and gives me a hug.

"Okay, okay," Andy says, though I know it's killing him to wait.

"Our guests will arrive in about an hour or so. We'll eat at noon," Mrs. Thacker says. "Would you like a beverage? Tea or water?"

"Is it sweet tea?"

"I wouldn't be a true southern woman if it weren't, now would I?"

"No, ma'am. I reckon not."

Mrs. Thacker leaves, and Collins takes my hand and pushes the walker aside. "You won't need that thing today."

"Uhhh…yeah, I do. I can't walk without it."

"You don't need it when you have me," she says as she puts my arm over her shoulder.

"And me," Andy says, grabbing my hand.

They help me into the kitchen, and Mrs. Thacker waits until I sit at the table before handing me the tea. "Thanks," I say and take a giant gulp. "It's delicious. Did you make it yourself?"

"Of course." Mrs. Thacker seems to lighten up a bit in her own home. Hopefully, Mr. Thacker will too.

About ten minutes pass and we all chat a little bit about the Panthers and football. Mr. Thacker shows interest in the fact that I played. "Anderson told me you had a chance to play for UNC."

"I did, but that's gone."

Mr. Thacker leans forward. Any hopes of him lightening up are shattered. "What are your plans now?"

I swallow hard and think about what I'm going to say. Something that will keep him from changing his mind about Collins and me. "I'm not sure, sir. Right now, I'm just trying to learn to walk again."

He doesn't skip a beat. "Sure. Sure. But after you walk again? College?"

"Dad, lay off. He just got here."

"It's fine, Collins. I don't mind." Even though he has me on the ropes and I'm fighting the urge to break out in cold sweats, I answer Mr. Thacker. "I've never thought much about college before, other than playing football. Nobody in my family ever went to college."

Mr. Thacker walks over to the counter and pours himself a glass of tea. "Collins told us a little bit about your family," he says, without looking back.

I look to Collins. "She has?"

She grips my hand. "I didn't think you'd mind, Dustin."

"I don't. Just surprised is all."

Mr. Thacker returns to his chair and continues. "She told us you're doing well with the work you have to do for your school. Is it true?"

I've been doing great with all of my schoolwork, so I don't hesitate to answer. "Yes, sir. I got all A's for the first time in my life."

He's not quite done drilling me. "That's great. So maybe you don't need football to go to college."

"I don't know, sir. I've never thought about it before."

"Okay, Dad," Collins interrupts. "He gets it. He needs to go to college."

What he means is I need to go to college if I think I'm going to date his daughter after I graduate high school. He fails to understand that I don't have the money for college. It's a great dream and all, but it's not my life. It's not what people from Flatbush do. Not most of us anyhow.

"James, leave him alone." Mrs. Thacker removes my empty glass and reveals his name for the first time. Mr. Thacker nods in agreement. "Anderson, why don't you show him your room now?"

"Finally," Andy says in an exasperated tone.

He and Collins help me to my feet and walk me to a towering set of steps in the front of the house. "Don't worry," Andy says. "We have this."

He opens a door that looks like it should be a closet and behind it is an elevator. Who has an elevator in their house?

We get to Andy's room, and it's massive. Bigger than my whole house. He has just about everything a kid could want. The boy loves sports. His baseball-shaped glove bed takes up one corner, and posters and pennants cover most of the walls.

Collins leaves the two of us alone, and I sit on the edge of his bed as he drags all sorts of things from shelves, closets, and anywhere else he can think of. He drops an autographed baseball in my hand and tells me about the last time he and his dad went to a game. He shows me pictures of himself and his family. The pictures he shows me are ones where he has hair. Brown like Collins' hair. He looks much different now. Thinner and paler. I reckon that's what life with cancer can do to a kid.

"Do you like my room?"

"Like it? I love it. It's even better than you said, buddy. And the good news is you may be able to come back home pretty soon, huh?"

"Yeah, but I'm kinda sad about it."

"Why? This place is incredible."

"Because I'll miss you." He hops up on the bed next to me.

Collins barges in without knocking. "People are here. Mom and Dad want us downstairs."

Andy and I get up, and the three of us head back down.

Chapter Thirty-Five

Dinner with Andy, Collins, and all of their family is fantastic. He's the center of everyone's attention all day long. It's incredible to see him so happy to be home. Even though I'm going to miss him like crazy, I can hardly wait for him to be able to come back home for good.

"See ya' on Sunday, buddy," I say as Collins gets ready to take me back to the hospital.

"I reckon."

"Take care of your sister for me."

Andy walks me to the car and Thomas opens the door. Collins follows behind. "Welcome back, sir," he says as I slide into the backseat. It feels odd having someone call me sir.

"Thanks, Thomas." Andy pushes my walker to Thomas. "Come here, buddy."

I lean over and give Andy a big ol' hug. So tight I'm afraid I'm going to snap his little bones in half.

"Are you going to be okay by yourself?"

"I'm going to be just fine, buddy. Don't you worry about me. I'm tough like you, remember?"

"I know." He drops his head to the ground; the bill of his hat hides his eyes. I'm sure they're wet with tears.

"It's only a couple of days." It's hard to say goodbye to him as he stands in the shadows.

He sneaks a quick kiss on my cheek and says, "Love you."

"Love you, too, buddy. Now get on back there with your family."

I pull the door closed, and Collins goes around to the other side where Thomas is waiting. Mr. Thacker gave her permission to ride back with me.

We kiss the entire way back to the hospital. My blood boils and my heart races. Thomas pretends not to pay attention, but I know he's not stupid. I'm sure he's going to tell Mr. Thacker when he gets back. I don't care.

Collins helps me back up to my room. "You still have half an hour before visiting hours are over."

I look at the clock on the wall and say, "Yep."

"Good." She shuts the door and moves me to the chair in the corner of the room.

"What're you doing?" It's a stupid question and I realize it as soon as it leaves my mouth.

"Shhh…" She puts a finger to my lips for a brief moment before reaching for me.

She removes my jacket and kisses me all over my neck and chest. My back arches as her hands slide down my back and her nails dig into me. Her mouth is hot and wet as she kisses me all over. She grabs my arms and wraps them around her waist. I'm about to burst, but I fight the urge.

She whispers, "I love you," in the night just before everything goes black and I swear I see stars. My body shivers as I run my hands through her long hair. She grips my shoulders like a vise and kisses me.

"Love you more," I groan.

Collins looks up at me in the darkness and stares into my eyes. She's the most beautiful person I've ever seen. She leans in and bites my bottom lip. My hands caress her back, and I sink my nose into the side of her neck. She lets loose a soft moan as she kisses me hard. We move together in rhythm as we kiss. For the first time in my life I know what it means to love a woman.

She sits in my lap, and I hold her. I'll hold her forever if she lets me. "That was amazing," I whisper in her ear. "You're amazing."

"So are you, Dustin." She gets up and checks herself in the mirror. "I better go, or Thomas will come looking for me."

"I wish you could stay longer."

"Me too," she says, as she buttons her blouse.

I put my shirt back on and turn on a light. Her hair is a mess, so she fixes it a little. She comes back over to give me a kiss.

"When will I see you again?"

She straightens her clothes a little more. "I won't be back until Sunday when we bring Anderson back." She sticks her bottom lip out and pouts like a baby. "Since all of our family is in town, mom and dad will want us all there the rest of the week."

"I get it. I figured that's what you were going to say. I had to ask anyway."

"Love you," she says as she gives me one last kiss.

"Love you more."

****

The next morning, I wake up but don't feel like getting out of bed. I don't have therapy because Brooke is off for the Thanksgiving holiday. She said something about going to Charleston to see her parents.

It's close to noon when I drag my butt out of bed and get cleaned up. My backpack hangs over my shoulder as I wander the halls of the hospital. There's nothing going on. A skeleton crew's working.

I decide to go to the garden and do a little writing and drawing. The only thought in my mind is Collins and last night. Remembering everything from last night sends a shiver up my spine. After finding an open spot, I pull out my pad and start drawing a picture of her. It takes me a couple of hours to get it right, and when it's done, I sign it like a real artist.

"Who's she?" A voice startles me back to reality.

"Jenny Lee. What're you doing here?"

"Answer my question. Who is she?" She points at the picture of Collins's face.

"Her name is Collins if you must know. Now answer my question. What're you doing here?"

"Isn't it obvious? I came to see you, babe."

Babe? Is she out of her mind? "I appreciate it and all, but won't Sully be mad you came?"

"That's kinda what I came to see you about." She sits on the couch beside me.

It doesn't surprise me at all that she came to talk about her own problems, rather than see how I'm doing. I decide not to mention it because I don't even care.

"What is it, Jenny Lee?"

"I changed my mind. I realize now that I made a huge mistake breaking up with you."

I raise my eyebrows and play along. "Sully dumped you, didn't he?"

"He didn't dump me," she insists. "It was mutual. Besides, Charlotte wouldn't stop hounding him until he went back to her."

"Whatever you say, Jenny Lee."

"It's the truth." She reaches her hand out and rubs my head. "What happened to your hair?"

"I shaved it."

"I can see that, babe. Why?" She's talking to me like she did when we were dating. She doesn't realize she's wasting her time.

"For my friend, Andy."

"Who's Andy?"

"I just told you. My friend. The kid you met."

"Oh yeah. I don't get it." I look in her eyes and realize we no longer have anything in common. There is zero connection.

"Of course not, Jenny Lee. I haven't seen you in months."

"That's not fair, babe."

Andy's words ring in my ear. "Life's not fair, Jenny Lee, and I'm not your babe."

Anger rises in her. "Is it the girl in the picture? What did you say her name is?"

"Collins."

"So you're going to treat me like this for her?"

"How have you treated me, Jenny Lee?"

"I love you, Dusty, and always have. I was just confused, and then the accident happened." Jenny Lee grabs me and presses her face to mine. She forces her tongue into my mouth.

"What're you doing?" I push her away from me, but the damage is done. Over Jenny Lee's shoulder, Collins stands in the lobby and sees it all. Tears well up in her eyes and she runs away.

"Wait!" I yell for Collins to stop but she doesn't.

"Who are you talking to?" Jenny Lee glances around in time to see Collins disappear through the door. "Is that her? Your girlfriend?"

I get to my feet, grab my walker, and go after Collins even though I know there's no way I'll catch her. She's probably long gone by now, but I still try. She has to know the truth. Jenny Lee kissed me and not the other way around.

"Let her go, Dusty." Jenny Lee pulls on my arm to get me to stop. "You're supposed to be with me anyhow. We're meant to be together."

I pull free from her clutch and keep moving. My jaw tighten as I say, "Jenny Lee, you need to go home. Those days are over."

When I get outside, Collins is nowhere to be found. Sitting on the bench, I wait in the cold, hoping she'll come back. A few minutes later, Jenny Lee passes by but doesn't say a word. After an hour, when there's no sign of Collins, I head back to my room and call her. Mrs. Thacker tells me she can't make it to the phone. She can make it, I'm sure, but doesn't want to. I ask Mrs. Thacker to have Collins call me when she can, but we both know it's not going to happen.

Chapter Thirty-Six

I call her twice a day for the remainder of the Thanksgiving weekend, and each time I do, I'm told the same thing. She's not available. When I ask Mrs. Thacker to let Collins know what she saw isn't what she thinks it is, she politely tells me she will, but Collins never calls.

Sunday night rolls around, and I go down to visit Andy. When he sees me, I can tell he knows something's different.

"Hey, buddy. Welcome back."

"Hey, Slaughter." His voice is less than enthusiastic.

"Did you have fun with your family?"

Andy doesn't answer. At first, I think he's going to avoid the question altogether. "Slaughter, why is Collins mad at you?"

The question is a hard one to answer even though the answer is so easy. "She came to the hospital to visit me."

"I know. She wanted to surprise you."

"I think I'm the one who surprised her, buddy. You remember me telling you about my old girlfriend, Jenny Lee?"

Andy nods.

"She came to visit me the same day, too."

"Even though Collins is your girlfriend?" Andy wrinkles his forehead.

"I didn't know she was coming, buddy. She just showed up. I swear."

"I believe you, but I don't think Collins will."

"I was afraid of that." I sit beside Andy on his bed. "When your sister came in, Jenny Lee grabbed me and kissed me."

"Why?"

"I don't know. She just did. And Collins came in right at the same time."

"Why don't you just tell her what happened?"

"She won't talk to me. Believe me, I've tried."

"Maybe I can tell her."

"Don't worry about it, buddy. Eventually, I think she'll let me explain what happened. For now, you just work on getting ready to go back home for good."

"Do you want to read me a story before I go to bed?"

"Sure. Which one?"

Andy has a stack of books on the shelf. He unzips his bag and pulls out the one I gave him for his birthday. "This one."

"I reckon."

Andy gets under the covers and I prop a pillow up and stretch out next to him. I read *Andy's Big Game* for the first time since I finished it. It's kind of funny reading it all these weeks later. The pictures I drew look pretty good, too.

About fifteen pages in, I hear the soft snore of a nine-year-old boy with cancer. I close the book and put it beside him as I get to my feet. He's battling so much, and now I've added one more worry to his plate. I curse myself for hurting Collins. And Andy.

A quick kiss on his forehead, and I go back to my room to write her a letter.

The next morning comes, and the morning after. Andy and I get right back into our normal routine as the days and weeks pass. We move on like nothing ever changed, but we both know something has. Collins still comes to see him but refuses to see me.

Every day, my leg gets stronger and stronger, and I walk a little faster. Brooke took my walker away and gave me a cane like old men use. It's harder to walk with it because I'm not used to it and it doesn't let me support as much weight as the walker. I ask Brooke to give the walker back, but she refuses.

Christmas is a few days away, and Andy wants to go back home. The doctors won't let him because the medication he's been on isn't working like it did the first few weeks he was on it. They're trying something different, but it doesn't seem to help. Andy hasn't been out of his bed in three days.

"Hey, buddy," I say as I sit next to him.

He's propped up on pillows and has all sorts of cords coming out of him. He fights to keep his eyes open, and his skin is paler than ever. "Hey, Slaughter," he chokes out. "No more walker, huh?"

"Nope. I gave it up a couple of days ago. I didn't give it up, actually. It's more like Brooke took it away from me."

Andy struggles to laugh. "My sister asked about you yesterday."

"Yeah? What did you tell her?"

"I told her you still love her. She still loves you, too, Slaughter. She's just being stubborn."

"Enough about me." I take my usual spot next to him and we talk. "What's going on with this new medicine?"

"You're looking at it." He waves his hand over his body. "Makes me sleepy, but the doctor said in a few days I'll be done with it and can get back to normal."

Normal is such a funny word, especially when his life is anything but normal. I guess it's normal for him.

"That's great. Then we can get back to watching the games. You know, the Bowl games'll be on in a little over a week."

"Yep." Andy taps his hat and points at mine. "Told you they'd make the Independence Bowl."

I forgot all about the conversation until he brings it up. "You sure did. Guess you won the bet."

He pauses a bit and then asks, "What's it like?"

"What's what like?"

"Playing football."

His question spins my head for a brief second. I've never had anyone ask me about playing football before, and never thought about it until just now.

"Geez, let me think." I close my eyes and run all of the years I spent on the field through my mind. "I started when I was about your age. I hated it at first. I was little, and there were big guys like you who kept tackling me hard. It hurt, and I wanted to quit."

"But you didn't."

"Nope. Mama wouldn't let me. She said Slaughters don't quit." When I think about her words now, I almost laugh. She was different then. Now, all I want Mama to do is quit using that junk.

"How come she doesn't ever come see you?"

He doesn't need to hear the truth, so I say, "She's too busy and we live too far away."

"That's sad. I don't know what I would do if mom and dad didn't come see me all the time."

"You're a lucky kid. You have all kinds of people who love you."

A weak smile washes over his face.

"Anyhow, I kept playing and got better and better. Figured if I didn't like getting tackled, I better learn how to avoid it. I grew bigger and bigger, and I got stronger. That helped a lot. The practices were horrible."

"I bet."

"Lots of running and pushups and crap like that. When I got to high school, it got even worse. We'd have early morning practices sometimes. Weight training and afternoon practice for like three or four hours. My whole life was spent on the field."

Andy laughs as he fights to stay awake.

"You need to rest, buddy."

"No, don't stop. I want to hear it." His words are slow, but clear.

"All of the hard work on the field is terrible, but at the end of the week it's game time. And the games make it all worthwhile."

"Tell me about them."

"First of all, I'm going to tell you something about me you may think is weird. I get real nervous on game nights. I get so nervous I don't know what to do other than puke."

"Gross."

"Told you it was weird. Anyhow, the first time it happened I puked into my helmet. You don't even want to know what it smells like on your head." He laughs again as he slides his little hand into mine. "I learned not to do it again, so I always know where a trashcan or toilet is. After I puke, I go to the back of the field house all alone and get myself together."

"Do you pray?" He waits for a split second, eyes fixed on me. "I do."

"Yeah, I guess that's what it is."

"Can I tell you something?"

"Anything, buddy."

"I pray for you every night."

My breath catches for a moment as his words register in my brain. "I pray for you every night, too." Honestly, I'm not sure if it's praying that I do because I never went to church too much growing up. I'm one of the few in Flatbush who isn't a member at one of the umpteen churches they have. All I know is that I close my eyes and make a wish that he'll get better.

Andy squeezes my hand. "Tell me more about the game."

"After I'm done…praying… I join the rest of the guys in the end zone. We wait behind a giant banner the cheerleaders put together for us to run through."

"Are the cheerleaders pretty?"

"Most of them are. But you want to know a secret? There isn't a single one of them who's prettier than your sister. She's the most beautiful girl I've ever known."

"Yeah, yeah," Andy says. "What happens when you run through?"

"Actually, right before we run through, there's a man on the PA system who gets the crowd all pumped up. There are thousands of people screaming and yelling. It's pretty cool. Then he says, 'Give it up for your Coosa County Eagles', and we break through the sign. My best friend and I…" It slips out before I realize it. "The quarterback and I run through first and the rest of the team follows us because we're captains."

"Cool."

"Yep. Then we run to the fifty-yard line and go to our side of the field. When the buzzer sounds and the ball flies through the air, my nerves are gone and I become a warrior."

"And you score touchdowns."

"That's my plan."

"Do you want to know why I pray for your leg?"

"You already told me. So I can walk."

"Yeah, but it's more than that. I want you to play football again, so you can go to UNC and be closer to me and Collins."

"I'm not sure it's going to ever happen, buddy."

"I know, but I pray for it anyways. It can't hurt."

"Nah, I guess it can't." I slide off the bed and kiss his forehead and tell him I love him as usual. "Get some rest, buddy. Maybe tomorrow you'll be back on your feet."

When I limp out of his room, a hand grabs me by my shirt. Collins stands next to the wall with tears in her eyes. "I love you," she says as she wraps her arms around me.

"I love you more."

"Did you mean what you said? About me being the prettiest girl you've ever known? And you better not say, I reckon."

"For sure." I pull her closer. "What you saw that night isn't what was happening."

"I know. Andy told me, but I couldn't get the image of you kissing another girl out of my head. Especially your ex-girlfriend."

"The key word is ex. I told her to leave and let her know we were over. For good. There is nothing there. Remember what you said to me a few weeks ago about living in the past?"

"Yep."

"My past is over. My future is you."

Chapter Thirty-Seven

By the time Christmas rolls around, Andy is back on his feet. His floor is full of families visiting their own kids. Santa came and left lots of wrapped boxes under the tree.

I'm up early and wait by the tree with Andy's parents and Collins when he drags his lazy butt out of bed and comes looking for his presents. He gives a half wave as he stares at us through sleepy eyes.

"Santa brought you lots of gifts, Anderson," Mr. Thacker says. "He piled them up over there."

Anderson walks to Mrs. Thacker and climbs up in her lap. She holds him as the twinkling tree lights spot his face with a variety of colors. Collins squeezes my hand.

"Merry Christmas, buddy," I say, breaking the silence.

"Merry Christmas." Andy's still half asleep.

"Want to go open your presents?" Collins jumps up and goes to the tree. "Looks like Santa brought you all sorts of things." She picks up a box and shakes it. It doesn't make a sound. "I wonder what it is."

This gets him interested. His eyes light up and he sinks in the floor next to Collins. Even though she's still in her pajamas and her hair is pulled back, she's beautiful.

"What is it?"

"I don't know. You better open it because it has your name on it."

His tiny fingers shred the paper before he pries the box open. It's a UNC hoodie. Andy puts it on, and it fits him perfectly. He digs through the pile of gifts and opens them all.

"Santa hooked you up this year, buddy."

Andy walks over to me and whispers in my ear softer than a whisper so nobody else can hear. "I don't believe in Santa Claus. I pretend so mom and dad are happy."

"Anderson," Mr. Thacker says. "What's this one say?"

Andy walks back to where all of his presents are. He leans down low and reads the label on a box pushed way back under the tree. "It says, to Dustin from Santa."

"Santa doesn't even know I'm here. How could it be for me?"

Andy pulls the box out and picks it up. I can tell by the way he carries it that it has some weight to it. "He found you. Here." He drops the present in my lap.

I'm suspicious about the package and wonder who put it there. Miss Bernice knew I would be here this morning. Maybe she's the one behind it.

"Don't just stare at it." Collins climbs onto the couch next to me. "Open it and see what he brought you."

I'm in shock when I open it up and a laptop stares back at me. "What the…" I can't believe they got me a computer. "It's too much."

"Looks like Santa wants you to have it," Mrs. Thacker says.

"I'd say so," Mr. Thacker confirms. "Maybe he wants you to use it for school and your writing."

"I reckon." I open the box and pull it out. It's the best laptop I've ever seen. Sleek and trim. I open the screen and it cycles on. I'm not used to it, so I screw a few things up right from the get-go.

"Let me show you." Collins pulls the computer into her lap and starts setting it up for me. She goes to the security screen first and sets up a login password. She types c-o-l-l-i-n-s. "Now you'll think of me every time you use it."

"I think about you all the time, even without a password."

Mr. Thacker goes to the nurses' station for a cart to carry most of Andy's stuff on. His hoodie, some books, and a few other things stay here with him. I help load the cart and add my new computer to the mix.

"Thanks for the laptop," I say to Mr. Thacker when we're on the elevator.

He presses number seven. "You don't need to thank me. You need to thank Santa. He brought it for you."

"Oh, okay. In that case, thanks Santa."

Mr. Thacker winks. "You're welcome, son." It occurs to me he calls me son. "Collins tells us how well you're doing in school now, and I know how hard it can be without a computer these days."

"I manage."

"Dusty, I don't want to get too much into your personal affairs, and I hope you don't mind, but Collins has filled me in on a few things about you."

The elevator bell dings and the door opens. He pushes the cart to my room. We drop my computer off and head downstairs.

Mr. Thacker starts talking again. "It just seems you've had a pretty tough life."

"I s'pose."

"I've never thanked you properly for all you've done for Anderson. You have completely changed his life for the better. All he talks about is you. And the way you shaved your head to support him speaks volumes. Don't get me wrong. Anderson has lost his hair before and it grew back, so we're used to it. Of course, we're hoping it'll grow back again once he's through this series of treatments and comes home."

"I'm sure it will, sir."

"It isn't just the hair, either. It's the way you treat him. I've never seen Anderson like this. You're like the older brother he never had. And the book you made for him is absolutely incredible. He carries it with him everywhere he goes."

"Yeah, I know."

"It is one of the kindest and most thoughtful gifts I've ever seen given to him or anyone else. You're quite talented, son."

"I'll be honest with you, sir. He's the one who got me writing. He had Collins bring me a composition book to write all my thoughts in like he does."

"Like he does? I'm not following you."

"You don't know about Excalibur, sir?"

Mr. Thacker pops the back door of a black SUV. "I have no idea what you're talking about, Dusty."

"He has a notebook he calls Excalibur. He writes in it when he's depressed or has things he wants to remember. He says it helps him when he's all alone in the hospital."

"Interesting." Mr. Thacker rubs his chin. "Collins knows about it?"

I nod. "He worries about you and Mrs. Thacker, sir. He knows how sad y'all get when you have to leave after your visits. He doesn't want y'all to know, though."

"The situation is hard on everyone. I'm sure you know already. His doctor told us he wouldn't be home for Christmas, and we were obviously sad, but he will be home by New Year's Eve."

"That's fantastic. I know he wants to get back home."

After loading the car, we wait for the elevator to arrive. "Sir, you don't have to worry about me. I'll be fine."

"I know you will, but Mrs. Thacker and I have gotten attached to you over these past few months. We've seen how great you are with Anderson, and Collins is crazy about you as well."

"I'm crazy about her, sir. She's smart and funny. She's amazing."

"I'm going to be blunt with you, Dusty. Collins is kind-hearted and sees how you are with Anderson. No offense, but it's one of her strengths and her greatest weakness." I'm not sure if he's being rude or not. "You're not the kind of guy we'd normally approve of for her to date."

"Yeah, she mentioned something about that." The elevator door closes. "As I'm sure you know, I'm not like y'all at all. Don't talk like y'all. Don't have money like y'all. The only thing we have in common is Andy."

"All of that's true, but I'm also a smart enough man to recognize potential when I see it. You're a good guy, and I believe you have talent you never knew you possessed. Here's my point. Her mother and I have discussed it and we're perfectly fine with you dating our daughter, but you have to do something if you plan to continue dating her."

"Anything, sir. What is it?" I take a deep breath and wait as his face tightens and his eyes narrow.

"You need to keep your grades up and plan on going to college. I don't care which college you pick, though I'm sure Collins would prefer UNC, but I do expect anyone who dates my daughter to have plans and a dream. Do you think you can do that?"

My pulse quickens as his words linger in the air like falling confetti. "I honestly don't know, sir. The only time I ever thought about college was so I could play football. The only reason my grades are halfway good is because I wanted a football scholarship. I only had to have a B average since I was a football player. Kind of planned to do the same thing in college and make it to the NFL."

He taps my cane as a gentle reminder of where I am. "Looks like plans have changed, so now it's time you change your plans."

"Yes, sir."

"One last thing." Mr. Thacker steps out of the elevator before me. "I've made arrangements for you to come spend a few days with us on New Year's Eve. If you want to."

"For sure. Thank you for the invitation."

"The way I see it, Anderson will be home for good by then, Collins will still be on break, and they'll both talk about you non-stop."

"Thanks…I think."

"Besides, Mrs. Thacker and I like having you around. Hungry?"

"I am."

"Good. We're going to have Christmas breakfast in the cafeteria."

His words swirl around in my head. I've never given any serious thought to college before. Not as a real student, but if that's what it takes to keep seeing Collins, then that's what I'll have to do.

After breakfast, everyone gathers back in the TV room. They pop one of Andy's new movies in the DVD player. Several of the other families join us. When the movie's over, Mr. Thacker goes back to the car and comes back with a bag full of gifts. He asks us all to go to Andy's room. I sneak away to get Collins's gift.

"We normally exchange gifts with one another, but since this is our first Christmas here we're doing things a bit differently." Mrs. Thacker hands Collins a gift and she opens it. She hands another to Andy. And one to me.

I unwrap the gift. It's an art set. "Thank you."

"Maybe you can do another book," Andy says. "I picked it out. Do you like it?"

"I love it."

I hand Collins the box and she opens it. "It's beautiful." She gives me a quick kiss on the cheek. She holds the framed picture I drew of her up to show Mr. and Mrs. Thacker. Andy moves over to get a good look at it. She scans it and puts her finger on it where I signed my name and the date. It takes her a second before she connects the dots. "I can't believe it. You did this…the day after Thanksgiving," Collins says. "I'm so sorry."

"Don't be. I'm the one who should be saying sorry."

"It's beautiful. I love it." She hands the portrait to Mrs. Thacker then wraps her arms around me. "Love you!"

"Love you more!"

Chapter Thirty-Eight

New Year's Eve falls on a Thursday this year. Mr. Thacker makes a deal with Brooke to let me skip my therapy on Wednesday. I have to promise to make it up the following Saturday.

Andy gets to go home today, and Mr. Thacker doesn't want to come back down tomorrow to get me. Fine with me. If I can get the heck out of this hospital for an extra day, I'm all for it.

"Are you excited to be leaving this place?"

Andy sits on one of the boxes the nurses packed up for him to take home. "Yeah, but I wish you could come with me, too."

"I'm coming up for a few days."

"I know. It's just that…"

"You fellas ready?" Mr. Thacker asks as he reaches down to hug Andy.

"Yes, sir," Andy says.

A few guys in white uniforms follow behind Mr. Thacker with a hand truck for the boxes. I don't have much; so one bag is all I have to carry with me for the weekend.

I have a hard time getting around because I still can't bend my knee, but I limp along well enough to get by. Dr. Riddell tells me to accept the fact that my leg is the way it is, but Brooke tells me to ignore him. She's confident I'll be walking without a cane one of these days. Says it may take a year or more, but she knows it's going to happen.

Andy and I have plenty of stuff to keep us busy until the party. We go out to Mrs. Thacker's stable to feed the horses. They have a couple of guys who work on their property, and the stable hand doesn't seem to mind us getting in his way.

"This one's my horse." Andy climbs up on a stall door. "His name is Edgar." Edgar nuzzles his giant nose against Andy's shoulder. "He already had a name when Mom bought him."

"Oh yeah?"

Edgar is big and black as a raven's wing. Pretty. I would guess he's extremely expensive, too.

"Guess who." Collins sneaks up behind us and puts her hands over my eyes.

"Hmmm…let me think about it for a minute."

"Not funny," she says. "What're you two doing out here?"

"Andy's showing me his horse."

"Mine is over there. Her name is Annabel Lee." A beautiful chestnut horse chews on hay, completely unaware that we're talking about her. "Maybe later we'll go for a ride."

"Not sure I can with my leg."

"That isn't a problem," Andy says. "Our horses are gentle."

"I don't think you'll be able to go, squirt." Collins tickles his belly.

"Uh huh. Mom and Dad won't care. I'm getting better."

"You can ask, but I don't think they'll let you."

Collins is right. It takes Mrs. Thacker about half a second to say no. It upsets Andy, but I know he understands because he asks me to ride Edgar.

Edgar towers over me. After one of the guys in the barn saddles the horses, Collins helps me climb on Edgar's back. It's a little difficult, and they have to adjust the strap so my straight leg will fit in the stirrup just right. Not a perfect fit, but good enough.

I'm a bit jumpy at first because I've never been on a horse. I've been around them at fairs and such, but never ridden one. Collins realizes I'm off to a slow start, so she grabs Edgar's reins and pulls him close to Annabel Lee. He settles down immediately, and Collins ties Edgar's reins to Annabel Lee's saddle.

"Thanks," I say. "I think I've got it now."

"You sure?"

"I think so." I hold onto the saddle for dear life, and Edgar does exactly what he's supposed to do. He's calm and relaxed as we make our way over the hill.

Collins takes us back into the woods, on a well-worn trail.

"Where are we going?" The clatter of the horse hooves against the ground forces me to yell a little.

"You'll see."

A bright sun shines overhead and rays of sunlight rain through the trees and splatter against the ground. The air is cool, but not cold. Edgar follows behind Annabel Lee. I don't have to do anything except not fall off.

We come out of the trees into another field. We're up on a knoll, and down below, a little pond glistens in the afternoon sun. There's a dock and a small cabin.

"Is this your property, too?"

Collins nods. "We have close to three hundred acres."

"Whew…big place."

"Dad stocked this pond for fishing a few years ago. He and Anderson come out here sometimes and spend the weekend. Dad calls it a men's weekend. Anderson loves it. Mom and I love it, too, because we go into town and spend the weekend shopping, getting manis and pedis and facials. You know, girl stuff."

We go down to the water's edge and Collins hops off. She drops the reins and Annabel Lee takes a big gulp.

"Don't you need to tie her up or something?"

"They won't go anywhere."

She helps me get down. I'm lucky I don't break my other leg, and Edgar isn't too happy about it at all, but somehow we manage. "It's going to be difficult getting me back up on him."

"We'll figure it out. Now come on."

I limp along behind her toward the cabin. She grabs a spare key hidden under a flowerpot and opens the door. It's rustic and sparse. Dust clings to every surface.

"I thought it would be fancier than this." The door creaks closed behind us.

"It's a cabin on a lake. How fancy should it be?"

"Just saying."

"We're normal people, you know?" Collins grabs me and throws me to the bed. "We just have lots of money."

"That's an understatement."

"Are you going to keep talking or are you going to kiss me?"

My decision is made when Collins plants her soft lips against mine.

My arms wrap tightly around her, and her head rises and falls as we watch the sun fading out of sight.

As I sit next to Collins, I catch myself dreaming about a life with her. Then the words of her father slam hard against my head. We come from two different worlds. Sure, it's easy to adjust to this world, but this world isn't real life for a guy like me. Real life has a mom on drugs, a house with holes in it, and trying to figure out what to eat. It's a life she's never known. I'm sure she's never even seen people like me.

Still, her perfume mixed with sweat from the hot sun drives me wild, and I dream. I dream I can offer her something other than a few months of fun. Eventually, I will go back home. She'll be here, and I'll be back on the mountain stealing wood to heat our house, hoping Mama's still breathing at the end of each day.

"Collins," I whisper. The shadows creep over us as the sun starts to set. "You know me and you are different, don't you?'

"What are you talking about?" She keeps her head pressed to my chest.

"I'm not like you. I don't have money like this."

"And I don't expect you to." Collins runs her finger over my belly. "I'm more like you than you realize. Even with all of this, my parents raised Anderson and me to love people and appreciate what we have. To give to others when we can. To give back, so to speak."

"Is that what you're doing now? Giving back?"

She pops straight up. Her eyes burn with fire. "Is that what you think? After all we've talked about. After these past couple months, that's what you think? Do you really think I think you're some sort of charity case?"

It sounds stupid when she says it like that, but I can't help myself. "Maybe."

She jumps up and grabs her jacket. "We need to get back. They'll be wondering what happened to us." A flash of anger washes over her face. Her wild hair refuses to be tamed.

I fumble over my words, trying to get her to calm down. "Don't get mad. I didn't mean—"

"Then you shouldn't have said it." She stomps around, and I slowly get dressed. "Say what you mean, and mean what you say. Words mean things."

"It's just that—"

"What? You're poor and I'm rich? My parents are together and your dad is in jail and your mom is an addict?"

"Something like that."

"I don't judge people for what they have or what their parents are like. I judge them for who they are, and if you can't see that then I'm not sure what to think."

****

Silence permeates the ride back and my leg throbs from getting back on the horse. I try to speak to her a couple of times but realize she needs a bit more quiet time.

We stable the horses, and she helps me off of Edgar.

"Dustin," she says as I hobble toward my cane. "I fell in love with you. Not what you have. Not what you don't have. You. Who you are on the inside."

I pull Collins to me. "I know, and I'm sorry." I press my mouth to hers. "It's just that your dad said—"

"What did he say?"

I regret mentioning what Mr. Thacker said. "Nothing. Don't worry about it."

"We don't do that, Dustin. We don't keep secrets."

"He just said if I'm going to keep dating you I have to go to college."

Collins doesn't even bat an eye. She lets me know that she already had the same conversation with her dad days earlier. Even when I tell her college isn't for me if I'm not playing football, she refuses to accept it. No matter what I say, she tells me that she believes in me. Not only that, she tells me Anderson does, too.

Chapter Thirty-Nine

It's time for the New Year's Eve party. We're going to some swanky country club where Mr. Thacker plays golf. Apparently, they throw a wild party every year. I don't look too bad in the tux they got me. Never been in a tuxedo before. Jenny Lee wanted me to wear one to last year's prom, but money was tight, so I borrowed a hand-me-down suit. I still looked pretty sharp, though.

Andy's downstairs playing games in the family room. When I walk in, he barely even notices me. "Must be a good game." I toss the couch pillow at him and it bounces off his head, taking his hat with it.

He snatches up the hat and throws it right back on his head. "Thanks a lot. I died."

My gut sinks when I hear his words. I know he doesn't realize what he says, but it still hurts. "Sorry, buddy. Just getting your attention."

He gets up from the floor and switches off the game. He puts the pillow back in its proper spot. Everything in this house has a proper spot and nothing is out of place. "Are you not going to wear your hat?"

I haven't taken my hat off since Mr. Thacker gave it to me. I didn't realize it meant so much to the little guy. "I didn't think we were wearing it with a tux, but if you want me to I will."

"I'll go get it." He races up the stairs. I guess that's my answer. I decide then and there never to take it off again, until Andy does.

"Here, Slaughter." He tosses the blue hat at me from the top of the stairs. Collins is right behind him.

"You look beautiful."

"Uhhh….thanks, I guess."

"Not you, Andy. Your sister."

"Thanks, Dustin," Collins says.

A blue dress clings to her body in all the right ways. Her curly brown hair is pulled tight against her head. A faint hint of lipstick enhances her beautiful smile. It's the first time I've seen her wear makeup. She's beautiful without it, but now she looks like a model. "I don't think I've ever seen anyone as beautiful as you in my entire life."

"Hush," she whispers as she comes down the stairs.

"I'm serious. You're gorgeous." I grab her around the waist and go in for a kiss, but she pushes me away.

"Not now, you'll mess up my face."

"The car's here," Mrs. Thacker calls out from the kitchen.

We all pile into a limo and take off.

I'm a bit out of place and know it. I hobble through the club as Mr. Thacker shows me around. He tells me all about playing golf with his buddies and asks if I've ever played. "No, sir," I say. "The only sport I've ever played is football."

"That's good, too, son, but a man tests himself when it's just him, a little white ball, and the course. I think it's the true test of a man's strength."

I don't see how walking around swinging a club at a little ball will do anything, but I don't argue with him. "I'm sure it is, sir."

"Let's go." Collins grabs my hand. "I want to dance."

For the next few hours, Collins and I dance. Actually, I'm not sure I'd call what I do dancing, but at least I'm on my feet like I promised. I have to take breaks every now and then because my leg throbs after being on it for any length of time.

Collins is good about it. Sometimes she hangs with me, but most of the time she's on the floor dancing her butt off. It's funny watching all the rich guys come up to her and ask her to dance. She politely tells them no and points to me. They give me a look that lets me know I'm not one of them and shouldn't be playing in their playground. Doesn't bother me though. I don't care about them. I'm here for Andy and Collins.

"Come on, it's time to go outside." Collins tosses my cane to the side and helps me up.

"What's outside?"

"It's a few minutes before midnight. They have a ball drop every year."

We walk out the backdoor. They've decorated the entire area like a winter scene. Fake snow and everything. Out on the golf course, a giant silver ball waits anxiously at the top of a post.

"Man, you guys go all out for everything," I say to Collins.

The rest of the family waits for us as we work our way through the crowd.

"If you're going to do something, best to do it right."

Easy to say when money isn't an object is what I want to tell her, but then I think about what she says. It's kind of true, I suppose, no matter how much money I have. No matter what I do, I always do the best I can. At least now I do.

"Two minutes before midnight," Andy says. The twinkle of the ball dots his face.

"I'm surprised you're still up, buddy."

Mr. Thacker puts his arm around Andy's shoulder and says, "Me too."

"Hey, I'm not a baby." Andy reaches for Mrs. Thacker's hand.

"Here you are, son." Mr. Thacker hands me a glass of champagne. Then Collins grabs one.

With thirty seconds remaining, we all start counting down to midnight.

"Ten, nine, eight..." we all say in unison. At the stroke of midnight, horns blare, and the band strikes up and plays the song everybody sings on New Year's Eve. Most of the people toasting and singing are blitzed, so they're just slurring words. Hardly any of the others know the words, but dang near everybody sings along. Including me.

Collins' warm breath finds my skin as she pulls my face to hers. We kiss for what seems like forever. "I love you more than you know,

Dustin," she whispers after catching her breath. "This year is going to be the best year ever. For you and me."

"And for Andy," I say. He's lost in the moment, so he doesn't hear me.

"Especially for Anderson." She takes my glass away and puts it on a nearby table. "Now kiss me, silly boy."

Chapter Forty

The rest of the weekend is amazing, and the time flies by too quickly. It's not long before I'm holed up back in the hospital going through the motions. Weeks pass and my leg still refuses to bend. Brooke tells me not to worry, but Dr. Riddell seems much more realistic.

"Dusty," he says. "You're progressing much better than anticipated a few months ago, but you aren't quite where we'd hoped you'd be."

"What does that mean, Doc?"

Dr. Riddell takes a long moment, pulls his glasses off his face, and leans back in his high-backed leather chair. "If you're ever going to have a chance to walk again, to walk without dragging your leg behind you, then we're going to have to operate one more time."

"Okay."

"It's not as simple as it sounds, Dusty." Dr. Riddell crosses his fingers. "We will have to go in and work on your knee, and the operation is quite extensive."

"It's fine. I don't mind." The reason I don't mind is because I'll be under and won't even notice.

Dr. Riddell sits up and leans on the top of his desk. "Dusty, the surgery is a complicated one. The best-case scenario is you'll have full mobility of your leg, but you'll still walk with a limp. With months of rehab. And that's if everything goes flawlessly."

"And if not, then I get what I've got. Believe it or not, Doc, I'm kinda used to it now." Those are words I never thought I'd ever say.

"Listen to me, son. If we aren't successful, you could lose your leg altogether from the knee down."

I take a few seconds to think it through and weigh my options. "You said I almost lost it the night of the wreck, right?"

Dr. Riddell nods.

"Then technically, I shouldn't even have it now anyhow."

"I wouldn't put it like that, Dusty." He stares me in the eyes. "Dusty, if you lose the leg, you'll have to be fitted for a prosthesis. You'll essentially have to learn to walk again. The technology is great now, but it's going to take you a considerable amount of time to get used to the new leg if it happens."

"If those are my two options, then I guess let's go for it."

"Those aren't the only options, Dusty." Dr. Riddell's face darkens with a cloud of worry.

"What's wrong, Dr. Riddell?"

"There's always the possibility we can lose you on the table."

"Lose me?"

"It's a risky procedure, Dusty. There are always complications that can arise. I just need you to understand all of the options, along with the risks. I'm telling you this as your doctor, and as the guy who gave you advice all those months ago."

"Thanks, Walter." I stand and stabilize myself with my cane. I work my way back to my room to think things over.

I grab Excalibur and start writing. A flood of emotion spills out on the page. The greatest risk, of course, is not waking up, but my life was spared once, so I have to have faith in Dr. Riddell again. Losing my leg wouldn't be the worst thing. I've adjusted to this new normal; I know I can adjust to a new normal again. Whether it means with a working leg or an artificial one.

My laptop comes to life, and I search artificial legs. There are all sorts of videos of people learning to walk again. Many of them are wounded soldiers from the war. They all seem to get along just fine. Some are doing pretty incredible things and staying active.

A deep sense of sadness filters through me as I grab my UNC hat off the shelf by my bed. I hold it in front of me and stare at the lettering and think about what life would be like now if Sully and Jenny Lee hadn't betrayed me that night.

With my eyes closed, I imagine I hear a voice on the PA system calling out my name as I run onto the Tar Heel field. Mama sitting in the stands, sober, cheering me on.

Then it occurs to me I wouldn't know Collins or Andy without the wreck. I'd never have known what love is or what courage is. Without Andy and Collins, I'd still be the poor kid up in the mountains hoping I'm good enough to make something of myself.

"Slaughter," Andy calls out, startling me back to reality.

"Hey, buddy." I high five him.

Collins follows right behind him and plants a warm kiss on my lips. "How's your day?"

"Not great," I say as I tuck Excalibur under my pillow.

"Why not?" Andy hops up on my bed.

"I had a tough day at therapy." I put my hand on his shoulder and give Collins a look to let her know there's more.

"It's okay, Slaughter. There's always tomorrow." The kid has more hope than anyone I've ever met. It seems like he's never had a bad day.

"I reckon."

"Do you want to go grab a bite to eat?" Collins dangles her keys in the air.

"Where?" The hospital lets me go out with Collins and Andy for dinner once a week now. It takes a little begging and pleading on my part, but I think it takes a few words and a check from Mr. Thacker, though he never mentions anything to me about it.

"I want pizza." Andy jumps to the floor. I can see little wisps of brown hair sprouting on his head from underneath his hat.

"Pizza it is then." I throw my hat on and out we go.

We go to a nearby pizza place with the best pizza I've ever had. The cheese is so gooey it stretches for miles. There's quite a wait, but it's totally worth it.

"Anderson." Collins hands money to Andy. "Why don't you go play?"

Without hesitation, he takes the money and disappears into a room full of video games.

"So what's the rest of the story?" Collins wraps her hand in mine from across the table.

"If I want my leg to ever have a chance of working again, I have to have another surgery."

"That's not so bad is it?"

"I don't guess so."

"Then what?" She rubs the top of my hand with her thumb. It's soothing.

"Dr. Riddell says there's a chance it won't work."

"And?"

"And I could lose my leg from the knee down." I don't tell her about the possibility of dying on the table.

Collins squeezes my hand with both of hers. "What do you want to do, Dustin?"

"Don't know. Kinda used to it the way it is, but if I want to walk again it's the only chance I have."

And before I know what I'm doing I say something I immediately wish I hadn't. "How will I be able to play with our kids?"

Collins freezes. I freeze. Neither one of us can believe what I just said. We both sit without speaking for an uncomfortably long time.

"I'm sorry." It's all I can think of to say. "I didn't mean that."

"What didn't you mean?" Collins chews on her lip. "You don't want us to have kids or you didn't want to say it out loud."

"Both. Neither." My face heats up. "I don't know. It's just…"

"It's fine, Dustin." She continues chewing her lip for a bit longer. "It's not like I haven't thought about it either."

My eyes widen like saucers.

"Don't get me wrong. I'm not thinking this year or even next." Collins takes a deep breath. "We'd both have to finish college and get jobs and stuff first." My eyes go big for a split second. "Yes, Dustin, you're going to have to go to college. Remember what my dad said?"

"I remember."

"It isn't just him, either. I want you to go. Not for me, but for you."

My conversation with Mr. Thacker bubbles to the surface on a regular basis. I've emailed UNC about information to apply to school. The lady who comes from my school with my assignments has already started talking with my counselor about what I need to get this semester to give me a chance.

Then there's the money. Even if I get accepted, there's no way in the world I'll be able to afford college. The advisor from UNC says they have financial aid for kids like me, but I'll have to be able to work. It's not going to be easy for me, since all my time will be spent on just keeping my head above water. At least I'll have Collins there to help me. As long as she doesn't get tired of a one-legged, ex-running back, broke kid from the mountains.

The server drops the pizza on the table. "Anything else?"

"This should do it."

"Let me go get Anderson." Collins follows behind the server.

I'm alone at the table thinking about everything that just happened. Kids. Marriage. College. It's more than I can handle right now. I just need to figure out what to do about my leg first.

We tear through a couple of slices of pizza and Andy heads back to the games. Collins pulls out an envelope and holds it in front of her. I chomp on a piece of ice thinking she's about to give me some information about college.

"What's that?" I crack another piece of ice.

"Promise you won't be mad at me?"

"How can I promise if I'm not even sure I can keep the promise without knowing what it is you're doing?"

"Just promise."

"Since I've never been mad at you a day in my life, I reckon I can promise easy enough."

"Remember you said that when I give you this." She waves the envelope in the air, and I realize it's not from UNC.

Immediately, I regret agreeing to her promise. I hold out my hand waiting for her to drop the envelope in it. She hesitates. "Just give it to me."

"I am, but you need to know I only did it because I love you."

She's getting serious now. Something is up. "I love…you too, but what's going on, Collins?"

"I did something without telling you." She tucks the envelope back in her lap. "You know how important family is to me, right?" I nod. "And you know how important you are to me, right?" Another nod. "Please don't be mad, but I found your dad."

My eyes bug out of my head and my hand falls to the table. "You did what now?"

"I found your father."

"My father isn't lost. He's in prison."

"I know." She slides the envelope across the table. I let it sit there. "I sent him a letter a few weeks ago."

"What kind of letter, Collins?"

"I told him I was your girlfriend, and I wanted to know if he was interested at all in talking to you. Kind of like a pen pal."

"Why did you go and do something like that?"

"I told you. Family's important to me."

There is no way in the world for me to be mad at her. She looks adorable sitting on the other side of the table from me. Besides, there's nobody else in my life who would ever take the time to do something so crazy like this simply because they love me. "What did he say?"

"Read it yourself." She pushes the envelope closer.

After a slight hesitation, I take the envelope and remove the letter. The words are poorly written, but for some reason it doesn't surprise me.

Collins,

It's crazy getting this letter in the mail from you and all, 'cuz I don't think I ever got a single letter from nobody ever since I been locked up. I am glad to know Dusty is doing alright. He was a good boy and I let him down. I don't know what you want me to say and all, but I reckon it's best to let him know there ain't been one day that's passed that I ain't thought about him. I reckon he's a man by now. If he wants to write me, it's alright by me, but if he don't I understand. Anyways, let him know I said hi. And tell him I still love him.

Sincerely,

Jason Slaughter

The smudged ink makes some of the letter difficult to decipher. It's hard to read something Dad wrote when I haven't seen the man in forever. He's just a story and distant memory to me. That's why it surprises me that his letter makes me sad and happy all at the same time.

"You don't hate me, do you?" Collins wears a look of worry on her face.

"Never, baby." I put the letter on the table and reach for her hand. "I can't hate someone who I want to spend the rest of my life with."

Chapter Forty-One

A week passes and the operation arrives. Thoughts of what I said to Collins and the letter from Dad thunder around like a storm in my head as they prep me for surgery. The entire Thacker family comes to stay with me.

"It's going to be okay, Slaughter." Andy grips my hand as he stands beside my bed. His eyes fill with fear.

"I know, buddy. You don't have anything to worry about. I'm tough, remember?"

"The toughest."

Collins stands on the other side of me and rubs my forehead. I've got needles and tubes in me all over. "You better be," she whispers as she kisses my cheek.

"I'll be back before you know it." The surgery is supposed to take about six hours or so. As long as there are no complications. If they have to remove my leg, it'll take longer.

"We're all here for you, Dusty," Mr. Thacker says.

"We'll be here when you get out." Mrs. Thacker walks over and presses her hand to mine.

It's clear they're all terribly worried about me. I have to admit I'm terribly worried about me, too. I'm having second thoughts, but I push them away. The reward is worth the risk because I want to live as normal a life as possible, and if it means surgery and rehab, then so be it.

"Time to go," a nurse from Dr. Riddell's staff says. She grabs my bed and unlocks the wheels. "He'll be fine."

"I know." Collins wipes her face and kisses me one last time. "He's got to be. We've got too many things to do together."

Andy tightens his grip. "You're getting stronger and stronger, buddy."

"Yep." Andy flashes a smile. "You've got this."

Within seconds they're behind me and I'm through the double doors to surgery. Once in position, Dr. Riddell comes in and explains everything once more. Everything except the death thing. Then he tells me to relax.

I do my best, but it's hard. The doctor with the knockout drugs comes in and starts setting everything up. It doesn't take him long before he slips a mask over my nose and mouth.

"You're going to start counting backwards from ten when I say. Got it?"

I give a shaky thumbs up.

"Then let's get started."

"Ten, nine, eight…"

****

Five seconds later I'm staring at a blurry face leaning over me. "Dustin. Dustin can you hear me?" The words are faint at first. My vision blurs and cobwebs fill my head. Either I'm dead or the surgery is over.

Dr. Riddell stands off to the side as the knockout doc keeps repeating my name. "Dustin can you hear me? Welcome back. You did great."

The room stops spinning and everything seems almost normal again. "How long?" I'm barely able to get the words out.

"Don't worry about that right now, Dustin," Dr. Riddell says as he moves closer. "You need to rest for a minute as they get you off the anesthesia."

I tilt my head forward but can't see anything other than a sheet. "Did it…work?"

"You did fine, Dustin," Dr. Riddell says. "Get your bearings together. I'll be back in about half an hour to discuss the results with you."

My head spins like a top, and thoughts of Collins come crashing in. I worry she's still sitting out there waiting to hear if I made it. I'm certain she's okay, but I want to see her more than anything in the world. It's funny that she's the last thing I think about before I go under and the first thing when I wake up.

I wiggle my toes but can't tell if they're doing anything because of the painkillers they have me on. I'm numb from the waist down.

"Dustin," Dr. Riddell says as he pulls up a stool next to my head. "Your surgery went much better than we anticipated. We were able to get in and take care of everything we needed to and we were able to save the leg. Again. We will have to wait a few days to see how well we did connecting the tendons and ligaments to determine how much use of your leg you will have."

"That's good, huh?"

"It's great, Dustin." He springs up from the stool like it's on fire. "You'll be able to go back to your room to recover in just a bit. They're all pretty anxious to see you."

So they know I made it. That makes me happy. "Thanks, Walter."

When the nurse wheels me back to my room, Collins is the first to jump up and rush to me. Andy is next. Mr. and Mrs. Thacker come in last.

"Hey, baby," Miss Bernice says. "I wanted to come down and check on you real quick befo' you get caught up with this pretty little girlfriend of yours and her family."

"Hey, Miss Bernice." My words float like soap bubbles through the air.

"You get better now, ya' hear?"

"Yes, ma'am. I will."

Miss Bernice pats my hand, says something to Collins I can't hear, and leaves.

Mr. Thacker slides up next to me. "Dr. Riddell says you did great, Dustin. That's wonderful news."

"I knew you were tough," Andy says. A smile beams across his face.

I hold out my fist for a knuckle bump. "The toughest."

"We were all worried about you, Dustin," Mrs. Thacker says. "Especially this one." She wraps her arm around Collins. "Come on, Anderson. Let's give them a few minutes alone."

Collins waits until Mr. Thacker closes the door before she pounces on me and covers my face with kisses. She slips her tongue in my mouth and kisses me like she's never kissed me before.

She takes a deep breath and says, "I was so worried about you, Dustin. It took longer than it was supposed to, and it made me sick. Nobody would come out and let us know what was going on since we're not your real family and all. Thank God Dr. Riddell came out when it was over to let us know you made it."

She kisses all over my face again. "I'm not leaving you, baby. Not in this lifetime," I say.

"Promise?"

"Promise."

Chapter Forty-Two

Weeks fly by and Brooke steps up my training. She works me harder than ever. Nothing she does seems to improve my leg. It's frustrating and harder than anything I've done before. Every night, I come back to my room with a throbbing leg and worry I'll never walk again. I'm back in the wheelchair most of the time now. Should be back to the walker in the next week or two, according to Brooke, but at this point, I'm not sure. Seems like to me my leg is worse now than it ever was before.

Collins comes to visit once in a while, but not as much now as she used to. She says it's because she's getting ready for midterms, but I'm not sure. I haven't seen Andy in weeks either, which is strange. He usually comes every Saturday.

I'm in the garden drawing when Collins finds me. The look on her face lets me know something isn't right. All the time away from her clues me in to what's about to come. I steel myself against the news she's about to lay on me and prepare to hear her tell me she's found someone else.

Whatever her reasons are, I'll accept them. After all, I can't say I blame her much. Who wants a boyfriend who can't walk and is stuck in a hospital? If the situation was reversed, I'm not sure I'd be able to stick around as long as she has.

She gives a quick wave as she heads across the lobby. I tuck my sketchpad next to my leg.

"Hey, stranger." I try to make light of her visit but know whatever she has to tell me isn't going to be pretty.

"Hey, Dustin." She leans over and gives me a hug and kiss on the forehead.

"Everything okay? You look like you've seen a ghost."

She's on the couch beside me in a matter of seconds. "I don't know how to tell you this, Dustin." She looks to the floor, almost as if she's ashamed to just go ahead and break up with me.

"Just tell me, baby. It'll be easier for both of us that way." I swallow hard and wait for her to speak.

"You know I haven't been by to see you as much lately."

"I've noticed. You said midterms."

"Yeah, that's true, but there's more."

She continues to stare at the floor. She clutches her hands between her knees.

"Just spit it out, Collins. I'm a big boy. I can take it."

"It's hard, Dustin. Give me a second." She looks up and I can see she's crying. Her bottom lip quivers and the dimples in her cheeks bounce up and down. This is not going to be good.

"What is it, baby?" I put my hand on her shoulder. "If you've found someone else, I understand. Just tell me." Now my bottom lip quivers a little.

"What?" She jerks her head up and cocks it sideways. "Found someone else? What are you talking about?"

"Aren't you here to break up with me? Isn't that why I haven't seen you in what seems like forever?"

She lets out a mixture of laughter and tears. "No, baby. That's not it at all."

I breathe a sigh of relief. "Then what is it?"

"You know how Anderson hasn't been by lately?"

"What are you saying? What's happened to Andy?"

"Nothing has happened to him yet."

"Yet? What does that mean? Where's Andy?" My heart beats with fury and my muscles tighten. "Collins, tell me. What's going on?"

"He's been sick the past few weeks." Collins buries her face in her hands. Her words are almost unrecognizable. "And…" She gulps air. "He's getting worse every day. They're bringing him back to the hospital tomorrow."

"What're you talking about?" I throw my head back and stare at the lights hanging from the ceiling. "He's getting better. His hair is growing back and everything. He's in remission."

Collins can't stop crying. "Not anymore. He can't get out of bed. His doctor says he may not make it this time."

"Stop!" I scream. "Don't say anything. You can't say that about Andy. He's tough. Tough like me. He's going to be just fine."

"They're sending an ambulance for him first thing in the morning. "He can't walk, Dustin. Mom and Dad brought in a nurse last week to help them. The new medicine isn't helping."

"I don't want to hear anymore. It's not true."

"It is, Dustin. That's why I haven't been here much. I've been there with him every day. I've even been skipping classes. My professors all understand, but I've barely left his side in two weeks."

I'm at a loss for words. I wrap my arm around her and pull her close. She squeezes me tight. We sit in silence. Every moment I've spent with that little guy flashes through my memory. The first time we met when he told me to take a picture. All of the football games. Excalibur. The book I made for him. Everything.

The night Andy told me he prays for me every night flutters in my head. He prays I get better and learn to walk again. He prays for me and not himself. The kid's unlike anyone I've ever known. He only thinks about others and never himself. I only wish I could be half the man Andy is. It's time I pray for him.

With my eyes closed, I start talking in my head to the man upstairs, asking him to let my best friend pull through this one. He's been here before and we both know it. I can't understand why he'd let a kid like Andy suffer with a pathetic disease like cancer. I scream out the words *it's not fair* in my head. Then Andy's words scream back at me. *Life's not fair*. And it isn't. I know it isn't, but he doesn't deserve to be sick. He needs to play in his room. He needs to grow up and hold a girl's hand. Get his first kiss. Play football. Go to college. It isn't fair, but it's life.

My hands wrap up inside Collins' curly hair and her face buries deep into my chest. She's quiet, but I can tell she's still crying. "You all right?"

She just shakes her head back and forth on my chest.

"He's going to be just fine. I know he is. He's a tough little guy."

She nods her head. I kiss her on the back of her head. "Dustin?"

"What is it, baby?"

"Can I stay with you tonight?

"Of course."

Chapter Forty-Three

The next morning Collins sneaks out of my room, and I go wait for Andy's ambulance to arrive. They won't let me get close enough to see him as they take him out of the back of the ambulance. He looks unconscious as they roll him inside the ER.

I wheel my chair back inside the hospital and find Miss Bernice. "When can I see him?"

"Slow down, honey. You're goin' to have time to see that boy."

"But when? Why won't they let me see him?"

"Listen, honey. I know you're wantin' to see that sweet baby, but they got to get him in his room first. The doctors got to spend some time with him to evaluate him and let his mom and dad know what to expect. The doctors goin' to have to get some medicine in him and start some chemo right away. It may be days before they let you back in there to see him."

"Thanks, Miss Bernice."

"No problem, baby."

I get my butt back up to Andy's floor to find Collins. She's not there. Most likely, she's off with her parents somewhere.

"How is he?"

"Too soon to tell." Angela leans in like she's telling me a secret. "I'm not supposed to tell you this since you're not family and all, but you're about as close to a brother to Andy as any I've ever seen, so I'm going to tell you. They're looking at doing several rounds of chemo and radiation. It seems his leukemia spread quickly, and they're trying to knock it back if they can."

"That doesn't sound good."

"It isn't, but it's possible they can catch it before it spreads more. I've seen it happen so many times."

"I hope you're right."

I wheel my way back to the elevator and down to my room. Collins is waiting for me when I get there.

"Where have you been?" she asks as she jumps to her feet and reaches for my hands.

"Went to see Andy, but nobody'll let me."

Collins drops her chin to her chest and sighs. "They won't even let me back there right now. Only Mom and Dad."

"Angela said they're doing chemo and radiation." The thought of it all brings a tear to my eye.

"They have to. It's not the first time he's been through it. And it won't be the last."

"How long will it take before he's back to normal again?"

Collins goes to the window and stares out at the parking lot below. "Dustin, you need to understand how this works. Anderson's been sick for a long time. This isn't the first time he's gotten like this. You've never seen this side of the disease."

"I saw him when he was sick in bed one time."

"They switched his medication. It's totally different. When he met you, he had already finished his chemo and radiation. He was past all the crap and was on the road to remission. When he's being treated, it's tough on his little body. He shrinks up to next to nothing and throws up all the time. It's awful. I hate to see him like that. When you first met him, he was looking great."

"He was pale and skinny when I met him."

"That's right. And that was a hundred times better than what he looks like when he goes through treatment."

"Okay. Okay. So what's the deal? How does it all work? When can I see him?"

"I don't know when you'll be able to see him since you're not family. They only let family in when he gets like this."

"So what happens?"

"He'll go through a few days of treatment, and then they'll wait to see how well it works. They'll know pretty soon whether it's successful or if they have to do another round."

Listening to her describe all of the crap Andy has to go through makes me want to throw up. If I could trade places with him, I would. He deserves a chance to live life. To live outside of these hospital walls. Outside of all the sickness.

"Will you tell him something for me?"

"Anything."

"Tell him I love him and want him to get better so we can hang out."

"I'll tell him." Collins lets go of me. "I have to go. I told my parents I'd be back. They don't like me being too far away when he's sick like this. It's why they wanted me to come home."

"I'll be here waiting."

Collins leaves me alone with nothing but my thoughts, Excalibur, and my sketchbook. I get to work.

The hours pass, and I draw a few pictures of Andy in all sorts of sports uniforms. He's a baseball player in one. Dunking a basketball in another. Playing tennis and stopping goals on the soccer field. I draw and color like there's no tomorrow. I want to give him my pictures as soon as he's better.

Still more hours pass without any word from Collins. Nothing at all. I don't hear from her or see her until the next morning when she comes to let me know he's awake.

"It's a good thing, right?"

"It's a great thing." She fights to hold back tears. "They let me in this morning to see him."

"Did you tell him what I said?"

"Yes, and he said he loves you, too."

"Good."

"That's not all he asked for. He wants the book you made for him. You know, he keeps it with him everywhere he goes."

"Still?"

"Everywhere."

"Did you give it to him?"

"Nope. Mom and Dad didn't bring it when they brought him down yesterday. Dad left about an hour ago to go get it for him."

"Cool." A grin surfaces. "Check these out. They're for him."

I reach for my sketchpad and open it up to all of the pictures I've drawn of Andy. There are a total of seven.

"These are beautiful, sweetie." Collins takes several minutes to look at each one of them. "You're an incredible artist. You are."

"They're just pictures. Not art."

"They're awesome, and Anderson's going to go nuts over them when he sees himself in all these sports scenes."

"You think so?"

"Are you kidding me? I know so. Hello…have you met my brother? He's a sports freak."

"That's just one of the things that makes him so cool." I watch Collins's eyes as she looks through the pictures again. "When do you think I'll be able to give them to him?"

"I don't know. Maybe in three or four days."

"That long?"

"Yeah, but if you want, I can give them to him for you."

I think about it for a few minutes but decide not to send them with her. I want to give them to him myself. "Maybe I'll wait until I can see him."

"Good. I think they should come from you anyhow. That's y'all's thing. He'd rather you give them to him."

"Don't give him any hints about it, please."

"I won't." Collins puts the pad back on the table. "Listen, baby. I have to go. I'll try to get down to see you tomorrow if I can. Mom and Dad are worried, and I feel like I should be there with them and with Anderson until he gets through all of this."

"I know. I understand. Don't worry about me. I'll be fine." Another of the few lies I've ever told. "Love you."

"Love you more."

Chapter Forty-Four

Two days pass and there's no sign of Collins. No word about Andy at all. I'm still doing my therapy with Brooke, but Andy consumes my thoughts.

Brooke says, "I need you to focus here if you don't mind."

Brooke doesn't know much about Andy, so I cut her some slack. She's just doing her job. "No problem."

"We're going to get you back on the walker starting right now. You've been using the chair long enough. If you keep using it, you'll never use your leg like you're supposed to."

Brooke removes the brace and bends my leg at the knee. It hurts but bends. I bite down hard and choke back a scream.

"It's not going to feel good at first." Brooke keeps bending.

"No kidding." I grab the handles of the wheelchair and squeeze.

She straightens my leg out and brings a walker over to me. I reach for it and position myself between the two handles.

"Listen to me, Dustin." She pushes the wheelchair to the other side of the room. "You need to walk as much as you can when you're not in here with me. You need to use your leg as much as possible. Plus, I want you sitting down and standing up all the time. Take about half an hour or so for as long as you can stand it a few times a day and just sit down and stand up, bending your leg. It's the only way it's going to heal properly."

"You got it."

"I'm serious. No slacking at all."

"I've never slacked on anything in my life."

"Good. Now let's try and get you to—"

"Sorry to interrupt, but they're looking for him." Some guy, a nurse from this floor, points at me.

"Who is?"

"I don't know who," the guy says. "I was just asked to come get you and send you to the tenth floor."

"That's Andy's floor."

"Who?" Brooke asks.

"He's a friend."

"Better get going then." Brooke points to the door. I look to the wheelchair because it's quicker. "Don't even think about it. You're on the walker now."

I hurry out of the room as fast as possible, which is slower than slow. Lucky for me, Brooke's chamber of torture isn't far from the elevator, and after a few stops on other floors the doors open to the tenth floor. Angela is waiting for me.

"Hurry, Dusty."

"What's going on?"

"Just hurry."

Angela leads me through the halls and into Andy's room. Mr. and Mrs. Thacker huddle together just to the right of Andy's head. Their faces are red and streaked with tears. Collins stands off to the other side.

"Come over here," she says. She leans in close to Andy. "Anderson, can you hear me?" Andy's eyes are closed. He's so skinny he doesn't even look real. "Slaughter's here." It's the first time she's ever called me by my last name. A strange feeling plunks into my stomach.

His little lips separate a tiny sliver and air escapes his mouth. He's trying to say something, but it's impossible to hear as I move closer. I slide up to the bed and use the handrail to get closer to his head. Collins grabs my hand to help me stay on my feet.

"Hey, buddy. It's me." His little fingers dance ever so slightly, and I reach out and take his hand. "I've got something for you when you're feeling better."

Mrs. Thacker loses control and starts sobbing for some reason. Mr. Thacker catches her before she falls. I look to Collins for guidance.

"He's dying, Dustin." Her voice is raspy as she whispers into my ear. "The doctor said it'll be within the hour."

Oxygen rushes from my brain. My legs go limp, forcing me to hold the rail tight. Collins puts her arm against my back. I shake my head back and forth and tears pour down my face. "Hey, buddy. You're the toughest kid I know. You're going to beat this. I just know it."

His little fingers seem to flinch inside my hand, but I'm not sure. His breathing is labored and his skin cold. I see the book I made him wrapped under his other arm. Collins notices when I realize it's there.

"When Dad got it here, Andy tucked it under his arm and hasn't let it go ever since."

"Can he hear us?"

Mr. Thacker's voice cracks a little. "I think so. They've got him on morphine to keep him comfortable, but I think he knows we're here."

Tears stream down everyone's faces. Andy's eyes flicker like he's trying to look at us, but the little guy doesn't have the strength to open them all the way.

We all huddle around him as the machines connected to him beep. His heart monitor blips slowly as time passes. Silence descends in the room and we all wait. I have no idea what's going through everyone else's minds, but I'm praying harder than I've ever prayed in my life. I'm just hoping the big guy upstairs will give this kid a break and let him fight through this, even though I know it's not going to happen.

Andy looks like he's completely at peace. His lips stretch in what almost looks like a smile. His UNC hat sits loose on his bald head. I reach up and touch mine as we wait. The cover of the book I made him stares back at me from under his tiny little arm, and I wish I would've sent the other pictures with Collins when I had a chance.

My heart sinks to know he didn't get a chance to see them because I was being selfish.

I've been in the room for maybe five minutes when Andy opens his mouth. Mr. and Mrs. Thacker press forward. Collins leans an ear close, and I follow her lead. Andy struggles for breath as his chest moves slowly up and down. His eyes bounce beneath his eyelids, but they never open.

"I…love…you…" Andy's words are hard to hear, "all." He sucks in a big gulp of air and his chest heaves. "Finish…the…game." One last breath and his heart monitor signal starts a nonstop beep.

Nurses rush in, and Mrs. Thacker collapses to the floor. Collins cries out with a scream that nearly bursts my eardrums. Mr. Thacker sobs uncontrollably as the doctor hurries to the bed and pronounces Andy dead at 5:30 p.m. I stand beside Andy with tears streaming down my face. Stunned.

Chapter Forty-Five

I'm as empty as a deflated birthday balloon as the hours and days leading up to the funeral pass. Collins goes home with her family, so they can get things in order. I stay in my room doing my best to figure out what happened three days earlier.

No matter how I run it through my brain, nothing ever makes sense. The coolest little kid in the whole world was vibrant and full of life a few weeks ago, and now he's lying in some cold funeral home alone.

Everything that's happened before I met him doesn't seem important at all. I've been going through the paces and getting nowhere. Andy showed me what a real friendship is. Even though he was barely nine years old, he lived a life I'd be proud of if I were given a hundred years. Now I've got to do something with my life to make him proud of me as he watches over me from heaven.

The envelope Collins gave me weeks earlier pokes out from under some other papers. I get up and grab it. I pull the letter out and read Dad's words again and again. I've never thought much about him since he got hauled off to jail. Now that I think about it, it's been a decade since I've seen him. It's almost like he's a stranger to me now.

When I read the letter he wrote, I can't help but think of Andy and Mr. Thacker. They had the kind of relationship all boys should have with their fathers. No matter what Jason Slaughter was or is, he's still my dad, and I can't have another in my life.

I take out a sheet of paper and start writing a letter telling him about everything that's happened in my life since he left. Before I realize it, I've written close to ten pages. I seal it in an envelope and address it to the state prison and take it to the nurses' station so they can put it in the mail.

Back in my room, I put on the suit I wore to Andy's house for the first time. Mr. Thacker asked me to because Andy wants to be buried in his matching suit. Collins told me Andy knew he wasn't going to make it this time. He also begged the doctor to let him see me, but they wouldn't. Collins didn't understand why.

I straighten my tie, grab my walker, and head downstairs. When I get off the elevator, Thomas is waiting for me. He rises from the couch and lays his newspaper on the table.

"Sorry, Thomas," I say because I was supposed to be down a half hour earlier. "Got caught up writing a letter."

He tosses my bag in the trunk of a black limo and then helps me in. We're on the road when Thomas lowers the music and says, "They want me to take you to their house first."

"Sounds good." My eyes meet Thomas' in the rearview mirror.

He turns the music back on, and I stare at the blue sky as we ride up the highway. People always say rainy and gloomy days are perfect for funerals because they're so sad. I've only been to one funeral before, so I don't know for sure. But what I do know is if they knew Andy, then they'd know the sunshine is just about perfect because that's the kind of kid he will always be.

"Stay here, sir," Thomas says as he exits the car. A few minutes later, he returns with Collins and her parents.

Collins slides in next to me. Mr. and Mrs. Thacker sit on the other row of seats across from us. "Hey, baby." Collins kisses my cheek. The makeup on her face is perfect now, but I know it won't stay that way for long.

"You look nice, Dusty," Mrs. Thacker says. "Anderson will be happy."

What a strange thing to say, even though I know what she means. I can't imagine what they are going through right now. I know what I'm going through, and I only spent six months with him.

"Thanks, Mrs. Thacker. I'm sure he will."

We ride in relative quiet, aside from a bit of idle chatter about some of the plans they've made for his service. Apparently, they bought family burial plots a few years earlier when they found out about Andy's cancer. They let Andy pick them out. Collins told me they knew this day was coming, but they didn't know when. Andy knew it too.

We're the first to arrive at the church, but it isn't long before their friends and family arrive. Many of the nurses and doctors from the hospital come. I go over to the coffin with Collins for the first time to get a peek.

"Are you okay with this?" Collins asks as she walks beside my walker.

"Yeah, I think so."

We move close to the coffin, and he's lying there like he's sleeping. It's obvious they've put some makeup on his face, but he looks happy. He wears a smile and his trademark blue hat. I straighten his tie even though it doesn't need it.

"You know he asked Dad to let him wear it?"

"Mr. Thacker told me."

"You're one of the best things that ever happened to my brother, Dustin. I want you to always remember that."

"He's one of the best things that ever happened to me." I put my hand on his bony little hand. "It's kinda funny, but I'm glad I wrecked my car that night. Without it, I wouldn't have met him. Or you."

She kisses my hand, and we move to the side to let others come closer. We join her parents out in the lobby as they're being consoled by friends and family members. There are so many people here for his funeral, but I'm not surprised at all. He touched so many lives in his short time here.

"You okay, baby?" Miss Bernice comes up behind me. She's wearing a Sunday dress with a big ol' hat and all.

"Yes, ma'am. I reckon I am."

"It's a sad day today. That's fo' sure. That baby is one of God's stars twinklin' in the sky from heaven above."

"Yes, ma'am."

"He's lookin' out for you too, baby."

"I know, Miss Bernice."

"I love you, honey. Now let me get inside and pay my respects."

The minister tells everyone the service will start soon and directs them to the sanctuary. A few of the men standing around in black suits go back inside.

I make my way toward the sanctuary, but Collins grabs my elbow. "The family goes in last." I scrunch my face. "You're family, too, Dustin."

Once everyone settles inside, someone starts playing an organ. Mr. Thacker puts his arm around Mrs. Thacker as a way to keep her on her feet it looks like. Collins walks beside them as I push my walker a step at a time.

We make it to our seats and the service starts. The coffin lid hangs open, and I can barely see the bill of his hat sticking up. Flowers surround the coffin and a huge pile of roses lay on top above his feet. An easel with the book I wrote for him sits off to the side. It's opened to the page where Andy scores the winning touchdown and jumps into his coach's arms. My face stares back at me from the pages as I hold Andy high in the air.

Part way into the service, the minister takes a moment to let a few people come up and speak. Collins talks about how much she loves Andy and her decision to stay close to him by going to UNC. Tears cut through her makeup. Mr. Thacker speaks for a few minutes. A few other people say a quick word or two, and then the minister asks if anyone else wants to come up and say a few words. There are hundreds of people in the sanctuary, so I'm kind of surprised nobody else gets up.

I stand up from my seat. Collins sees me and immediately reaches for my walker, but I push it away. If ever there was a time to start walking this is it. I take a step forward and almost fall. Collins jumps up, but I hold out my hand to let her know I'm okay. Tears fill Mr. Thacker's eyes.

A small, unstable step becomes another, and then another. Eventually, I make my way to Andy instead of the podium. I take a few moments to get one last look at Andy. He's wearing his hat like he always does. I take mine off and reach over to kiss his forehead one last time. Even though I break a promise I made to myself, I need to leave a part of myself with Andy. Instead of putting my hat back on my head, I lay it beside him and say, "I love you, buddy. Always will," then walk back to my seat.

Chapter Forty-Six

Collins and I walk through our days like zombies for weeks after Andy's death, but we walk them together. Most days, anyway.

The day of his funeral let me know that I can walk on my own, and I walk everywhere I go without a walker or cane now. It took a couple of months and many hours of hard work with Brooke to make it possible. The day they put Andy in the ground will always be a day I'll never forget. It's the day I decided to make Andy proud of me.

I spend weeks working as hard as I can on school. I have A's and my counselor tells me if I can finish the school year with all A's I'll have a good shot at getting accepted at UNC. If not, I'll find a community school somewhere and transfer in a couple of years. It's not the ideal situation for Collins and me, but it's better than her being here and me working in Sully's dad's place. Andy opened a whole new world for me. When he gave me my own Excalibur, he gave me a gift I never dreamed of.

Turns out I'm a pretty good writer. I write all the time now. Everything that comes into my mind goes into Excalibur. Actually, I'm on my seventh Excalibur. Most of what I write is about Andy or Collins. I've written many poems for her, though I'm not sure they're good enough to be called poems. Either way, I've only given her a few of the ones I've written for her. They're mostly for me.

My greatest accomplishment so far, I think, is the essay I wrote for admission to UNC. I send in my completed application package this week, since we just finished spring quarter. Until then, I'll keep my fingers crossed and hope they take pity on a nobody from Nowhere, North Carolina.

Football remains as much of a distant memory for me as Jenny Lee. They're like parts of me that'll always be there, but they're not as important now as they once were. Don't get me wrong. I miss football like crazy. I want nothing more than to be able to run across the goal line one more time, but my new limp lets me know it's nothing more than a dream. So I quit dreaming that dream and pick out new ones.

Collins told me once before that people without a future live in the past. Her words seem so prophetic now. My eyes are always looking forward to a better day on a different path. I'm just thankful she's there to walk the path beside me. And for those times I have to walk alone, I can always count on her to be down the path a ways waiting for me to get to her.

I let my hair grow back out after Andy's death. I didn't know for sure if I would, but I realize it's what Andy would want. He lived for the future and would want me to do the same.

I'm in the garden writing when Collins walks in carrying a couple of pizzas. It's one of the things we do now for the kids at the hospital.

"Hey, sweetie," she says with a kiss over the top of steaming pizza.

"Smells delicious. Missed you."

"Missed you more."

We work our way upstairs and are immediately mobbed by about twelve kids, including Katie bug.

"Dusty, Dusty, look at this." Katie bug twirls like a little ballerina, and I notice a red ribbon clinging tightly to a few strands of blonde hair.

"Beautiful. You're absolutely beautiful."

Katie bug continues to twirl in circles, and her smile grows with each spin.

"Ready for some pizza, Katie bug?" Collins sets the boxes on the table.

"Smells yummy."

"It is." I scoop her up in my arms, and she plants a giant kiss on my cheek.

"You're scratchy."

"He's been lazy hasn't he, Katie bug?" Collins pokes me in the chest. "He needs to shave, huh?"

"It's okay, Dusty. You're still my boyfriend."

"Hey, now!" Collins tickles her tummy the way she used to do Andy's.

Katie bug giggles. It's a running joke she and Collins have had for the past few weeks. "Let's go eat, you two."

Katie bug helps me hand out slices of pizza, and Collins fills little cups with soda. Angela peeks in to make sure we're set. This has become our new Wednesday routine. It's a nice bump in the middle of the week for most of them. A week is a long time to go without seeing your parents. I should know. I haven't seen Mama in about eight months.

After we put the kids to bed, we go back down to the garden.

"I'll be right back." Collins rushes to the door. I have no idea what she's up to.

I take out my sketchpad and start drawing. I draw almost every night. Especially after I spend time with the kids. They love it when I give them pictures of themselves.

"Where'd you go?" I ask Collins as she comes back in.

"I had to get something."

I notice an envelope in her hand as she sits on the couch next to me. She pulls her legs under her and leans in close.

"What's wrong with you?"

She gives me her sad hound dog eyes. "You have to promise not to be mad at me."

"The last time you asked me to promise you gave me an envelope from my dad. I sent him a letter, remember? We're writing back and forth now, so it can't be from him."

"Not from him." She flips the big envelope over so I can't read it. "By the way, I meant to ask you how he's doing."

"Fine. He keeps asking me to come visit him."

"Are you going to?"

"I don't know. I'm not sure I'm ready for a visit yet." I tap against the envelope. "Quit trying to change the subject."

She puts out her bottom lip and pouts. "I'm not changing the subject. I just want to make sure you won't get mad."

When I ask her why I'd get mad, she tells me how much she loves me. When she asks me if I love her, too, I shrug my shoulders, so she slugs me in the arm and tells me I better watch myself. I laugh and say, "Yes, I love you with all my heart."

When she asks me if I trust her, I get a bit nervous and tell her to stop beating around the bush. She pulls out an envelope, letting me know that whatever she's talking about has already been done. "Spit it out, Collins."

She tries to convince me that whatever is in the envelope is a good thing. Collins takes a deep breath and pulls the envelope to her chest and gives it a giant bear hug. "You remember the writing contest I told you I was thinking about entering?"

"From a month or so ago?"

"Yes. That one."

"I can't say that I do."

"Ha, ha. So funny. Anyhow, I decided to enter it."

"And you won. Congratulations, baby. That's awesome."

"Settle down, Dustin. I didn't win. In fact, I didn't even come close."

"Then what's with the giant envelope and the secrecy?"

"It's that…" Collins pauses and flips the envelope around. I don't look at it at first. "You won, Dustin. You."

"How did I win? I didn't enter."

"Here comes the part you have to not get mad at me about."

I search my mind wondering what she used to enter me. One of the poems I gave her, maybe. But there's no way I'd win with those. "Spit it out."

"I entered *Andy's Big Game*."

I'm stunned when she tells me what she did. "You did what?!"

"I entered the book you wrote for Andy." She pulls the letter from the envelope and puts it in my hand. "And you won first place. Read it."

The official UNC seal stares back at me as I prepare to read the letter.

Mr. Dustin Slaughter,

Thank you for your submission to our contest. Your artwork and storyline are incredible, and we're pleased to let you know you've won first place. As a result of winning the University of North Carolina Fiction Writers Association Young Writers' Contest, you've also been awarded a $1,000 cash prize. We will present you the check this weekend. Thank you for sharing your work with us, and we wish you all the best in your publishing pursuits.

Sincerely,

Dr. Phillip Rosenthal

I ask Collins what the letter means, and she jumps into my lap, kisses me, and tells me how proud of me she is for winning the contest.

I have no idea what a thousand dollars even looks like. I've never had more than about fifty bucks in my pocket at any given time. "I don't know what to say." I read the letter again. "I'm not sure if I should be angry or happy."

"This is a good thing, baby. It means you're a writer and artist. A real, award-winning writer. I told you the book is amazing. Why do you think Andy loved it so much?"

"Because it's about him."

"Because it's about both of you." Her face lights up and her eyes sparkle with happiness. Her eyes remind me of Andy. "It's cool that you won. I'm so proud of you."

"It's cool and all, but I don't want to get carried away here. Just because some college professors and English students like it doesn't mean anyone else will. Besides, I only meant for Andy to see it."

"Fine, grumpy Gus. Be that way." Her eyes continue to sparkle. She's not going to let this go. "At least you'll be able to take me to dinner after the ceremony with the thousand dollars you have."

Chapter Forty-Seven

Mr. and Mrs. Thacker join us for the award ceremony and take us out to eat afterward at their country club.

"We're proud of you, Dusty," Mr. Thacker says. "Any word about UNC yet?

"No, sir," I say, choking down a piece of steak. "I just submitted my application online yesterday. I should know by May."

"Dusty," Mrs. Thacker says, "He loved your book more than anything."

"Yes ma'am, I know."

"We almost buried him with it," she says. "Collins talked us out of it." Collins squeezes my knee under the table. "Now we know why."

"I hope Andy's proud of it. Proud of me."

"I am sure he is proud of you, Dusty." Mr. Thacker calls the waiter over and orders a second glass of wine. "Winning the contest with his book is something Mrs. Thacker and I never would have imagined. I just wish he could've lived long enough to see it."

A tear creeps into my eye. "He's a great kid. I miss him something terrible."

"We all do," Collins says.

Mr. Thacker raises up his glass. "To Anderson and Dusty." We all raise our glasses and clink them together.

"So when do you leave the hospital?" Mr. Thacker is full of questions. I'm kind of used to them by now, so it isn't a big deal. He's a serious guy and expects a lot for his daughter. Boyfriend included.

"By the end of the week. Coach is going to come down and get me."

"Are you ready to go back home?"

"To be honest, sir, I'm not." Mr. Thacker looks at me sideways. "It feels like years since I've been home. I'm more at home here than I ever was there. My family and all, ya' know."

Mr. Thacker rubs his chin as if in deep thought. "Collins has told me a little more about your family. Seems like they're having some difficulties."

Difficulties? "That's one way of putting it, sir. Mom's a mess, and I don't really know my dad."

"But he's been writing him for a couple months now." Collins lays her fork on her plate and turns to me. "My father suggested it, and I think it's a good idea if you go visit him."

"Are you serious?"

"Family is important, Dusty." Mr. Thacker swirls the wine around in his glass. "It's one of the things we believe strongly about. Family is family, and everyone deserves a chance to be forgiven."

"I reckon."

He continues to swirl the glass like he's looking into a crystal ball and says that Collins told him about Mama's addiction. I tell him it's true, and he asks if I'd mind telling him about her.

I do mind, but after all this family has done for me, it's the least I can do. So I tell him about how she used to be a real good mother. And how I remember Daddy and Mama laughing and joking around. We'd go places and do things. We were never rich or anything. Heck, I've been poor my whole life. But we were happy once. That's what I want Mr. Thacker to know.

Collins moves her chair a bit closer.

I admit that maybe it's because I was a kid and all, but things seemed pretty good. Up until the plant closed and he lost his job and started drinking real heavy. It surprises me how hard it is to tell Mr. Thacker about how my dad landed in jail and how it wasn't too long after he went to jail that Mama got all depressed and started drinking, too. Tears well up when I tell him about getting off the bus and finding her drunk already. Everybody knew it. It was embarrassing.

"I'm so sorry, sweetie," Collins says.

"It's okay. Ancient history. It wasn't until about high school that she got started on the pills. Some lowlife she was running with got her hooked. She hasn't been the same since."

Mr. Thacker's eyes lock on me like a laser. "Well, your life's going to be changing soon, son." He leans back and takes a sip of wine this time. "You'll get accepted to UNC and leave all of it behind you."

"I can't just leave Mama, sir. Somebody's gotta look out for her."

"That's true, but you can't look out for her by hanging around your old town going nowhere. You have to get out of there and make your own path. We can figure out how to get your mother some help, but it's going to take a professional."

"It's funny that all the time I've been in the hospital only a few people visited me. Coach and a few guys from the team."

"Don't forget your girlfriend." Collins raises an eyebrow at me.

"Ex-girlfriend."

"Don't worry about that so much Dusty." Mr. Thacker shifts in his seat. "It's not an easy drive back and forth. People get caught up in routine. Just like you did at the hospital. They'll accept you with open arms when you return next week."

"It's going to be like walking into a brand new school all over again."

"I reckon," Mr. Thacker says. The three of us stare at him like he's lost his mind. He laughs. "What? It reminds me of Anderson, and I kinda like it." He drains the last bit of wine from his glass.

Chapter Forty-Eight

"**A**re you ready?" Coach wastes no time once he arrives.

"I reckon."

It's bittersweet packing up my stuff and getting ready to head back to Flatbush. Only two boxes, my backpack, and laptop are all I have to my name. It's kind of funny that I spent so many months in this hospital with so few things. Then again, it's a lot like my life back home. I reckon that's why I don't mind.

"Fancy suit." Coach points to the small closet.

"Oh yeah, I almost forgot about it."

"You wouldn't want to do that. It looks expensive."

Miss Bernice comes in with a wheelchair.

"What's the wheelchair for?"

"For you, honey."

"I'm walking outta here."

She throws her hand on her ample hip. "Don't argue with me, baby. You know hospital rules say you gots to be taken outside in a chair. I don't like it no more than you do."

"Whatever." I sit in the chair, and Miss Bernice wheels me out. Coach pushes the cart with my stuff beside me.

"They're awful excited to see you, son." Coach mashes the elevator button. "It's been a long time since you've been in Flatbush."

When the door opens, Collins is standing there waiting on me with a huge bundle of balloons.

"Sneaky girl." She leans over to kiss me. "Thought you couldn't make it. Test, my butt."

She giggles. "I have to keep it interesting, now don't I?"

"I reckon." Coach taps me against the shoulder. "Sorry. Coach this is Collins. My girlfriend."

"Nice to meet you. Do you mind if I call you Coach, too?" Collins sticks out her hand.

"Not at all," Coach says. "You're mighty pretty, young lady. How did you end up with Slaughter here? You don't look hurt."

"Long story, Coach." I jump in real quick so Collins doesn't have to bring up Andy.

"It's okay, Dustin. I don't mind." She hands me my bouquet of balloons. "My brother, Anderson, was a patient here. That's how we met."

"I see. He's gone home already then."

"In a manner of speaking, Coach." Collins grabs my hand as Miss Bernice pushes me. "Anderson passed away several weeks ago. He had leukemia."

"I'm sorry. I didn't know." Coach drops his eyes to the floor.

As we round the corner, there's a group of folks from the hospital waiting on me. Angela and several of the kids from upstairs are there in their pajamas. Katie bug isn't there because she went home a couple weeks ago. She's in full remission, and that makes me happy. Angela promises me she'll keep in touch and let me know how Katie bug's doing. Her parents say Collins and I can come visit her over the summer.

"Dusty, it's been some ride, huh?" Dr. Riddell reaches out his hand to shake mine.

"That's one way of putting it, Doc."

"Who knew a brief encounter that morning in the parking lot would have us forever linked?"

"No kidding. Life's a funny thing, isn't it?"

"It sure is. You keep working your leg, and keep your follow-up appointment with your doctor back home. I've already sent your records to him, so you shouldn't have any trouble."

Brooke leans over and gives me a hug. "I'm going to miss you, Dusty."

"I'm not going to miss all the pain you put me through, but I am glad you never gave up on me."

"I've never given up on any of my patients." She pokes me in the chest. "Not even the huge pain-in-the-rear babies like you."

After saying all my goodbyes to people from the hospital, Coach takes my stuff out to his truck.

"Okay, baby. You can get up now." Sadness fills Miss Bernice's words.

"I'm going to miss you most, Miss Bernice." I stretch my arms around her and kiss her chubby cheek. "I don't know how I would've ever made it without you. You're an angel in a nurse's uniform."

"Hush, baby. You goin' to make Miss Bernice cry."

"I love you, Miss Bernice."

Miss Bernice pulls Collins in close. "You'll take care of him for me, won't you?" She nods. "He needs a good woman in his life." Miss Bernice squeezes Collins. "I'm goin' to miss you too, honey."

"Me too."

Miss Bernice wheels the chair back inside, and Collins and I wait for Coach to bring the truck around.

"Looks like this is it for a little while," I say as I stand in the warm spring sunshine.

"It's only temporary." I put my arm around Collins as she nuzzles her head against my chest. "I'll be up to visit you soon enough. And I'll be at your graduation in a few weeks."

"Hopefully, I'll hear from UNC by then, and we can start making plans for the fall."

"You'll get in, Dustin. I just know it." She squeezes me lightly. "You deserve it. You've worked hard."

"I couldn't have done it without you."

"Yes, you could have."

"I wouldn't have, though. You make me want to be a better person. You make me want to be somebody. I don't know what that somebody is yet, but whatever it is, it's in the future, not the past." I wrap my arms around her and squeeze her tight.

"There's Coach." Coach pulls up in front of me. He comes to the passenger side and slings open the creaky door. "Guess you better go before I start to cry." Collins peels away from me and plants her lips on mine. She gives me a long kiss, forcing Coach to turn his eyes to the sky. "Love you."

"Love you more."

We walk to the truck and I get in. She pushes the door shut and stands on the curb with her hands to her mouth and blows me a kiss. I put my fingers in the I-love-you position, blow her a kiss with it, and then hold up my I-love-you fingers and wave for her to see as Coach pulls out of the parking lot. I don't stop waving until she's out of sight.

After giving me some quiet time, Coach says, "Seems like a nice girl."

"The best."

"It's a terrible shame, son, what happened to you. UNC wanted you real bad. It broke my heart to have to tell them what happened."

"It's okay, Coach. That's the past. I've got a new path now."

Chapter Forty-Nine

oach puts my stuff just inside the door. Mama waits on me to get out of the truck, and it appears she's sober. It's only noon, so she hasn't had time to get her daily fix yet. I give her a quick hug and kiss on the cheek. Then I walk Coach out to his truck.

"Thanks for coming to get me, Coach."

"No problem, son. Glad I could help." He eyes Mama. "Need anything else?"

"No, sir."

"Slaughter, I know you haven't got it easy here. I've been knowing it for years. You've had it a thousand times better at the hospital. Anyway, what I'm trying to say, son, is if you need money for food or anything, let me know."

"It's all good, Coach. I'll be fine." I don't tell Coach about the thousand dollars and the contest I won. I won't tell Mama either, or she'll steal it to get high. It would be enough money to put her in the ground for sure.

"Okay then. I'll be by to get you first thing on Monday."

"See ya, Coach."

He slaps my shoulder and drives away. I head back in to deal with Mama. It's time we have a talk.

"Mama, can you sit down a second? I got a few things I need to say."

"What is it, Dusty? I got to go meet a friend in a minute. Can it wait?"

Mama squirms and fidgets and her eyes run wild with desperation. She's jonesin' for a fix so bad she can hardly stand it. That junk has a hold of her, and there isn't any way to get her clean.

"No, Mama. It can't wait. Sit down." I guide her to her ratty recliner. She reaches for a cigarette and lights it up.

"What do you want?"

"This Mama." I pick up an empty pill bottle. "You've got to quit using."

"I barely even touch the stuff, Dusty. You know that."

Even though I know one of these days I'm going to come home and find her dead if she doesn't stop using, she says she has it all under control. She fidgets in her chair and sucks on her cigarette. I drop my head to my hands, elbows on my knees, and tell her I've been talking to my dad. She looks at me with wild eyes, and moves just enough to take another drag of her cigarette and blow out the smoke. Her face a blank canvas.

"Ain't you going to say something, Mama?"

"What do you want me to say?" She puts out the cigarette in an overflowing ashtray and lights up another one. "Ain't much to say, now is there? You're a grown man, and if you want to talk to your dad there ain't nothin' I can do to stop it."

When I ask her why she won't talk to Dad, all she says is that it wouldn't do any good. Mama puts out the cigarette without finishing it. She gets quiet and serious. "He's locked up for ten years now and got twenty more to go for killing the preacher man's wife. When he lost his job, things was bad enough. When he went away, it was all I could take. I begged him and begged him to stop drinkin' but he wouldn't."

"Kinda like what I'm doing with you now."

Mama doesn't like that. "We had no money, and I had you to feed. Things just got too hard. And I couldn't get your disappointed face out of my head."

"That's why you started with the drugs?"

"There's more to it, Dusty. Stuff I'm not proud of and you don't need to know about, but I had to put food on the table the best I could and clothes on your back. One thing led to another and here we are."

I let out a heavy breath. "It doesn't always have to be that way, Mama. Things can change."

"Can they, Dusty? Can they?"

"You never even came to see me in the hospital, Mama. Not even once."

"Coach came and told me you was doin' alright. Said you'd do better if I didn't come."

It makes no sense why Coach would tell Mama that. No matter how bad off she is, she's still my Mama. Why can't she see that? "Mama, I applied to college."

Mama cackles and reaches for the unfinished cigarette and lights it back up. After a puff of smoke escapes from her mouth she says, "People like us don't go to college, son. Look around you and see what your future looks like."

"I'm going to college, Mama. I have a new girlfriend who believes in me. She goes to UNC. I'm going to go to UNC, too."

Another cackle. "We'll see, Dusty. We'll see."

"What do you mean?"

"I believed in your father once, and you see where all those promises got me."

"I'm not him. I've got hope."

"Hope ain't no plan, Dusty. It's just a dream."

Mama's words hit hard. She's right, and I know it. Guys like me don't go off to college. We work at the factory and talk about when we were in high school. I'm not going to be one of those guys. This town almost killed me once before I got a chance to get out. There isn't any way I'm going to let it have a second shot at me.

"Collins and I have plans, and they don't include Flatbush. But Mama, you've got to get better."

"I'm just fine. Don't be worryin' about me, Dusty. Besides, when your girlfriend gets one look at who you really are, she's going to go runnin' right back to her fancy school and forget all about you."

Tears well up in my eyes as this shell of a woman sits and puffs away on her cigarette. She picks at her skin and moves around in the chair like it's on fire. This is my life, but it will not be my life forever.

There's more out there than this, and I'm going to do whatever it takes to find my place.

"You're wrong, Mama. She loves me and I love her. You'll see."

Mama gets up from her chair and slips on a pair of bedroom slippers. "I've got to go now, Dusty. I'm glad you're all better and back home. I missed you."

She slides out the door and heads up the road.

Chapter Fifty

Coach is right on time and we're at school much sooner than I want to be. I don't want to go, but Coach helps me out and we walk in through the front door. There's a huge banner in the lobby that says, WELCOME BACK, SLAUGHTER.

Music blares as some of the marching band starts to play. Guys from the team are there to greet me, along with the cheerleaders. "Welcome home, Slaughter," Coach says.

It's funny how it doesn't much feel like home anymore. "You did all this?"

"No." Coach raises a finger. "It was mostly her idea."

Jenny Lee stands in the middle of the cheerleaders holding a sign saying, I MISSED YOU! Sully lurks over on the side. He stands still like he's afraid to move. "Great," I say. "Just what I wanted."

"I thought you'd like it, Slaughter." Coach squeezes my neck. "You're still a part of the Coosa County Eagles. Always will be for as long as you live."

"I reckon."

Jenny Lee and Charlotte come over to me with a smile on their faces like nothing ever happened. Sully stands like a statue.

"Hey, Slaughter," Charlotte says. "Welcome back. We all missed you." Charlotte is still sweet as ever. "Even Sully. Aren't you glad to be back?"

Jenny steps between us. "Of course he's glad to be back. This is his home. This is his life."

I glare at Jenny Lee.

"I missed you, too, *Charlotte.*" Jenny Lee crinkles her nose when I hug Charlotte and not her. "Guess I better get on to class. Takes me longer than it used to." I pat my damaged leg.

I turn to walk to my first class and just like I expect, Jenny Lee walks beside me. It's not like I can run away from her. She twirls her hair and flashes her best impression of a sincere smile. "We need to talk."

"I told you back at the hospital we don't have anything more to say to each other." I do my best to step around her. "Jenny Lee, I knew coming back here wasn't going to be easy, but you're making it a whole lot worse by dragging up the past. I told you I have a new girlfriend." I stop walking and turn to look her in the eyes. "And quite frankly, a new life."

"You're still with that girl?" I remain silent and start walking. "Trust me. She won't last. She'll forget about you as soon as she can, and then you'll be back. You'll see. I'm the only one who loves you."

"You don't love me, Jenny Lee. You love the idea of what I used to be." My feet move slowly down the hall as I make it to my first class. "Jenny Lee, I need you to listen to me once and for all." She tries to hold my hand, but I pull away from her. "I forgive you."

Her face blanches with confusion. "What?"

"I forgive you."

"That's gre—"

"Let me finish. I forgive you, but I will never forget what you did." Jenny Lee starts to say something, but I stop her. "I'm not done. I'll never forget you, either. In fact, I should thank you for doing what you did because if it weren't for what you did I would be the same person now that I was back in September. And you know what?"

"What?"

"That would be sad because I'd never have met Collins or Andy if you hadn't betrayed me like you did." She tries to talk again, but I stop her. "Andy taught me what it means to live life, and Collins is teaching me what it means to love someone deeply and truly. And to be loved in return." She throws both hands on her hips and huffs. "So thank you, Jenny Lee. Thank you for showing me there's more to life than this small town."

Without a word, she storms off, and I go to class. The day progresses as well as expected. My teachers all rave about how well I did with the work they sent me. They all apologize for my accident as if they were somehow personally responsible. It's funny how people react when they don't know what to say.

Toward the end of the day my counselor calls for me over the intercom. She wants to see me for some reason. "Go ahead and take your stuff," McDougal says.

I throw everything in my backpack and head to her office.

"You wanted to see me, ma'am?"

"Have a seat right there." She points to the only other chair in the room. "So you applied to the University of North Carolina a few weeks ago, right?"

"Yes, ma'am."

"I sent your transcripts from the midterm."

"Yes, ma'am, I know."

She reaches into her drawer and pulls out an envelope and lays it on her desk. The UNC seal waves at me from the top left corner. My stomach twists into knots. "They've already made a decision."

"That's pretty quick, right?"

"It is. I was surprised to get it so soon."

"It's okay, Mrs. Hill. You can go ahead and give me the bad news."

"I'm sorry, Dusty." She slides the envelope to me. "You need to read it for yourself."

I cringe as I pick it up. She's already opened it, since I gave them the school's address. My eyes race over every word written on the page. There's some information I don't understand that I'll need to ask Mrs. Hill about, but the important word pops out at me like a neon light in the dark. "I'm accepted?"

Mrs. Hill's face beams as she looks over her glasses at me. "Seems so, Dusty. Congratulations."

"But how? What does contingent mean?"

"You're accepted to start in the fall depending on your grades at the end of the school year. If you maintain all A's then you'll be accepted as a full-time student. You'll be a Tar Heel like me." She nods back over her shoulder to a framed piece of paper hanging behind her.

"This is so cool. I don't know what to say."

"Just say you'll finish with all A's and make us proud."

"Yes, ma'am. I will. I can do that."

I get up to go but she stops me. "Don't forget this." She waves the envelope in the air.

"I can take it?"

"It's yours."

I snatch the envelope and shove it in my bag. I can't wait to tell Collins the good news, so I rush out the door and pull out the phone Mr. Thacker gave me. "Hey, baby."

"Hey," she says. "Everything all right? Shouldn't you be in class still?"

"Yes, but they called me to the counselor's office and guess what?"

"What?"

"I'm in."

"Are you serious? That's awesome. I'm so happy for you, baby."

"Me too." I limp through the hall as quickly as possible. "It's only official if I keep A's."

"You can do that. There are only a couple of weeks left."

"Yep. I'll call you later."

"Sounds good."

"Love you," I say.

"Love you more."

I rush to see Coach before the bell rings. I want to show him for some reason. Before I get there, Sully stops me.

"Can we talk?"

I tuck the phone in my pocket. "Not sure there's anything to say, Sully."

"It's just that..." Sully shoves his hands in his jeans like lead weights. "I can't get that night out of my head, man."

"Yeah, that makes two of us." Anger rises in me, but I think of Collins and relax. "Don't worry about it. Seriously."

"It's because of me that you'll never play football again, Slaughter. Coach told me that North Carolina wanted you."

"It doesn't matter now." I don't tell Sully UNC still wants me. Just not for football.

"The thing is, Slaughter..." He hesitates. "I'm sorry for everything. I know you'll never forgive me, and I don't blame you, but I wanted to let you know I'm sorry. What I did was wrong."

Time for me to swallow my anger once more and think of Collins. "Sullivan, listen man. I forgive you." I don't tell him how I should thank him like I did with Jenny Lee. I simply forgive him and move on. "I've got to go see Coach before the bell rings."

"Yeah, that's cool. I am sorry, Slaughter. Maybe one day we can be friends again."

"Maybe." I work my way down the hall, leaving Sully behind.

I push Coach's door open and see him sitting at his desk, nose buried in some papers. "Got a second, Coach?"

"I've always got time for you, Dusty. Whatcha need?"

"I wanted to show you this." I toss the envelope on the desk.

After he reads the letter, Coach stands up and comes around to my side of his desk. I stick out my hand, ready for him to shake it, but Coach does something I've never seen him do before. He pulls me up in his arms and lifts me off my feet. After he puts me back on the floor he says, "That's great, Slaughter. I knew you had fight."

"I've still got exams to get through, but it looks like I'm going to finish with all A's."

"Fantastic." Coach hands the letter back to me after putting it in the envelope. "Any idea how you're going to pay for it?"

"I applied for financial aid and loans. And I'll have to get a job. Mr. Franklin said he'll give me as many hours as possible over the summer, which will help me save some money."

"What does your pretty little girlfriend think about it?"

"She's excited."

"You like her, huh?"

“I don’t like her, Coach. I love her. She’s the best thing that’s ever happened to me. I slid down this mountain backwards, and she helped me figure out a way to get back up it together.”

“You may not believe this son, but my wife’s the same way. If it wasn’t for her, I don’t know where I’d be. Take care of that girl, ya’ hear?”

“That’s the plan, Coach.”

I turn to leave his office, but he stops me. “Dusty.”

“Yeah, Coach.”

“You were the best football player I ever coached. You had NFL written all over you, son.”

“Don’t worry about it, Coach. That’s the past.” The bell rings and I leave.

Chapter Fifty-One

Graduation comes and goes without a hitch. Mama stays sober long enough to watch me limp across the makeshift stage they set up on the football field. It's the first and last time I've set foot on the field since my accident.

Collins and her parents make sure to come up for my graduation, which is a nice surprise. Mr. and Mrs. Thacker are nice to Mama, and Mama likes Collins. Mama doesn't have anything to give me for graduating, but I don't mind much. The fact that she stays sober long enough to even be there is enough for me.

The summer flies by, and I save a little money working for Mr. Franklin. After a few weeks of saving and the money I won from the book contest, I'm able to buy another Honda. It's newer and in much better shape than the green monster, even though it has a few dings and dents. Still not fancy, but good enough to get me back and forth to work.

I heard Sully and Charlotte's trip was successful. He gave her a promise ring while they were overseas. There's a rumor she's pregnant, even though she says she isn't. For Sully's sake, I hope she isn't because he'd give up his fancy college scholarship and come home to be with her. Either way, it isn't any of my business.

The summer sun shines hot on my face as I drive into Chapel Hill again for the second time in my life. Excitement bubbles to the surface, but under much different circumstances this time. I'm meeting Collins and her parents at the school for some sort of announcement Mr. and Mrs. Thacker want to make. They're both graduates of the school, so they give a lot of money. He's getting some award or something, I think Collins said.

I pull into the parking lot and see Collins standing by her convertible. When she sees me, her face lights up like it always does.

"Hey, baby," I say as I get out of the car.

She gives me a hug and a kiss. "Hey, sweetie."

She tugs at my arm. "Come on, I need you to see somebody."

"What's the rush? Doesn't your father's thing start in an hour or so?"

"It's something else." She cuts her eyes at me as she pulls my arm. "It's a surprise."

We go inside the English building and snake through the hallways to an office, which reads *Dr. Rosenthal* on the door.

"This name seems familiar," I say to Collins.

"It should." She knocks on the door.

"Come in. It's open," a man's voice calls out. As soon as I hear his voice, I remember who he is.

"Hey, Dr. Rosenthal." Collins enters first.

Dr. Rosenthal springs from his leather chair like a jack-in-the-box. "Oh my," he says. "It is a pleasure to see you again."

I look to Collins to figure out why I'm here, but she simply shrugs her shoulders. He offers us something to drink, but we both refuse. After he settles into his leather chair, he tells me that he submitted *Andy's Big Game* to some agents he knows in New York on my behalf. Collins gasps in surprise.

"Uhhh…okay," I say.

Dr. Rosenthal clicks on his computer for a few seconds and then twists the monitor around for us to see. "Read the email."

We both read the email in silence. Collins is a faster reader than me, so she finishes first. "It just keeps getting better and better, baby." She pulls my face to hers and gives me a kiss.

"It is incredible, Dustin." Dr. Rosenthal flips the monitor back around. "It's only one, though."

"Only one?"

"Yes, there are two agencies who sent emails letting me know they'd like to represent you."

"Represent me?" I'm still not sure what the heck's going on.

"They want to be your agent, baby."

"I'm confused, Dr. Rosenthal." I suck in a big gulp of air. "They want to make my gift to Andy a book? A real book?"

"Yes, Dustin. They liked it so much they want to represent you. They want to pitch your book to publishers to see if someone will buy it and publish it. You'd be a full-fledged author. Isn't it incredible?"

"It's something for sure."

Dr. Rosenthal laughs. "You will have to contact both of them to decide which one you want to represent you. Collins can help you with it. We discussed a bit about the process in my fiction writing class, so she has some experience."

"Thank you, Dr. Rosenthal."

"Yeah, thanks," I say as I shake his hand.

Once we're out of the building, Collins jumps up and down and screams like she just won the lottery.

"I can't believe it. Dustin, do you know what this means?"

"No," I answer.

"It's the most incredible thing I've ever heard. You're going to have a chance to sell your book. To sell many books."

"I reckon." It's easier to talk about Andy now, but it hurts like crazy to know he's gone forever.

"I just thought about something."

"What?"

"If you get the book..." Collins looks up to the blue sky above. "When you get the book published, it'll be like Anderson will live forever."

"Yeah, you're right. All the kids will," I say as I stare at the sky with her. "I like that."

"I like it, too."

Chapter Fifty-Two

We enter the lobby of the auditorium and it's crowded. I look around for Mr. and Mrs. Thacker and spot them off to one side talking with some old guy in a fancy suit. It's a formal thing, so as usual, I'm wearing the only suit I own.

"Dustin, great to see you, son," Mr. Thacker says as he shakes my hand.

Mrs. Thacker is less formal and gives me a hug. "You look handsome."

"Thank you, ma'am. You look lovely, too."

"Dustin, I want you to meet Dr. Andrews. He's the Dean of the School of Medicine here at the University of North Carolina.

I reach my hand out. "Nice to meet you, sir."

"Nice to meet you, too, Dustin. Mr. and Mrs. Thacker speak highly of you. Nice to see you again, Collins."

She gives him a hug. "Hi, Dr. Andrews."

He chats for a few minutes before being dragged away by someone else.

"Mom. Dad." Collins says after Dr. Andrews is gone. "Dustin has something to tell you."

"What is it, Dusty?" Mr. Thacker asks.

I clear my throat. "It seems the little stunt Collins pulled in the spring by entering me in the writing contest keeps on going."

"What are you talking about?" Mrs. Thacker asks.

"The guy in charge of it…"

Collins interrupts. "Dr. Rosenthal."

"Yeah, him. Seems he sent some letters—"

"Query letters," Collins adds.

"—To some people in New York and a couple of them want to be my agent."

"That's fantastic, son." Mr. Thacker slaps me on the back.

"It's great news, Dusty," Mrs. Thacker says. "Anderson would be so happy."

"Collins, have you asked him yet?" Mr. Thacker squints his eyes.

"Asked me what?"

"We were talking about your mother and her addiction."

Normally, I get angry when someone brings Mama up like this, but not anymore. "What about it, sir?"

"We've decided…" Mr. Thacker stops and grabs his wife's hand.

"If you're okay with it, of course." Mrs. Thacker says.

"We've decided to pay for your mother's treatment if she'll agree to go to rehab. It's already taken care of. All she has to do is be willing to go."

"Are you serious? You don't have to do that, sir." I'm floored by their generosity. I don't know what to say.

"We know we don't have to, Dusty." Mrs. Thacker smiles. "It's something we want to do, but it is completely up to you."

"Your mother seems like a sweet woman," Mr. Thacker says. "She just needs a helping hand."

"Uhhh…yeah, I'm okay with it. Not sure about her, though. She doesn't think she even has a problem."

"We'll worry about it later." Mr. Thacker looks at his watch. "We need to take our seats."

There are four seats reserved on the front row. I'm not even sure what's going on, and when I walk past Miss Bernice, Dr. Riddell, and Angela, I'm even more confused.

"What're they doing here, Collins?"

"I have no idea," she whispers as we head up front. "Dad, what's going on?"

"You'll find out soon enough."

We sit and Dr. Andrews takes the podium. He speaks about the work they're doing in the School of Medicine and the partnership they have with the Children's Hospital where Andy and I met.

After he speaks about numbers and projects for way too long, Dr. Andrews calls Mr. and Mrs. Thacker up to the stage. A screen comes down and there's a picture of Andy smiling back at us.

"As most of you know, this is our son, Anderson. He lost a tough battle this year with leukemia."

A few sniffles cut through the silence.

"He was a rare treasure among so much dullness in this world. He was the kind of kid who maintained strength through all adversity. If there was ever a kid who deserved a second chance in life, it was Anderson."

Mrs. Thacker starts crying and someone rushes tissues to her. She dabs her eyes. Mr. Thacker kisses her on the cheek.

"Anderson never once complained about his sickness or his eventual death. What he did instead was give and do for others."

Mr. Thacker clicks the remote in his hand and the image changes. There's a picture of Anderson and me sitting on the couch together. Both of us wearing our hats over our bald heads. Collins squeezes my knee.

He shuffles through a whole series of pictures of Andy. Some in the hospital and many before he got sick. The slideshow continues for about fifteen minutes and nobody says a word.

At the end, the same picture he started with is back up on the screen.

"I've spoken with Dr. Andrews and people at the hospital about an annual scholarship Anderson's mother and I would like to start in Anderson's name. It's going to be called the Anderson Charles Thacker Memorial Scholarship or the ACT Scholarship. And it'll cover all tuition and other expenses for four years of college for the student chosen."

Everyone in the audience applauds.

"This scholarship will be open to any student in the state of North Carolina, but there is one catch. This student has to have shown a willingness to work with children in rough situations throughout their high school careers."

More claps.

"Specifically, the students need to work in some sort of charitable capacity. This can be with children who have cancer or any other life-altering situation children encounter such as abuse. Their ACT of kindness will be the determining factor. Dr. Andrews and I will get together to work out all of the particulars later, but it's basically a scholarship for someone who has been selfless and put others' needs ahead of their own. Just like our son did."

A thunder of applause fills the auditorium.

"I want to thank you all for coming out this evening to be a part of our gift to the school and to the students of North Carolina. It's important to my wife and me that Anderson's spirit and memory never fade. This way, he'll be around long after we are gone."

Mr. Thacker switches the projector off and the screen rises to the ceiling. Behind the screen is a poster board on an easel with a picture of Andy and information about the scholarship.

"You've all been invited here to be a part of the presentation to the first recipient of the Anderson Charles Thacker Memorial Scholarship."

The silence is deafening.

"The person we've chosen was brought to our attention by Anderson. He's a young man who seemed to stumble into Anderson's life. According to the reports from the hospital, he and Anderson were connected at the hip. As I mentioned earlier, Anderson never got his second chance, but now, with this scholarship, Anderson will be able to give one incredibly important young man the second chance he deserves."

Mr. Thacker continues to talk and my body shakes uncontrollably.

"He was the big brother Anderson never had. He gave Anderson hope, and I believe Anderson did the same for him. An unlikely pairing to be sure, but one that came with a bond that'll never be broken. In the short time this young man spent with my son, he lifted his spirit more than we ever imagined possible. And I'm certain Anderson did the same for him as he recovered from a horrific accident that almost took his life."

Mr. Thacker gets a bit choked up. "And just before coming up here, I found out the book Dustin Slaughter made for Anderson's birthday may end up getting published. So without any more rambling, it is our honor to award Dustin Slaughter with the first ever Anderson Charles Thacker Memorial Scholarship."

The auditorium erupts in applause and cheers again. I hear Miss Bernice blubbering louder than all the others saying, "That's my baby. That's my baby," over and over again.

"Come on up, Dusty," Mrs. Thacker says. Her smile reaches across the stage and pulls me to her.

I make my way up the steps and shake Mr. and Mrs. Thacker's hands. He hands a plaque to me. "I'm proud of you, son," he whispers in my ear.

"I don't know what to say, Mr. Thacker. I'm blown away. You didn't have to do this."

"Yes, we did, Dusty. It's the least we could do for all you did for Anderson."

Mrs. Thacker hugs my neck. "He loved you so much, Dusty. You're all he ever talked about."

"I loved him, too."

"I know. We all know. Make him proud by representing him with this scholarship."

"Yes, ma'am, I will. I promise."

Chapter Fifty-Three

I'm finally moved into my dorm and ready to start a new chapter in my life. It all feels so unreal. So much so, that I have to pinch myself every once in a while to make sure I'm not dreaming.

It's the final weekend before classes start, and I'm more nervous than I've ever been about anything in my life. This past year has been one of the toughest I've ever had to endure, and as I drive down the road I can't help but wonder what all of it means.

I ease into a parking spot and get out of my car. And even though it's old and damaged just like me, we both still have many more days ahead of us.

After I grab my backpack with the pictures I drew for Andy, some flowers, and a UNC football from the passenger seat, I limp across the lawn to Andy's grave. Tears well up in my eyes when I see his headstone. Three balloons flutter in the breeze, so I know Collins and her parents have been here. A stream of sunlight shines on it as if he knows I'm here. I know in my heart he does. Because I know in my heart he's always beside me. No matter what.

"Hey, buddy," I say as I reach down and remove the old flowers. I push the new bouquet into the permanent vase. "I've got something for you."

I toss the miniature plastic football in the air a few times, doing my dead-level best to maintain my composure. Even though I come visit him once a week, I still can't get used to the fact that he's gone on to a better place. I know he's no longer suffering, and I'm happy about that, but I would give anything to have one more day with him.

"I know I told you about the scholarship and all, and that you were right all along about me going to college." My words stick in my throat for a moment. "UNC is a beautiful campus. But you already knew that."

There's a bench at the foot of his gravesite, so I ease myself down. My elbows press into my knees. "My leg's healing up pretty good, buddy. It'll never be the same again, and my football days are over." My lip quivers like always when I'm talking to Andy. "It's okay, though, because I got so much going on. I wish you were here to see it."

Andy's face is etched into the marble. Not the face of a kid with cancer. Instead, it's from a picture they took of the two of us wearing our hats. When he was getting better and his hair was growing back. Even still, he wanted us to wear our hats anyhow. He's so handsome.

My cheeks are wet, so I wipe them with the back of my hand. "You're not going to believe this, Andy," I say, "but I decided on an agent who is planning to help me sell your book. Can you believe that? *Andy's Big Game* may someday be on bookshelves everywhere. You're finally going to be the superstar you always were."

I stand up and walk to the headstone, tossing the blue ball in the air.

"I owe you my life, Andy. Without you, I wouldn't be the person I am today. You'll never know how much you mean to me. How much you mean to everyone you ever met."

I slip the pictures out of my bag. "I want you to see these since you never got the chance." The pictures rest in a folder, so I pull them out one at a time to show Andy. "You're a tennis player here, and dunking a basketball here. If everything goes like I plan, you'll be the most inspirational athlete the world has ever known."

After a couple moments, I pack the pictures back in my bag, lean over and place the football at the base of his headstone. "This is for you, buddy. I thought I had my life planned out. But it wasn't until I met you that I realized I didn't have a clue. I realize now that you were put in my life to make me a better person. To make me the person you knew I could be no matter what."

I take my cap off my head and tuck it under my arm. "Thanks for seeing in me what I couldn't see for myself. I love you, buddy!"

Chapter Fifty-Four

"So how did your first day of classes go, college boy?"

I limp over and drop my backpack on the grass next to Collins. "Not bad, I guess. My first couple of classes don't seem like they're going to be too tough."

"Yeah, yeah. Just remember you said that when midterms get here."

I sit down beside her and give her a kiss. "That's what I've got you for, right?"

"Whatever. You're on your own now, smart guy."

I stretch out in the grass and soak in the setting sun. It's warm on my face. "Mama called today."

"What did she say?"

"She said she's doing great and the withdrawals are over."

"That's great, sweetie."

"It's too early to cheer just yet. It's only been three weeks. Six months is an awful long time for Mama to be there. I just hope she can make it through and be like she used to be."

Collins and I lie in the grass and watch the stars come out. One in particular catches my eye, and I think of Miss Bernice's words at the funeral. We talk about anything and everything. Mostly, we talk about Andy.

"Today was a good day. Tomorrow will be a better one."

"What are you talking about, Dustin?"

"What you said about the past."

Collins doesn't remember and that's all right with me.

"The past is gone. We have a future."

"Yes, we do." Collins wraps her fingers in mine. "Love you."

"Love you more!"

Acknowledgements

First and foremost, I want to thank my lord and savior, Jesus Christ. Without Him, this would not be possible. I want to thank my editor and team around me to finally be able to bring this project to life. I want to thank my mother, Margaret, and father, Jonas (JD), for working hard all those years to make sure my brothers and I received a great education. Without their efforts, this book would never have been possible. I want to thank my amazing daughter, Talon. If it weren't for her blessing my life, there is no telling where I'd be. It's because of her that I've been blessed to be a teacher. I want to thank my best friend, Ronald, for always being there these past thirty plus years. Your continual support and encouragement know no bounds and is greatly appreciated. I would like to thank all of those who read various versions of *Love You More*, though it wasn't titled that in the beginning. Your encouragement and love of the novel was and will always be an inspiration to me as I continue to write. There are many who are part of this group, and you know who you are, so please allow me to simply say, thank you. I'd like to thank my dear friend and mentor, Robin, who was one of the first to read the manuscript. Thank you for providing such amazing literary insight. I'd also like to thank Danielle for always being willing to read everything I write. Your support for my writing is greatly appreciated. Last, but certainly not least, I want to thank my wife, Roxie, for always supporting me in my writing. Even though it was scary when you read the manuscript for the first time and has become a story to tell, I am so grateful you loved it as much as I did. Thank you for continually reading all my writing and giving me honest feedback.

For my grandfather, Steve Bobo Jolley. Although he had to drop out of school in the eighth grade and go to work, never learning to read and write, he has been and always will be an inspiration. He watched *Wheel of Fortune* and *Jeopardy!* every night, and it demonstrated to me that there is an innate desire within us all for the written word. Miss you, pop!

I want to thank all of you who took the time to read my debut novel. Though *Love You More* isn't the first novel I've written, it is the one closest to my heart. Once you fall in love with Anderson and Dusty, please take the time to leave a review. It will be most appreciated.

Please check out my contribution to *A Girl Dad & and a Few Wise Men.*

Running with My Heart, Seasons of Love, and other titles will be forthcoming.